# DOMINANCE

*To: Beverly*

*Enjoy!*

*S. Holiman*

## SHARON HOLIMAN

Paperback-Press publishing
an imprint A & S Publishing, A & S Holmes, Inc.
Springfield, Missouri

ISBN: 1-945669-20-9
ISBN-13: 978-1-945669-20-0

## ACKNOWLEDGMENTS

I would like to give special thanks to the following people as each has contributed in some way to the book.

Judy Givens
Carol Lawson
Pat Elliott
Tina Sandstrom
Mallory Holiman
Alan Miller
Don Lueke
William Smith
Cathy Anderson
Sharon Kizziah-Holmes
Cathy Burgos
Charles Holiman
Norma Eaton
Tina Vyborny

# PROLOGUE

In the midst of the 17<sup>th</sup> century, with years of conflict and coexistence, the signing of the Indian Removal Act made it necessary for various Indian tribes to migrate west.

Rising Starr knew her strong, powerful husband, the tribal Chief, had great empathy and concern for his tribe's well-being. He far surpassed any other chief of his day. He stood over six feet tall and was strikingly handsome with his sparkling, black, magnetic eyes. She cherished him.

While sitting today abreast his favorite red and white paint, River Dancer, he shared his deepest concerns with his people. "We need to move soon and search for a new homeland."

Pride and love soared in Rising Starr's heart as she and her son, Aadi, listened intently to her husband speak, she knew this was real. As the chief observed the faces of his people standing before him, she couldn't help noticing the sun's rays dancing across his deeply tanned face.

"It will be winter soon," the chief let them know. "We have a long journey ahead of us."

Rising Starr's heart wasn't filled with joy. This was the land where she was born, where her mother and father were buried on the mound. She had spent her entire life on this land. After looking around, she took a deep breath. She understood it was time to begin her preparation for the passage and leave her home behind.

The actual day was soon upon them. She and the chief joined the tribe, and they all stood hand in hand, silent. With tear-filled eyes, the people gazed upon the land they were about to walk away from. When their leader's voice broke the serenity of the moment, Rising Starr turned toward him. "It is time." Hunting Bear let go of her hand.

Studying his friends and family members, his tribe, as they started their journey, Hunting Bear addressed Rising Starr still standing beside him, "I am amazed at their strength."

"Truly, they gather most of it from you."

"No, they are strong on their own. Look at them. They are uprooted and dispossessed, but they move on, heads up, taking with them all they have."

The sick, the old, and the small children rode in travois, along with blankets, cooking pots, and additional belongings. Others traveled on either foot or horseback. The chief couldn't have been more proud, but he knew there would be troubled times ahead. "It is too close to winter."

"It is, but with your guidance, we will be fine."

The chief smiled and looked in her direction. For the first time in a long time, he noticed her dark, black hair glistening in the sunlight from the colored dust she used. In awe, he realized how much he really loved and depended on her. This average stature, strong, unyielding woman, respected among the tribe was his rock.

Bringing the chief back to the present, she said to him, "Look at our son. He is tall like you and handsome. He rides a horse well, too."

He was proud of Aadi. "In no time he will be of age to join the hunting parties."

Hunting Bear laughed and lifted Rising Starr onto the horse that pulled their travois.

"We'd better go," he smiled, "before we are left behind."

As they plodded along on their journey, the rains came, and with them came cold weather. Then, after the fatigue of each day, the tribe camped for the night. They used animal hides for shields from the inclement weather, and the cold, wet ground for their resting place.

Weeks had passed since they had left their homeland. Hunting Bear wished he could see into the future but had confidence the Great Spirit would show them the way. He was pleased the band had managed to keep their momentum and excitement for the journey intact.

Unfortunately, the day came where they were forced to stop their journey. They stood face-to-face with a frozen river being too icy for canoes but not frozen enough to walk across.

After being stranded for a surmountable time, Hunting Bear felt the day finally came when they were able to cross and continue. "Spring is near. We shall pack and be ready to move forward at sunrise."

As he feared, the road ahead proved full of misery and heartache. There was sickness and death. Hunting Bear, along with the tribe, sorrowed at their losses, but they pressed on.

The chief rode ahead of the tribe on many occasions. This day, he topped a hill and gazed down upon a fair land of rolling hills, stony bluffs, and great plateaus. His heart soared; he smiled, glanced back to see his people close behind and waited for them.

Rising Starr was the first to reach him. "It is beautiful." She saw a sparkle in the chief's deep-set eyes. Never had she loved him more. When he spoke, his voice was deep and held authority.

"We have come to the end of our journey. I believe we have found the perfect place to live. We will make this place ours." Hunting Bear was pleased with the new village.

Time seemed to pass quickly and with spring came new life on the land. No one was happier than he was, except perhaps, Rising Starr.

She had taken to riding River Dance around the hillside. What a wonderful sight it was. He would sit beneath his favorite Oak and watch her more times than she knew.

She dismounted, picked wildflowers, and enjoyed the earth. In all her beauty, she mounted again. He knew she would bring her treasure into their home to display. He had thanked the Great Spirit for her many times. Her warmth beside him each night was something he couldn't imagine being without. He was sure she was his for eternity.

The chief turned when he heard someone approach. There stood Aadi. He had grown from the boy that followed his father everywhere into a young brave. He stood tall, and sat strong and straight on horseback. The young man had become swift and sure with the bow and the spear. One day he would take his place as chief. "My boy, what brings you to sit with me today?"

"I would like to join tomorrow's hunting party."

Hunting Bear nodded. "I see. What makes you think you are ready for the hunt?"

"Father, it is time I am freed from spending hunt days in camp with the women. I want to follow in your footsteps. If I continue to hang on Mother's skirt, I will be unable to do so."

Laughter escaped the chief. "Yes, I have been where you are." He studied the brave beside him. "We will make it so, my son. Tomorrow you will join the hunt."

The next morning before the sun came up; the chief woke with an uneasy feeling in the pit of his stomach. Today the braves would hunt, but he could not dispel the uneasiness that gnawed at him. Was it because Aadi would join the party? No, it was something else. After having wrestled the thought in his mind for some time, the chief decided to share his concern with Rising Starr.

He wrapped his arm around her. When she stirred, he watched her beautiful brown eyes flutter open. She was his life. "Good morning."

She smiled. "You should be getting ready to hunt."

"I know, but the Great Spirit has put a bad feeling in my gut. I do not want to leave you this morning."

With great confidence, she gently caressed his lips. "There is simply nothing for you to worry about. When you return, we will celebrate my thirty years of life."

Midway into the hunt, a formless foreboding riddled the chief's thoughts. His mind's eye returned again and again to Rising Starr. Lastly, his sense of darkness broke like a storm. He knew he had to get back to camp. He rode hard doing so.

When he turned his mount around the last corner, the camp was in full sight. His heart immediately fell to his feet.

"No!" the chief shouted. A squaw in blood-soaked clothing quickly ran up to him.

"Renegades overtook us! We grabbed whatever we could to defend ourselves, mostly rocks and cooking vessels."

The chief's heart thumped hard in his chest. His gaze frantically searched the camp. "Where is Rising Starr?" The woman shook her head. He didn't like the look in her eyes.

"Rising Starr fought with conviction and courage," she tried to explain, "but somehow, during the confusion, she simply vanished. The few who managed to escape the horror hid among the rocks and trees. I am sorry, I do not know of Rising Starr's whereabouts."

The chief suddenly dropped to his knees. With his fist lifted, he began to wail. Then making his way to the top of the hill, he shouted words meant for Rising Starr. "You are who I am! How can I be me without you?"

The many failed attempts over the next few days to locate her left the chief distraught, empty, and cold inside. How could this happen? How could she be gone? It was still hard for him to believe or accept.

On the morning before the attack, he had teased her about her age, even though he was many years her senior. Now, she had simply vanished, leaving him grief-stricken. He felt helpless and old. His life was nothing without her. She wasn't gone, she couldn't be.

Feeling powerless, Aadi stood quietly in the shadows observing his father age day by day. On one occasion, he found him quite ill. While sitting by his bedside, the now frail chief slipped into a trance-like state. In a short amount of time, he could be heard babbling, as though he was communicating with Rising Starr.

"We will be together forever on this land, I promise you."

As Aadi sat holding his father's hand, he couldn't help thinking he would be glad the day his father joined the Great Spirit and have his heart healed. Then a soft, faint-like murmur came from the fragile chief.

"Don't worry, my son. My destiny lies on this land. I will wait here for your mother."

Those were the chief's last spoken words. On the following morning, his father, the great leader, was prepared for his final journey. Per protocol, an Eagle's feather was placed upon his body. He was then laid to rest near the top of the hill in full view of the old Oak. Now, the tribe's future, their destiny, rested in Aadi's hands.

With his father's lingering words still haunting him, Aadi felt compelled to share his vow, and for all purposes, it seemed Hunting Bear's spirit was indeed on the land. It would remain there for centuries as just an unfulfilled legend without validity until the middle of the 20<sup>th</sup> century.

\* \* \*

On the coldest February morning in 1948, at a small-isolated farm just sixty miles east of the legendary Indian land, a newborn child of Cherokee heritage took her first breath. That innocent cry from the baby girl, Julie, drew the attention of none other than the spirit of Chief Hunting Bear himself.

Over the next thirty years, he continued to stand vigilant as he watched her mature and struggle, to find her identity, to find her self-worth.

Then in the month of February 1978 on those infamous rolling hills, stony bluffs, and great plateaus, Julie's world collided with that of the chief.

This by-chance meeting, or pre-designated introduction, set the path for the fulfillment of the centuries-old legend. It would be the chief's continued vigilance and dominance that would ultimately change the direction of Julie's life, her destiny, and her happiness.

# CHAPTER 1

*The time was mid-afternoon, and the temperature was warm with a slight sweet but wild breeze. A Native American woman pulled her vehicle alongside a lone mailbox. Immediately, she saw a terraced stairway surrounded by various colored wild flowers where Mother Nature had strategically placed them to be noticed. This oasis seemed to welcome her as if she belonged.*

*She got out of her pickup not fully understanding what was happening; nevertheless, feeling a compelling draw, the woman began to trek up the alluring flight of steps. About halfway up, a red and white paint stallion stood beside the stairway. Without hesitation, she climbed upon his back and rode to the top of the hill. From there, she rode around the perimeter of the beautiful property time and time again. Her long, white dress and dark, black hair flowed in the wind as though on wings.*

*Her heart soared with pleasure. What...no, where was this place? It seemed so familiar, yet not. There was something missing but what?*

*After having enjoyed this newfound freedom for a period of time, she rested beneath an old Oak. The stallion grazed nearby. When the sun's final rays began to set and shine through the sweeping branches, an Indian brave graciously approached and knelt beside her. She looked into his deep, black eyes and his voice was but a whisper. "You are who I am. How can I be me without you?"*

*"What's your name?" He smiled. A giant hand grasps at her heartstrings and takes her breath.*

*"What's your name?"*

*"Julie."*

At the same time she spoke, she heard the buzz of her alarm clock. She quickly reached to shut off the irritating sound before grabbing the nearby pillow, placing it over her face.

Had she met this brave before? Her mind raced to understand. Was she an innocent observer in someone else's dream? Was it a dream? A dream or...no, she was thinking crazy thoughts, but could this in some way be her own reality? She was Cherokee, was it her own destiny she saw?

The questions remained but Julie managed to push herself out of bed. While she made her way down the hallway, her steps were soundless against the carpet. She stopped and turned. "What's happening to me?" her lips mimicked into the hall mirror.

She rubbed her forehead in a last-ditch effort to gain control of her thoughts. She went to the front door, unlocked the dead bolt, turned the doorknob, and stepped out into the brisk morning air to retrieve Sunday's newspaper.

While she sat at the kitchen table somewhat dazed, she began to sift through the paper. Words surrounded by a bold black frame caught her attention. "Oh, my gosh how bizarre." Somewhat mystified at what she was reading, she shifted her weight and became unbalanced, nearly falling from her chair.

As if the confusing dream hadn't been enough to unsettle her nerves this morning, this ad surely was. Julie continued to read aloud, "FOR SALE: 125-acre farm with many trees and a small farmhouse."

Maybe a house was what was missing from the land in her dream. Her adrenaline kicked in. She regressed back to her own childhood. Before her birth her mother had been left in the city on her own to take care of herself and two other young children. Therefore, not being able to receive any kind of support from her estranged husband during this childbirth, she went to stay in the country with her sister, Mary Etta.

Since Mary Etta didn't have children of her own, she jumped at the opportunity to adopted Julie, so to speak, at least during the coming summer months. However, when Julie got older she secretly felt as though she had been pawned off, separated from her siblings for no reason. She never quite understood the arrangement between her mother and her aunt.

Why? She often wondered. It didn't matter so much now, but during that severance period, Julie bonded more with her aunt's unique little farm than with her aunt. She felt welcome on the land as if she had something special like a gift or just an understanding.

Many times since then, she reflected back to that young girl running barefoot across the countryside chasing butterflies and hiding in her own little sanctuary sandwiched among the tall, old Oaks, her protectors from the outside world. Even though Julie was now approaching her 30th birthday, she often questioned how she personally fit into today's society.

Now, this morning with all that had happened, she couldn't help but wonder if this farm might somehow be the missing link in her life. While still in a state of confusion, she needed to talk to someone. She probably should call her boyfriend, Slate, but instead she dialed her best friend, who was a tomboy like her.

"Good morning, Bailey," she blurted, not really

knowing quite how to begin the conversation.

"What's going on?"

Apparently, Bailey heard the anxiety in her voice. How was she going to phrase this? The best way was just to say it. "I kind of feel like someone's playing mind games with me."

"How so?"

She chuckled, realizing she had surely confused Bailey this morning with her outburst, though none of it was funny. "That makes two of us. I had a realistic dream this morning about some beautiful land, and then I found some similar farmland advertised in the morning newspaper."

"So?"

"I know I can't expect anyone to understand, but you know me...there's always something out of the ordinary happening in my life."

"That's for sure. Try giving me a little more information. I'll see if I can wrap my head around what you're saying."

It was impossible to explain. She didn't really know what had her so wound up. "My mind is going in fifteen different directions right now, if that's even possible. I'm pacing the floor like a lion in a cage."

"Julie, take a deep breath and slow down."

She stopped where she stood, took in a deep breath and let it out slowly. "Well, at least I stopped pacing."

"I'll come over."

Somehow, she had to sort this out herself. "Thanks but it's not necessary. I'll calm down here in a minute. Maybe a brisk walk will clear my head, along with a cup of caffeine."

"Are you sure?"

"I'll be fine. My imagination just went wild for a moment." She still questioned if it was real or a dream. "Thanks for listening. I'll talk with you later."

She hung up the telephone and paced. No matter how

hard she tried to suppress her thoughts, she couldn't. Therefore, racing down the hallway, she entered the bathroom and quickly threw her nightclothes aside. She put on a pair of loose fitting jeans, a light blue tee shirt, and a pair of tennis shoes. Her hair tied back, she grabbed a jacket from the hall closet.

The ad secure in her hand, she started for the door before stopping short in her tracks. What was she doing? Was she really going to go look at this farm? It was crazy, but she ignored her incredible turmoil, went into the garage, and started her pickup. She backed out of the driveway and headed toward the familiar, yet unfamiliar, destination.

Still being a little apprehensive about her choice to move forward, her gaze kept returning to the rearview mirror. Now, her only companions were the thoughts racing through her mind. Why was she chosen to live this life? Was there a reason she was here? She asked the questions over and over.

Maneuvering her pickup over the winding country road, Julie found herself quietly singing as the sun glistened above the treetops. When she approached a forthcoming hill, from nowhere, a small deer leaped out in front of her. "Nooo!" She slammed on her brakes coming to a full stop.

While sitting there, wide-eyed and trembling, her mind reflected on her friend, Wapa. A deer, according to his medicine cards, meant *to apply gentleness to your present situation, and it will melt the heart of the demon and your path will clear. Fear cannot exist in the same place with love and gentleness.*

"Whew, that was far too close for comfort."

Seeing a dirt driveway just ahead, she made the decision to turn around and abandon this adventure. She put her pickup in reverse but for some reason, a feeling inside her made her have a change of heart. *This must be some kind of a farm to have this much control over me.*

From having looked at the directions, Julie knew she was getting close. Then within seconds, she again brought her pickup to a standstill. "No way!" She sat there staring at a familiar mailbox, the one in her dream. A cool quiver ran down her spine.

Finally, a form of normalcy returned and the shock subsided. Julie began to broaden her gaze. Her vision encompassed a small farmhouse approximately a couple hundred feet from the road. The screen door was flapping from the blowing wind, and in the front yard stood an old, rickety rail fence with the remains of a rambling rosebush climbing through it.

Inhaling deeply, she continued to study the area before she spotted an elderly farmer standing nearby. He was dressed in a pair of faded blue overalls, a long-sleeved, red-plaid flannel shirt, and a dilapidated straw hat. She rolled her window down. "Hello."

"Good afternoon, young lady, are you lost?"

Cautiously holding up the newspaper, Julie managed to find her voice. "I think I've found what I'm looking for."

"Well, then pull into my driveway. Over there by the 'For Sale' sign will do nicely."

Julie quickly obliged and before stepping out into this new adventure, secured her camera.

The farmer extended his hand. "Hi. My name is Ervin."

"Glad to meet you, I'm Julie. I'm excited about being here...I think."

"Well, since you're here, would you like to look around?"

"Yes. Your farm has set off a gamut of emotions in me this morning. I'm eager and fearful at the same time."

"Nothing here to be fearful of," he responded. "We can start with the house, if you like. It's as good as any place to begin. You know, I actually built it for my wife many years ago."

"How cool is that." A labor of love, she liked it.

After about fifteen minutes of looking and talking, Ervin conveyed, "Well, that concludes the inside tour. Let's go outside, and I'll show you the rest."

"Great." She stepped out the backdoor and gasped. Her heart raced at the sight. "Where does that path lead?" She pointed barely able to contain herself. It was like the pathway in her dream, so familiar.

"That up there," Ervin glanced into the direction the walkway led, "is like walking into another dimension or level of self-consciousness." He looked in her direction. "If you believe in that kind of thing," he said. "Anyway, at the very least it's the highest pinnacle and the most beautiful spot on the farm as far as I'm concerned. Would you care to see it?"

"Yes, most definitely." She fought to keep her composure. This was the weirdest thing that ever happened to her. She followed Ervin to the beginnings of the path. Her anxiety began to mount, and she desperately tried to calm herself. She held up her camera. "Is it okay if I take pictures?"

"Be my guest, take all you want."

She listened intently as he proudly talked to her about his farm life. Then something made her stop walking. Ervin's voice brought her back from her thoughts.

"What's the matter, did you hear something?"

"No. I was just wondering." This was going to be a stupid question. Somehow she already knew the answer. "Isn't this about halfway?"

After a quick survey, Ervin commented, "Yes, I'd say so. Do you need a rest?"

"It's not that." She glanced around the hillside. "I was kind of expecting to see a red and white paint stallion standing about here." She chuckled but was only half-joking. Her dream was still in the frontal part of her brain, and she wasn't sure what was reality and what wasn't.

"Oh, you mean ole Pete?" He smiled. "I put him over in the pasture this morning. Although, he's a brown horse with a black mane."

Julie shook her head. This was so strange. She immediately resumed her trek up the hill, snapping pictures with nearly every step. Her emotions were running wild; she wanted to get as many pictures as she could to keep her memory fresh.

"See the big Oak over there," he pointed. "The one on the very edge of the clearing?"

"Oh my. Oh my!" Julie verbalized looking at the recognizable tree. What's going to happen next, her mind raced to understand? She struggled to focus, to maintain her sanity.

*The one who had stood vigilant on this land for many, many years, the one who was waiting to fulfill his age-old prophecy, observed her every movement. It was happening.*

*While watching Julie, a grin had its beginning on the chief's weathered face; and why shouldn't he smile? After all, she had finally arrived with her similar attributes too, of all people in the world, his beloved Rising Starr.*

*As the chief enjoyed the smile that spread across his face, he couldn't help but study Julie's grin. She possessed a similar, seductive one he knew in times past. Losing the woman who bore that smile broke his heart and left a burning memory deep inside his mind.*

"Let's go over there." Julie started toward the tree.

Ervin graciously obliged. "My wife and I used to come here every once in a while and have a picnic. It was an opportunity to relax and spend time together, a kind of connection we had to the land."

"I fully identify with what you're saying." She smiled. "As a small child, I also had my own special connection with the land. I hope to someday have it again. Maybe your farm can provide that for me."

"I'd like that."

Julie glanced down the other side of the hill. "Ervin, what happened to those trees lying on the ground? They look like a fallen army that lost its battle."

Sadly responding, with his head slightly bent, he began, "I have medical bills to pay. I had to sell the timber. However, I requested this one old Oak be spared." He glanced up at her. "By the way, if you would buy this farm," he said, with renewed hope. "I wouldn't have to cut another one."

"Okay. Okay," she muttered.

Her attention focused, once again, on the lifeless trees. She became curious. "Ervin, could those be Indian mounds I'm seeing beneath the timber?"

"It's an age-old legend that they are. Oops." He hadn't planned on bringing that subject up. "This won't keep you from wanting to buy the farm will it?"

"No, it only makes it more intriguing."

"Whew." He gave a sigh of relief when Julie didn't pursue the issue of the mounds or the legend. Most people would tuck tail and run from an Indian burial ground on any property not owned and cared for by the People.

However, Ervin had no way of knowing about the reception of the warm breeze that blew across Julie's shoulder about now making her feel welcome, as well as giving her a sense of security.

*And little did Julie know, she was experiencing new found feelings that would become a vital part of her everyday life for years to come, while the chief was simply standing by on the sideline watching his plan unfold.*

Following their discussion of the fallen trees, Ervin proceeded to answer other questions or concerns Julie had. She decided not to bring up the young brave she had seen in her dream. She figured the old man would think she was crazy. Still, she'd felt a presence by the Oak tree, and where had that breeze come from?

"Well, that just about ends the tour, any last minute thoughts?"

"I don't think so, but I am rather anxious to talk with my boyfriend."

"Tell him you can buy all this for a modest down payment."

"I will most definitely tell him that. Here." She handed him her telephone number. "Call me if you think of anything else."

"I'll gladly do that." He placed it into his shirt pocket, then opened her door for her.

"Thanks for showing me around." She got in her pickup and Ervin stepped back.

"Yes, ma'am." He waved goodbye to the potential new owner of his beloved farm.

*Returning to the city, Julie was unaware of what lay ahead. It's just as well, though, for you see, there's no way to prepare one's self for this type of journey. That is, not unless your name is Julie, a very strong-minded woman of Cherokee heritage.*

After dropping off her film for developing, Julie pulled her pickup into the garage. She was riddled with uncertainty. She fought to shut down the feeling. Unable to, her thoughts transfixed on an endeavor to find a way to finance the farm. Not just any farm, it had to be the one she visited this morning. There was something stimulating about this one. She couldn't put her finger on it, not right now anyway, but it would show itself.

She ran several scenarios through her mind, and not really deciding on any specific solution, Julie thought of Bailey. A light bulb flashed in her mind. The answer was right in front of her.

Her friend was temporarily living with her parents, and she had expressed a desire to be out on her own. Julie could see the potential of solving both her and Bailey's dilemma. With a feeling of urgency, she picked up the phone and dialed her friend. Her hopes were high.

"Hello."

"Bailey, you need to move to the country. I took several rolls of film, and I'm waiting for them to be developed. Soon I'll be able to show you what you're missing. I know you can't say no."

"Wait a minute, wait just a minute, Julie. Catch your breath and start from the beginning. Does this have anything to do with our earlier conversation?"

"Maybe, the farm's only about twenty miles from here. I will buy it. You can rent from me. I want the farm so I can visit there on weekends."

"Hmm, I don't know."

"Call me when you make up your mind."

"I will. I promise," Bailey assured her.

Hesitating a moment before placing the receiver into the cradle, Julie pondered about rushing headlong into such an investment over a dream and an ad in the Sunday's paper.

That same question rippled throughout her mind, plus, the realization of Slate not being included in any of the decision-making. She knew he would like the farm, but this dream was really hers and hers alone.

She and Slate had met one Saturday evening in a bar at the lake. Standing 6'4", he was her knight in shining armor. That night he stopped her from making a bad decision. For some reason, she felt he had sheltered her. He vowed to stay with her through the entire weekend, and he kept his word. Because of this, Julie learned to trust him. Something she had a hard time doing.

The telephone ringing startled her and pulled her away from her thoughts. It was probably Bailey with her decision. She picked up the receiver and heard Slate's deep voice.

Have you missed me? I'm in a hunter's paradise."

Julie couldn't help but smile, a paradise indeed. "Of course, I've missed you, and I think I've found my own hunter's paradise."

"Where's that?"

She didn't want to break the news over the phone. "Oh, it's a surprise. I can't say anything just yet."

"Okay, I guess I can wait. Hey, I'll be home in time to celebrate your birthday."

"That's great but don't hurry on my account. Just enjoy yourself. In fact, it will give me more time to get things lined out here." She heard Slate groan on the other end of the line. "This can't be good."

Julie giggled. "Why do you say that?" He would never guess what she had been up to.

"Because I know you. Are you sure you can't even give me a hint?" he asked rather sarcastically.

"Nope, you'll find out soon enough." She held her breath hoping he didn't push the matter. She didn't want the conversation to end in an argument.

"Okay, then. I love you, and I'll be home soon."

"I love you, too, bye." She did love him, and it might be selfish, but this was her fantasy.

# CHAPTER 2

As Julie stood brushing her hair in front of the bedroom mirror, a tap on the front door brought her back to reality. She hurriedly smoothed her hair and headed toward the sound. She peered through the tiny peephole. The image she saw was that of a Cherokee medicine helper known as a hollow bone. To her, he was her good friend, Wapa.

He had long hair, was strong built and possessed an old soul. He sometimes lived out of a bread van, a true hippie. Even so, he had taught her to love and embrace her Indian culture. He walked the walk and talked the talk. Part of his job was to restore hope, understanding, confidence, harmony and health through the resources of nature; fur, skins, bones, crystals, shells, roots, and feathers.

She had never seen Wapa without his medicine bag hanging from around his neck, and he had yet to reveal the contents.

If someone would listen, she could talk for hours about the experiences she and Wapa had shared over the years. He was actually the first person to take her on a vision quest. He would hold a special place in her heart for eternity.

"Oh, my gosh! What a nice surprise," she said, opening the door. "It's been a long time since I've set eyes on you.

What brings you out today?"

"When I woke up this morning, I seemed to be getting a vibe from you. So, here I am."

"Well, come on in." She led the way to the living area. "Have a seat."

Wapa sat and relaxed against the chair back. "What has happened that you are sending out these feelings?"

"Where do I begin?" Julie sat across from him and met his gaze. He always had the uncanny ability to know what she was thinking. She hesitated a moment as her emotions began to surface.

"Go ahead."

The best thing to do was just tell him everything. He would see through anything less. "It all started, believe it or not, with a dream." She told the details as she remembered them and ended the saga with, "Can you make any sense out of this?"

Wapa, being a man of very few words responded in his own wise way. "Julie, only you will know the answer. It's inside you. Follow what you feel, and you will find it."

He reached into his pocket. "Maybe the countryside is calling you home. In the meantime, I think it's time for you to have your own animal cards. Maybe they will help you to understand animal spirits and their medicine. Perhaps, they may even have a lot to say about this matter."

She took his words to heart. "You mean it? They're really mine?"

"Yes." He smiled. "Happy early 30th birthday, my friend. Call me if you need me. I mean anytime."

"More than likely you will be hearing from me." Julie smiled, confirming his words.

She waved goodbye, stood in the doorway, and watched her dear friend drive out of sight. After shutting the door, she returned to the kitchen, wondering why Bailey hadn't called. She had to find out what was going on with her friend, so she dialed her number.

"Bailey, I couldn't wait any longer. Have you made up your mind?"

"Yes. I have. I want you to know, I've already finished a full pot of coffee."

"I've never known you to drink so much."

"I know. I thought it would give me courage. I don't want to stand in your way, but it's not right for me."

"It's okay, really. I understand."

"But I don't want to be the reason you can't realize your dream."

"I will find another way," Julie assured her.

"I feel better now. Oh, by the way, I'm going to the pharmacy. Is that where your film is?"

"Yes."

"Do you want me to pick up your pictures?"

"That would be great, thanks."

It would be early evening before Bailey knocked at Julie's front door. Anxiously, Julie motioned her in.

"Okay." Bailey handed Julie the packet. "Now, let's see what has you so stressed out."

Julie promptly spread the pictures out on the table for better viewing.

"Looks like your normal, typical farm," Bailey acknowledge. Although, as she began to scan across images, she selected one of the photos and questioned, "Julie, what's this little white spot over Ervin's shoulder?"

"That's strange." Julie peered at the picture. "Maybe my film was old. Of course, the spot would have to be on this particular picture."

Bailey suddenly gasp! Julie glanced at her friend. "What is it?"

"When you look real close, it looks like there's a face in this picture." She placed it back on the table. "Julie, I don't like this at all."

"Let me see." Taking a look for herself, a thought went

through Julie's mind. "What do you know about orbs?"

"Very little, actually nothing at all."

"I don't think it's the film that's bad. I believe those spots are orbs. Slate will not believe this."

"I don't either." Bailey hesitated. "Are you sure you want to pursue this farm?"

"Yes." Her mind was made up. "The orbs just add a little hint of mystery. Don't you think?"

"Not for me, no way." Bailey looked at her watch. "I need to be going. Talk with you tomorrow."

"Goodnight. Thanks for picking up my pictures."

"You're welcome."

*Julie was unaware how her fascination of the orbs would have a very profound effect on her life for a very long, long time.*

## CHAPTER 3

It was the morning of Julie's 30<sup>th</sup> birthday, and she couldn't sleep. She waited for the sun to come up and could only imagine how different her life would be out on the farm.

Walking past her kitchen window, she noticed a glimmer of morning light; disappointed she couldn't see the actual rays. There were far too many buildings in the horizon for that.

Alas, the congestion and noises of the city had taken over her peace, along with the ringing phone that interrupted her last moment of serenity. "Hello."

"Happy Birthday to you. Happy birthday to you," came the greetings through the earpiece. The voice brought her back into the realm of reality. "Aren't you up a bit early this morning, Bailey?"

"I guess so. I just wanted to be the first one to recognize your birthday, and of course inquire about the farm. Have you made a definite decision?"

"I'm not one-hundred percent sure. Although, before you called, I was feeling a draw in that direction. Maybe it stems from my troubled childhood, the fascination of the orbs, or perhaps it's just my destiny."

"Well, I'm confident in the end you will make the right

decision."

She knew Bailey wanted the best for her. "Thanks. And thanks for the birthday song." She hung up in time to hear the doorbell ring. She looked through the peephole and was surprised to see a florist. She opened the door and eyed his beautiful arrangement.

"Good morning, are you Julie?"

"Yes."

"Then these are for you." He handed her a bouquet.

She accepted the beautiful gift of a dozen red roses. Returning to the kitchen, she placed them into a tall vase on the center of her table and sat down to read the attached card.

> *You make my life complete*
> *I will always, 'til forever*
> *protect and love you*
> *HAPPY BIRTHDAY*
> *Slate*

She smiled and read the card two more times. Then laying it side, she was reminded of a comment his mom had made to her the day they met.

"One thing you will soon learn about Slate is he never misses an opportunity to send a friend a card. He more often than not chooses to show his love and affection through unspoken words."

What a true statement. She reflected back to the many other cards Slate had given her. Then jolting back to the present with a piercing sound, Julie picked up her receiver.

"Happy 30<sup>th</sup> birthday."

"Thanks, Slate." It was amazing the last couple of times she had him on her mind, he called. "I was just thinking about you. You caught me admiring your roses and your very sweet, touching card. Thank you so much."

"You're welcome and many, many more."

She put the card down on the table. "Okay, that's

enough reference to my 30th milestone, plateau, or whatever it's called these days."

"Party pooper, I'll see you around 5:00 o'clock this evening. Are you hungry for barbecue?"

"Are you going to make it with all the trimmings?"

"I am, just for you."

"I will be hungry and waiting for you."

"Okay, see you then."

Having some time before his arrival, Julie grabbed her coat from the hall closet and stepped outside to go for a walk. The air was crisp and there were a few scattered snowflakes, just enough, so she could track her footprints.

The snow had intensified. When she finished her stroll, she found herself covered from head to toe in white fluff. She went into the garage, removed a small whiskbroom from the wall, and brushed away the clinging snow. It had been a refreshing walk, and no sooner had she hung the broom back onto the hook, she heard a horn honk in her driveway. Immediately, she saw Slate step out of his truck.

"I'm so glad you're here," Julie squealed, rushing into his arms. When the last linger of his kiss faded from her lips, she met his gaze through dancing snowflakes. "I can't believe all the things that have happened in your absence."

"Well, before you clue me in..." He handed her a small red box.

Julie accepted his gift. Her hands trembled as she opened the package. She was pleasantly surprised to see the matching bracelet to a necklace he had given her on Valentine's Day. "Oh, Slate, it's beautiful. Thank you." She stood in front of him, waiting for him to close the clasp around her wrist, and was oblivious to the intensification of the snow. Slate finally spoke up, spitting the feathery stuff out of his mouth.

"Maybe we should continue this conversation inside."

"I couldn't agree more."

"I brought lots of barbeque. I'll get it."

Julie watched him walk back to his vehicle and retrieve their meal. Once he climbed the porch steps, she held the kitchen door open for him. "See your flowers?" she pointed. "They're the most beautiful long-stemmed red roses I have ever seen. I'm very impressed."

"Hopefully, this meal will be just as impressive." He placed the food on the table.

"I'm sure of it." She inhaled the aroma. "I can hardly resist the tantalizing smell as we speak."

"You know, when I started preparing this meal, there was hardly a trace of snow."

"I understand. There was just enough that I left footprints this afternoon. I kind of felt like Hansel and Gretel who left breadcrumbs behind to find their way home." Then she hesitated. "Hmm. Maybe this journey is all about finding my way home?"

*From only a short distance away, the chief couldn't agree more. Julie had only touched the tip of the iceberg, so to speak. She would experience many peaks and valleys before she would be able to put all the pieces together. However, he would guide her every step.*

Slate scratched his head and took a seat at the table. "Did I miss out on something? What journey are we talking about?"

"As I mentioned, a lot has happened in your absence. So much so, I can't even begin to explain; especially, the part where I feel, at times, someone or something is manipulating me. Anyhow, I'll bring you up-to-date after we enjoy this delicious barbeque."

"Sounds good to me." Slate filled his tea glass. "By the way, thanks to my marksmanship, our next cookout will be venison."

She was surprised he didn't press the subject. "That's great. I know the perfect place for the event."

"And where's that?" Slate anxiously asked.

"A place I've wanted for a very long time. A place that would never disappoint me and ask little of me in return." She saw the suspicious glint in his eye. "What? Don't look at me that way. You know how unhappy I am living in the city."

"Tell me what's going on in that devilish mind of yours?" He wiped away the excess barbecue from his mouth. "I get the feeling sometimes you only want me around, because I can cook."

There was some truth in his statement, but she smiled in his direction and said, "Don't be absurd. You have many good qualities. Any woman would consider herself lucky to have you in her life."

"Oh, is that so." Slate pushed his chair back and excused himself from the table. "I'll be right back."

Returning shortly, he instructed, "Now, with your eyes closed, make a wish and blow out the candles on this cake in one breath."

"Here goes." She inhaled deeply; not wanting to leave one lit candle.

"Great job," he smiled as the smoke drifted toward the ceiling. "Your wish will surely come true. Care to share it with me?"

"Well, maybe..."

"Out with it. I'm in suspense here."

She took his hand. "Okay, sit down. It's time I let you in on my little secret. While you were out of town, I looked at a far–." The telephone ring brought her confession to a halt. She wanted to tell him her experience, but it would have to wait awhile longer. She stood and retrieved the receiver.

"Okay. Okay," Slate heard Julie say walking out of the kitchen with the telephone cord trailing behind her.

What was going on? He got up and walked to the doorway. He saw Julie go into the bedroom swinging and waving her arm, stretching the telephone cord to its limits.

"It isn't going to go any further," Slate shouted down the hallway. "You're going to pull the phone right off the wall."

She walked back toward the kitchen. "Okay, thanks for calling. I'm so happy right now."

Seeing the smile on her face, Slate asked, "What's going on?" The smile he thought was so beautiful lifted the corners of her mouth.

"I just bought myself a birthday gift." She sat down and gave a sigh. "I just bought a 125-acre farm."

"You did what?" Slate's brows knitted. "I get it. It's a joke, right?"

"No, I'm afraid not. I had a dream about a farm. After seeing Ervin's, he's who I bought it from, I knew it was the one I had dreamed about. It was that simple."

Slate reached over and placed his hand on her forehead. "You don't seem to have a fever."

"You don't understand. It's the hunter's paradise I told you about over the phone."

Slate shook his head. None of this made sense to him, but he was willing to humor her. "I suppose you do have a plan to finance this endeavor?"

"Not exactly, but I've been working on it. I only need a five-thousand dollar down payment."

"Hmm." He sighed, still trying to make sense of how the dream farm and the real farm were one and the same.

Julie stood up, put her arms around his neck and pressed a kiss to his lips. "You'll love it. I know you will," she whispered.

"The hunting part sounds good. Give me a minute to let all this soak in. I didn't see you for a few days and look what happened." He sat down and shook his head in disbelief. "I can't even imagine what would happen, if I left you alone for a month. You understand we are a long way from retirement?"

She realized how surprised Slate must have been. "Yes,

I know. This farm just came out of nowhere, and I can't seem to let it go. If I don't get to show it to you this evening, I won't get one wink of sleep tonight. "I have to return to work tomorrow. That fork-truck isn't going to run itself, you know."

Slate shook his head, stood up then pushed his chair under the table. "A woman driving a fork-truck."

She saw his mind was made up. He wasn't going to go to the property tonight, but at least he could look at the photos. "Oh, wait a minute. I almost forgot the farm pictures." She walked over and took them out of a nearby drawer, spread them out on the table, then watched him shuffle through them. "Well, what do you think? Pretty neat farm, huh?"

Slate studied the images. "I have to say you have sparked my interest."

"What about the spots?" Julie persisted, "Are you intrigued?"

Picking up a picture, he looked more closely. "I wouldn't go that far. Was it raining the day you went out there?"

"No. It was a pleasant, clear day."

"Well, then maybe the spots are from dust particles, or could be your film was bad." Slate laid the pictures aside, pulled Julie close and gave her a kiss. With her in the comfort of his arms, he gave her a rather sheepish smile, "Julie, there's no one like you, and I wouldn't have you any other way, but take a look outside. If the weather permits, tomorrow before your shift begins, I'll take you to this farm of yours."

Slate had made a good point. She could see the snow hit the windowpane and hear the wind howling outside. "It's just I'm excited, and I want you to see it."

"I know you're anxious, but you can wait a few more hours, can't you?"

"Okay, I guess. I'll see you early in the morning, and

thanks again for making my 30<sup>th</sup> birthday extra special. You know, I wasn't looking forward to leaving my twenties behind. You made that transition less painful. I love you for that."

"You're welcome. By the way, congratulations on the beginnings of your new journey. I can't wait to see where it takes you." He walked to the door, opened it, and gave her a final goodnight kiss.

"Neither can I." She closed the door behind him and leaned her back against it. "Neither can I."

With thoughts of uncertainty still dancing throughout her mind, Julie returned to her den and seated herself comfortably on the couch. Within seconds, various impulses had organized themselves into a last minute revelation. Therefore, wasting not another minute, Julie made an anxious call.

"Hello, Dad, how are you?"

"Jewels, I'm fine. What's going on?"

"Oh, Slate just left for the evening, thought I'd call."

"I'm glad, just a little surprised, that's all."

"Actually, Dad I was wondering if you could help me out."

"May I ask what you've gotten yourself into?"

"You know me much too well, I'm afraid."

"I should, my blood runs through your veins. So out with it."

"Oh, I'm so wound up! I've found a farm I want to buy. My plan is to rent it out and let the renter ultimately make the monthly payment for me."

"How can I help?"

"Dad, the owner of the farm has made me a fantastic offer. My problem is coming up with the down payment."

"Jewels, your call couldn't have come at a more convenient time."

"How so?"

"Well, I've been pondering the moving idea myself."

"Really, that's great."

"Tell you what I'll do. I'll come down and look at this farm of yours, maybe even rent it from you."

"Oh, Dad, I would simply love that."

"Me too, Jewels."

As Julie returned the receiver to its cradle, she felt a sense of peace. She hadn't seen much of her dad after he divorced her mom and moved away. Now, besides buying the farm, it seemed she might have the opportunity to bond with him again.

She was still reeling with excitement, so she once again picked up and dialed her dearest friend. "Guess what? I hope it's not too late to call, but I have to share the news with you. I've committed to buy the farm."

"Congratulations. I know how bad you wanted this to happen. I'm glad, really, but..." Bailey managed to say. Although, in her heart, she had reservations regarding this venture.

In fact, the orbs in Julie's pictures had made her have an uneasy feeling in the pit of her stomach. She had taken it upon herself to do a little research.

She'd found a leading theory stating orbs are not spirits themselves, but energy being transferred from a source to the spirit, so they can manifest. Securing this information did little to ease Bailey's mind. However, she wished the best for her friend. She was especially grateful that she wasn't the one making the move to the country.

"But what?"

"I don't know. Those orb things just creep me out. Are you sure you want to go ahead with this?"

"I'm sure. And guess what else?"

"What?"

"I think my dad may be my renter."

That relieved Bailey's mind somewhat. "I think that's great."

"I think so, too. Well, I'll let you go, just wanted to

share."

"Goodnight."

Julie leaned back into her recliner. She closed her eyes and allowed her memories of her little retreat on her aunt's farm to play repeatedly in her mind.

*At the same time, with a somewhat pleasant look on his face, the unrelenting chief was doing the same.*

# CHAPTER 4

On an early Monday morning, with her anticipation at its highest level, Julie received the call that would virtually shape the next thirty-five years of her life. Little did she know she was about to embark on a wild journey. Willing or not, she was going to be a key player.

"Hello." She heard Ervin's voice on the other end.

"Meet me at the title company. We're going to close today."

Her heart raced. "Be there soon." She was more than ready to turn the page of her life to a new chapter.

When all the papers were signed, Ervin placed the long awaited farmhouse key into Julie's hand. She clutched it tightly and threw her arms around him. "Thank you so much!"

She waved goodbye, returned home, and sat at the kitchen table contemplating on whether she had moved far too fast with the purchasing of this 125-acre paradise. With those thoughts darting in and out of her mind, she ran her fingers up and down the long, tubular-shaped key. It was of a dark gray color and looked old and mysterious. Julie quickly became aware of the hollow-tapping sound it made when she lightly struck it on the edge of the table.

*What kind of secrets have you been keeping locked up*

*all these years?* She stared endlessly at its unique shape. Unable to suppress her anxiety, she felt like she was merely wasting time. She climbed into her pickup and headed down the country road toward the farm.

As she rounded the last curve, she swerved. "No!" A group of horse riders were on her side of the road. The sudden swerve soon headed her toward the ditch. Quickly slamming on her brakes, she found herself teetering on the edge. Nervously looking around, she noticed one of the riders approaching.

"Are you okay?" His eyes were huge. "I'm so sorry. We only stopped for a moment to watch Madelyn work her jumpers. Everyone in the neighborhood knows she's a well-known horse whisperer. However, that's no excuse for our carelessness. I sincerely apologize."

"I'm fine, really," she insisted. "No visible harm done."

In a calmer more relaxed voice, he said, "Then let me introduce myself. I'm Alex. I live up at the crossroads with my wife and three children. Those guys are friends of mine, Bill and Alan."

"Glad to meet you. I'm Julie." She extended her hand. "I'm your new neighbor. Ervin spoke highly of both you and Madelyn."

"Have you met her?"

"No, I haven't, but I'm glad to learn you both love horses. Someday, I plan to have one of my own."

"A farm isn't complete without one, you know. Well, you have a nice day now, and again I am so sorry for our carelessness." He waved goodbye.

Shortly, Julie pulled her pickup onto the little dirt driveway. A thrill of expectation surged throughout her entire body. "Well, here it is. It may need a little work, but it's beautiful to me." Tears of joy spilled from her eyes. She'd had this dream for such a long time. To have a farm, and finally through some kind of spiritual happening, it was a reality.

"I can imagine this little house with some new paint, possibly a porch swing, a farm dog, a new barn, and last but not least, a beautiful horse in the pasture."

Julie opened her door and stepped out. She was immediately sheathed with a warm, welcoming breeze, reminding her of her first visit. She smiled as it embraced her.

*The powerful Hunting Bear, of the infamous legend, stood just inches away in a different realm. He was content with knowing that Julie would occasionally make an appearance on the farm.*

It was around 4:00 o'clock when the sound of Slate's truck finally caught Julie's attention. She stepped out on the porch and watched him get out of his vehicle.

"How are things going?" he asked.

"Better now that you're here." She loved the way he made her feel safe and alive at the same time.

"I thought you deserved a break." He smiled just before pulling her close.

At last he released his hold, grabbed a picnic basket he'd brought, and headed inside. Soon the couple was sitting in the middle of the kitchen floor enjoying their meal. Among the topics of discussion were Julie's thoughts about her farm improvements along with her explanation of the harrowing event, which had led up to her meeting Alex.

"Well, I see your first day will be one to remember."

"You could say that. Apart from nearly crashing my pickup, I really do feel at peace here."

"I'm sorry the timing isn't right for us to move out here."

"You're not half as sorry as I am. I envy my dad getting to enjoy this country lifestyle, while I have to wait several more years."

*The chief, on this 28<sup>th</sup> day of February 1978, couldn't agree more. Therefore, as he watched the couple drive away, the wheels were already turning in the mind of this persistent, powerful one. No one would ultimately interfere with the fulfillment of his vital goal, no one.*

# CHAPTER 5

On this brisk Saturday morning as the couple pulled into the farm driveway, Julie spotted her dad.

"Good morning, Jewels." He waved.

Catching up to him, she asked, "Would you care to join us for a walk?"

"Not right now. You kids go ahead."

Nearly every weekend a walk or some fun project, of sorts, was on the agenda. When they were in season, Julie enjoyed hunting Morel mushrooms. If an abundant supply were found, she would either freeze or share them with friends. They were one of her seasonal favorites.

Of course, she never missed an opportunity to climb up on the farm tractor her dad bought. It fit her like a glove. She was soon pushing and pulling down trees damaged from ice storms; thus, allowing her to make trails that ran across and throughout her entire farm.

If there were one disappointment about this farm, it would be the fact she could not find a naturally fed spring. After a good rain, you would find her removing rocks from the wet ones. She always hoped to hit the jackpot and discover a lasting one. It did not seem quite fair. Her neighbor, Madelyn, owned fewer acres, and she had two. Nevertheless, Julie cherished this simple time in her life, and she was not going to let anything distract her for very long, not even the harsh winter, which was currently coming to an end.

After walking deeper into the woods, Julie motioned Slate to stop and rest for a moment. They sat on the remains of an old Oak discussing their future and all at once, Julie's focus changed. She stood up and shouted, "This is it. This is the spot!"

"What spot are we talking about?" Slate looked strangely at her.

Julie pointed while walking to a nearby area. "This right here," she motioned, "reminds me of my little retreat on my aunt's farm."

## CHAPTER 6

It would be a late fall afternoon that Julie received a nice surprise. The sky was a vibrant, sapphire color, with a slight breeze that carried the fallen leaves about. The snapping of small twigs made rabbits freeze in their tracks, then dart for cover.

In the distance, Julie and Slate watched as a reddish-brown fox nearly ran right in front of them before disappearing out of sight. While being somewhat mesmerized with nature at its best this morning, Julie suggested they sit for a minute longer. Nonchalantly, Slate took her by the hand.

"I have a Christmas surprise for you." He smiled with excitement. "I can't keep it a secret any longer. I'm building you a cabin on this very spot."

"What?" She gazed into the eyes of the man she loved. "You're serious!" Julie screamed in a high-pitched tone. "You really, really mean it?"

She stood up, ran around in circles, kicked up the fallen leaves, and pushed Slate to the ground, landing right on top of him. "Thank you from the bottom of my heart. Do you realize what this means?"

"No, not really, but I'm sure you're going to enlighten me."

"We'll be able to spend more time here. I can't believe it's finally going to happen."

*She was ecstatic and at that very moment, she was not the only one. The chief, himself, could not be happier with this news.*

The actual construction of the cabin began the first week in December 1983. It would bring Julie's childhood back into her adult world. The one-room, cedar-slab cabin was located in a valley surrounded by trees which would hide it from the world.

It had a long front porch and a large back window allowing a nice view of the hill that stood between it and the river. Yet, most importantly, Julie helped to construct a nearby fire ring making the area complete. After Slate had driven the last nail, she took a step back and admired his labor of love.

"It's so beautiful!" she shouted. "Don't you just love it out here?"

Before answering, Slate paused. A whitish-like shadow rushed passed his vision. He rubbed his eyes and shook his head. "I do, but if I lived to be one-hundred years old, I couldn't possibly love it to the degree you do."

Seeing Slate rub his eyes, Julie merely thought he was tired. She actually had no way knowing the tension mounting on this somewhat puzzling farm of hers.

*Each day, the chief patiently watches and waits, in the shadows, to fulfill his legacy.*

"I'm the luckiest woman." Julie smiled at Slate's accomplishment. "I never want our life to change. I want to stay here forever and live the simple life like my ancestors."

That evening as the darkness approached, the couple

nestled around a rather relaxing campfire. At the same time, Slate admired her handiwork. "By the way, how many trips would you estimate it took you to make this fire ring?"

"Too many to count but each trip was made with love. I cannot even imagine this little cabin without it. Can you?" While looking in his direction, Julie hesitated. "I don't know what could make me any happier. It is a beautiful night, and I'm sitting here around this charming campfire with everything I ever wanted." Julie caught a glimpse of the Big Dipper twinkling overhead and sighed. "What more could a girl ask for?"

Slate raised his head and looked intently at her. Julie caught a slight sparkle in his eyes radiating through the reflection of the flames. Then a grin began slowly and widened to a smile. Julie's breath caught in her throat. She began to tremble inside. His love for her was evident in his expression.

"Julie, we've known each other for some time now." He took her by the hand. "In the beginning of our relationship, I never imagined this moment. I never really thought I would say these words to you. I want you to marry me. I love you. Will you marry me?"

His words lingered in the quiet night, just long enough for a cool puff of air to stir the embers and whisk them into flight. She had never seen anything like it. Speechless and totally taken by surprise, Julie could hardly find her voice. "You have made my life complete, Slate, but marriage? I'm not sure I'm ready for that." She cleared her throat. "You know we have to be realistic. First, there is the fact I am older, and don't forget about my desire to embrace my Indian culture. Right now you're okay with the differences, but what about the future?"

No sooner had the words left Julie's mouth than a slight rain began to fall, masquerading her tear-filled eyes. It seemed such a joyful occasion had turned sad. With the rain intensifying, the couple quickly stood up and ran to the porch for cover. Seeing a blanket on the porch swing, Slate quickly grabbed it and put it around her. He then leaned over and whispered, "Do you have any idea what it would mean to me to hear you say yes? Just so you know, I don't have plans of giving up."

*The chief smiled. "Neither do I. Neither do I."*

# CHAPTER 7

Author's note: *Each year many couples travel to Hot Springs, Arkansas, to be married. In fact, Congress had previously set aside the popular site as a federally protected area. Cool mineral water continues to flow, even today, from the magical springs. Legends tell us tribes at war often laid down their arms for the healing waters in the valley of the vapors.*

It was no wonder Julie, being of Indian descent, would choose Hot Springs for her big day. Slate was pleased he had finally won the battle, more than pleased. Her saying yes made his life complete. However, he knew Julie had a hole in her heart. Something was missing. He understood he might never find the key in healing this void, but he had to at least give it a try.

A week prior to their wedding day, the couple went to the city shopping for their wedding bands. After looking at several, they mutually agreed on matching gold and silver ones. Picking out the rings that evening brought Julie's emotions to the surface. Slate had softened her heart, and she felt the time for marriage was right.

On the morning of September 14, 1985, Julie rose early. "You do look sharp." She playfully flirted with Slate, squeezing his cheeks with both hands and planting a kiss on his lips. "Come stand by me in front of the mirror. I want to see how we look as a couple. Well, what do you think?" She studied their reflection.

"You know, I fell in love with a lady wearing blue jeans. I can surely marry her dressed that same way."

"Thank you." She gushed. "My pink blouse does go well with your pink shirt, don't you think?"

Putting his arms around her, Slate replied, "I do."

"No. Don't say that just yet," she interrupted. "Save those words for the minister."

*The chief, who was watching from his vantage point, could only shake his head. Would Julie's marriage somehow place a wedge into the fulfillment of the prophecy he was so destined to bring to an end? Only time would tell.*

# CHAPTER 8

What a whirlwind day it had been. The sun's rays had faded away, and the newlyweds were enjoying the fruits of one of Hot Springs famous spas. No one felt more pampered than Julie did. She closed her eyes in contentment, her mind transfixed to a few hours earlier. She had nervously stood before Reverend Reid holding a red bouquet.

"I'm a very lucky lady today." She leaned back into the moment of solitude and indulging pleasure. She had received from Slate his promise of continued love and protection. In return, he had received what he had wanted for a very long time, her hand in marriage.

After having spent a surmountable time enjoying the spa treatment, they decided to continue their exploration of the town. Two days of enjoying the sights ended. The couple had participated in, among other things, a midnight swim, a climb to the highest tower, a viewing of the alligator farm, and the checking out of a few flea markets.

Alas, it was time for them to return to their house in the city. Upon pulling into their driveway, Slate pointed. "Is that what I think it is? It sure looks like a banner hanging across the front door?"

Julie couldn't help but laugh. "Oh, how funny. It really

is a homemade banner. I bet my sister, Carol, is responsible."

They both stood, for the longest time, chuckling at the butcher paper draped across the front door bearing well wishes.

"You know," Julie began, "on a similar note, Carol sends me a homemade birthday card every year. She is so creative."

"You want to see how creative I can be?" Slate moaned against her lips. Then sweeping her into his arms, carried her across the threshold.

The following morning, the couple rose bright and early.

"Hmm. Is this how being married in 1985 feels?" Julie asked.

"Pretty much so, I guess."

Julie shivered with overwhelming pleasure. She couldn't be happier. She had married Slate, the man who vowed to protect her as long as he lived. She knew their mutual love for one another would grow more and more through the years. What could ever shatter the blissful feeling she had waited for so long to receive?

* * *

The next two months flew by. Julie spent her weekends secluded in the midst of wilderness in her personal little hideaway.

One night, while gazing at a midnight blue sky, with only a sliver of a moon present, Julie brought up a lingering question. "Do you know what's missing at the farm?"

Slate scratched his head and thought a moment before answering. "Nothing as far as I'm concerned."

"Don't you remember last week? My dad brought up the subject."

"Oh, now I recall. I agreed then, and I agree now about getting a dog for the farm."

"Think we can go look for one tomorrow?"

"Sure, but right now, I have something else in mind." He smiled and took her into his arms and kissed her passionately.

The following morning, Julie was primed and anxious. She could hardly wait to visit the Humane Society. "Are you ready?"

"Can you, at least, let me take a shower first?"

"Okay, if you insist but please hurry."

Once they were on the way, the couple discussed a variety of names. Ultimately, they agreed on Tonka, a beloved pet name from Julie's childhood.

Upon arriving at their destination, Julie and Slate were escorted to a large room filled with several rows of cages.

In the second row, a three-month-old black German shepherd caught Julie's interest. It was pretty much love at first sight. Shortly thereafter, Julie carried their newly acquired ten pounds of joy to the truck.

She smiled and looked down at their new addition. "I don't think the thirty-five dollar investment was too bad."

He noticed Tonka snuggled under her arm. "Me either and since we're in town, I'd like to go by the Honda dealership. I want to see what kind of a deal I can make on a four-wheeler."

"Okay, then we'll need to buy some puppy supplies."

What a hectic day. They had not only added a puppy to the farm but also a four-wheeler. Julie was extremely happy. That night a new family member snuggled at the foot of their bed.

The next morning, to their astonishment, the ground was covered in snow. Julie took Tonka outside and set him down into the white, downy stuff. His paws sank in, and the snow nearly embellished him. Julie laughed at the little black spot trying to navigate throughout the yard.

Suddenly, Tonka halted at an outburst of an unfamiliar noise. She picked him up and tried to comfort him.

"It's okay. It's only Slate playing with his new toy. You'll soon get used to hearing that sound. Slate, wait for us," Julie hollered above the noise.

The couple, along with Tonka, spent over two hours that day riding throughout the hills and hollows of the farm, enjoying every minute of this new adventure. Julie was happy with this new life. She was living in the country, or at best on the weekends, married to a marvelous man, and of course, she had just added a final addition named, Tonka.

*Nonetheless, the chief had yet to secure his own happiness, and his patience was at an all-time low.*

# CHAPTER 9

Julie wanted to spend more and more time on the farm. You might say she was becoming addicted to the soaring Eagles overhead, and the nightly sounds of those mysteriously distant beating drums. Where were they coming from anyway, plus the warm breezes? Somehow, they offered her comfort and a sense of protection.

"Slate, I've been thinking about quitting my manufacturing job and going into business for myself."

"Really, where did that crazy notion come from?"

She heard the shock in his voice. "I want to spend more time here in the country."

"So, you're just going to throw away nearly fifteen years of retirement? Let me see if I understand." He sat up in a more attentive position. "You want to start a business of some sort. What did you have in mind, a dress shop or something like that?"

"No, a concrete company."

"In case you haven't noticed, women these days don't own concrete companies. Did you factor that into your equation?"

Unfortunately, Slate had no idea how much control the chief was beginning to have over Julie. In fact, because of his religious background, he would never concede to there being a spirit of any kind on the farm. Therefore, unless Julie had some hard evidence otherwise, she might as well save her breath.

She ignored his skepticism. "Yes, I did plenty of factoring, and I'll become the first WBE or Woman Business Enterprise construction owner in our state. You can work for me. That's if you don't have a problem working for a woman."

"I don't see a problem. You can have all the glory, all the headaches." He glanced across the table at her. "Now that the shock has somewhat subsided, your idea doesn't sound half bad. By the way, that's only because you would have the best foreman in the state working for you."

"Really." She smiled at his challenge.

While lying in bed that night, Julie spent several restless hours tossing and turning. Her mind just wouldn't shut down. However, all that business talk hadn't caused Slate to lose one wink of sleep.

Much to Julie's surprise, she woke up early the next morning, with little remorse from her decision. By the time Slate made his way into the kitchen, the wheels of progress were already set into motion. "I've started putting things together for the business."

Slate took a seat at the table. "That's great. I'm proud of you."

She smiled and gave him a kiss. "Thank you."

* * *

Weeks had passed since Julie applied for certification. She had just about given up on the whole idea, when the letter came. Her hands trembled. She nervously opened the envelope. It was official! She was certified!

She'd been checking out established companies. Soon she had secured a thriving business. Her dream of spending more time at the farm materialized, and she was quite happy with her new lifestyle.

"It's really good to hear the confidence in your voice," Bailey told her one afternoon. "In looking back, I can admit I was wrong about the whole farm idea. It seems to complete you."

*However, the chief was but a mere distance away contemplating a sinister plan. One which would send Julie's life into a tailspin of unimaginable proportion.*

# CHAPTER 10

*Julie's world of contentment escalated beyond her control in the summer of 1988.*

She hummed under her breath. She loved being on the farm with Slate. The sound of Tonka barking filled the air. She turned to see what was going on.

"Tonka get over here," Slate shouted.

Julie saw a man appear from the woods. He barely even acknowledged her but focused his attention on Slate. What was he doing in the middle of the woods?

"Good afternoon." The man stuck out his hand. "My name is LJ. I'm your neighbor from down the road apiece. I was hunting the river. As I grew nearer to your cabin, I got a whiff of charcoal. I assumed from a grill or something."

"It's nice to meet you," Slate said, shaking the man's hand. "This is my wife, Julie."

"Hello."

"Hi." She wasn't at all sure she liked this man. However, she really didn't have a reason not to. Slate's voice drew her attention.

"Would you care to join us for lunch?"

"I wouldn't want to impose; however, those burgers sure smell inviting."

Slate pointed. "Pull up a lawn chair."

Looking around the cabin site, LJ continued, "You two sure must like your privacy."

"We do." A cold chill came over her. She did not care for the way the man was studying their place. It was almost as if he was casing it for further reference.

From day one of meeting LJ, Slate began to distance himself from her. Only a few weeks had gone by since then, and she could not put her finger on what was going on. Her husband's personality seemed to be changing. He was not his happy-go-lucky self.

Looking for, and needing support, she turned to Bailey. "You were right to have doubts about this farm." She sniffed and wiped tears from her cheeks. "Everything began changing since LJ came into our lives. Why, I don't understand?"

"I'm so sorry. Is there anything I can do?"

"I don't know. I just don't know." A hollow ache welled up inside her. She was afraid she was going to lose her husband, but what did LJ have to do with it?

Feeling desperate one morning at the breakfast table, she decided to confront Slate about it. "You look like you're carrying the fate of the world on your shoulders. What's wrong, Slate? Anything you care to share with me?"

"Nope, I'm good." She found the cheeriness he interjected into his voice simply a put on.

His response was irritating. She knew he was lying, but she wouldn't push it, not right now. However, it made her plunge headlong into the other concern plaguing her mind. She took a drink of coffee before setting her cup down. "There's something else."

Slate glanced up from his newspaper. "Yes? What now?"

"What's going on with you and LJ?" An uncomfortable look flashed across Slate's face.

"You won't admit it, will you?" Clearing his throat and

crumpling his newspaper, he spoke with a cynical voice.

What was he talking about? She gulped. "Admit what?"

"That you let LJ get under your skin for some reason. That's all."

Julie's eyebrows arched from the anger building inside. Was Slate defending LJ or demeaning her? As she readied herself for a verbal battle, Slate tried to bring their conversation to a screeching halt.

"Is there anything else, or can I finish my paper?"

Fuming at his arrogance, Julie bit the soft inner flesh of her cheek. She pushed back her chair and paced the floor in a vain attempt to disperse her frustration. "That's it?" She couldn't believe it. "I think we need to have a serious talk."

"Okay." Slate watched her walk to the other end of the table before sitting down again.

By now, she could barely control the tapping of her right foot. It was a sign of nervousness she hated.

"Well, come on, spit it out. I don't have all day."

She glanced down at her wedding band. Was she doing the right thing? She was aching for the feel of him against her, yearning for his warmth, his protection, not an argument. Remaining silent, not knowing what to say, she glanced across the table at him. Her broken heart was nearly beating out of her chest.

With one eyebrow raised, Slate leaned back on his chair. "Don't blame this on LJ. You just have quite an imagination. By the way, since you started this conversation, my employees have been digging me a little bit about my authority, or lack of, on the job site. Seems I have very little power, since you're the boss. I can't even write a check or make a decision without your say-so. I'm the foreman who has to call his wife for permission to do my job."

Suddenly, Julie felt an electric shock coiled up her spine, forcing her to sit at attention. Slate presented a good argument. Few men had to deal daily with a female boss and even fewer had their wife as a boss.

Julie slowly cleared her throat before speaking. "Slate, I had no idea. However, I can see it has put a wedge in our marriage. I'm okay with transferring the business over to you. Is that what you want?"

"It would be a start anyway." Slate quickly jumped at the opportunity.

For several days, Julie wrestled with the idea of allowing Slate to take over her company. She finally came to terms that, just perhaps, the arrangement could work out in her favor; so the next day she called her attorney.

Upon leaving his office, Slate looked over at her. "Thank you for your confidence. It is so important to have the respect from the men working under me. I didn't think it would be an issue in the beginning, but I was wrong."

Julie had been willing to try everything to have her old life back, even walking away from her own company. However, it wasn't long before she had second thoughts about her decision. The relationship between them had definitely not improved, and she was worried.

# CHAPTER 11

One morning, Julie woke up in a cold sweat. She had just dreamed Slate was doing drugs. His mood did seem to change daily, and she was suspicious. In fact, her dream could very well be a reality, with LJ being his pusher. Since her patience was growing thin, she decided to investigate.

She began her search today by going through dresser drawer after dresser drawer. Not finding anything, she walked into the living room. There, on the end of the couch, lay Slate's work clothes where he had evidently left them by mistake. If he wasn't going to work, where was he going?

She picked up his clothing and something fell onto the floor. When she looked down, she saw a spoon and a syringe needle. "No, not Heroin," she screamed. While still standing there in a daze, she heard Tonka bark.

LJ barely had time to step up on the porch when Julie approached him. "You got my husband involved in drugs, didn't you? We were doing just fine before you came along. Why can't you leave him alone?"

LJ gave her a sheepish grin and looked pleased with himself. "I can't. He's one of my best money sources, thanks to you."

Julie's throat went dry. What did he mean by that?

Inhaling deeply, she tried to maintain her control as she watched the smugness on his face. At that instant, her mind rushed to thoughts of her company.

Feelings of ice ran from the bottom of her spine to the top of her head. She dropped everything and hurried to her pickup, leaving LJ standing on the porch with a self-satisfied look. Her mind was now like an explosive battleground of emotion. She frantically burst into the office.

After spending several hours looking over records and placing numerous telephone calls, Julie was devastated to learn Slate had lost contracts, sold equipment, and virtually had the company in bankruptcy.

Gripping the arms of her chair, she tried to force her mind into acceptance. A jagged pain stabbed through her heart. With tears streaming down her face, she somehow managed to reach the nearby phone. Crying profusely, she mumbled to herself, "Please pick up. Please pick up, Bailey."

Julie stood and forced herself against the wall. Her knuckles turned white from her tight grip. She tried slowing her racing thoughts down by taking in sips of air and exhaling. It had been seconds but seemed like minutes before hearing a familiar voice.

"Hello."

"Bailey."

"Julie, what's wrong?"

As she spoke, her voice trembled. "How could I have been so stupid? How could I have walked away and let Slate ruin my company?"

Without hesitating, Baily said, "I'll be right there."

In a matter of minutes, Bailey came rushing through the door. "I'm so sorry, Julie."

"Now I can see that moving to the country was a mistake." She wept as she informed her friend of the ugly truth about her company and Slate's involvement into the world of drugs. "You were right. I should have listened to you." Realizing there was little she could do, Julie hesitantly walked over, flipped off the light switch on her once promising, productive company, and closed the door behind them.

"Thanks for coming," she sobbed. "There are so many thoughts and emotions darting in and out of my head right now. I just need some quiet time to process and put it all into perspective."

"Remember, Julie. I'm only a phone call away."

"I know," she said, giving her friend a hug. Upon climbing behind the wheel of her pickup, Julie looked into her rearview mirror at her swollen eyes. Music began blaring; she immediately reached to shut off the sound. She needed total silence.

Once, she arrived and entered the security of the little cabin, she opened the windows and doors in an attempt to allow the crisp night air to clear her mind. Catching a glimpse of her wedding photo sitting nearby, she wanted to scream.

Memories started rushing in and out of her mind at warp speed. She loved so many things about Slate, now she was about to lose him and everything else. She stepped outside for a moment trying to calm herself down. Before long, she had a flashback of her actual wedding day and how happy and carefree they both were.

As they were driving along the busy highway to Hot Springs that day, Slate suddenly pulled to the side of the road, just feet away from a small creek. They looked at each other, rolled up their pant legs, and waded right into the flowing, cool creek-water, stumbling over moss-covered rocks as they searched for crystals. She allowed herself a small grin reflecting on Slate in his wedding clothes trying not to slip and fall. Life seemed perfect then.

As she continued to reminisce, she remembered how

Slate had showed her the way to live, love, and be happy every day. Yet, here and now, she was feeling lost and out of place. She longed for the comfort of his embrace, the safety of his touch. She wanted him to take her into his arms and protect her.

She yearned for the mere contact of his lips on hers, being unpredictably, unquestionably sensual.

Unable to cope with this rollercoaster feeling, she went back inside and threw herself onto the bed. Then using her pillow as a punching bag, she pounded away at it while wishing the cabin would cave in and end all her pain and misery.

In a final, desperate attempt to shut out all the light, the sounds, and her throbbing mind, she buried her head deep inside.

Unable to control this restlessness, she tossed the lifeless pillow aside and walked back outdoors. Before long, she caught a glimpse of the full moon and its draw to the familiar pathway. As she began a somber walk in that direction, her shadow silhouetted the ground along with Tonka's who had quietly joined her. She silently bent down and acknowledged her loyal companion. He seemed to understand her plight.

Sometime later, she reached her private sanctuary and gave vent to the long held-back frustrations holding her mind captive. She was not only angry about her failed marriage, her failed company but also her failed attempt at finding lasting peace on the farm she had grown to love.

She desperately needed, almost craved, a form of reassurance that she wasn't a failure. She felt like nothing without somebody. Then from out of nowhere, her mind flashed back to her previous dream of the young brave who told her he was nothing without her.

Slowly but deliberately, Julie's mood of anxiousness subsided, and she became aware of the silence surrounding her. She had never witnessed phenomena of this magnitude.

Had the noises been quieted in order to listen to what she had to say? Had they somehow felt her pain? Her only response was a mere trace of a sound coming from her beating heart and even that sounded wounded.

Looking toward the heavens for a form of acknowledgement, Julie noticed how the full moon had now taken refuge behind shred-like clouds. It seemed to be afraid to glow at its full capacity. How sad it looked to her, how vulnerable. It really did seem to emulate her pain.

While helplessly standing there on the hilltop searching for answers, a warm, gentle sensation began to encase her shoulders, eventually sheathing itself completely around her body. Succumbing to the warmth and protection it provided, Julie's mind momentarily relaxed. That was until Tonka licked her hand, bringing her back to consciousness and the realization that the night noises had suddenly returned.

Then, from the now enhanced moon's glow, Julie's attention was drawn to the dancing trees. They seemed to have come alive with their native shadow dancing. As she watched their spectacular performance, she wondered if she would ever be able to embrace and enjoy dancing with them again. Finally, a smile had its beginnings and even though there was chaos and indecision still going on inside, she somehow felt a form of peace. Before long, she began her trek back down the hillside.

The next morning arrived much too soon. Julie stirred only slightly before turning her head. Tears, more of frustration than fear, trickled down her pale cheeks. She again realized she was alone. Looking in the mirror, the words I have to go on with my life, silently moved across her lips.

It wasn't long before she opened the cabin door and stepped out into the morning's light. As usual, Tonka was there to greet her. He wagged his tail and patiently waited for her to scratch behind his ear.

"Good morning," she began while touching, with teary eyes, all the things that mattered to her and wished them a final, heartfelt farewell.

For the first time, the land was sad, or at least it seemed that way to her. The birds were singing a different song these days, and she missed their joyful sound. With every tear that fell, Julie's connection with the land grew stronger. However, she had the urge to run back to the city and away from the place that had brought her happiness yet so much pain. The city now seemed to be her destiny but was it?

She quickly considered the fact she may never find happiness again on the farm. Was it somehow responsible for her misery? She wished she knew and then, perhaps, it would help the nagging feeling inside her vanish. It was, at that moment, she looked up and saw her dad coming down her driveway. She managed a wave in his direction.

He waved back. "Good morning, Jewels."

Walking closer, Julie let it all spill out of her mouth. "Dad, you know that Slate and I haven't been real happy for some time now. He has changed, particularly since his friendship with LJ. Well, I've come to terms my marriage is over."

Not allowing her dad to interject, she wanted him to know about her decision. "Last night, up on the hill, I vented out most of my anger and, in saying that, I've made up my mind to return to the city."

"Are you sure, Jewels?" He saw the heartache in his daughter's eyes. "What can you do in the city to make your life better that you can't do out here in the country?"

"I don't have it all figured out, yet. I'll let you know once I do."

"Are you planning to leave soon?"

"Yes. I plan to leave this morning."

"Well, give your dad a hug." He embraced her, shook his head, and watched his daughter disappear out of view.

At one time, she had been strong, successful, and confident. Nevertheless, in a single moment of time, a snap of the finger, her life had been altered. Nothing would ever be the same. All that was left was to pick up those shattered dreams and move on. Slate had promised to love and protect her forever. In her heart, she still believed that was true, but she hoped to someday know real love.

*It's only a matter of time, the chief wanted to blurt out as he observed the tears trickle down her cheeks. How could he convey to her that her life's journey was scripted, that her failed business and ultimately failed marriage were merely Chapter one of a carefully choreographed manuscript.*

# CHAPTER 12

Unexpectedly, on Julie's 40th birthday, a work opportunity came along. It ultimately sent her on the next leg of her journey. Bailey's sister had opened a small bar north of town and since the business started slow, Julie volunteered to help her for only the tips she would receive.

Nonetheless, the expenses of running the bar were greater than the income. It was soon evident, the bar wasn't going to survive. It was during this time; Julie was introduced to George, a regular customer. He told her he was sorry the bar was going under, but he would like to give the business a try himself.

"You're a natural, come work for me," he suggested to Julie. "All I need to make it a reality is an investor."

It only took Julie a moment. "I'll be your investor."

"Great." He shook her hand. "You got yourself a deal."

Unfortunately, George was not a good person, and his bar was also soon headed for closure. One night, having reached his wits end, George simply walked away from both the bar and Julie. Therefore, accepting the challenge set before her, she turned the failing bar into a successful nightclub.

Although, after the first year, its fast pace and bright lights began to drain her spirit. Therefore, to get away momentarily, Julie found herself slowly returning to the farm. Needless to say, she was again greeted with a warm reception that had a way of welcoming her. She was temporarily able to set the past aside, at least for now.

As time went on, Julie began making more and more frequent visits, which was just fine with not only the chief but her dad and Slate, as well.

Living back in the city and trying to move on took a toll on her. However, she came to terms with the realization even though marriage wasn't right for her; she and Slate could still be friends. He was off drugs and almost back to being his old self. She was proud of him for that.

In a roundabout way, they developed a long-lasting friendship better than their marriage. Slate continued to protect her from the sideline. Many nights they could be found still sitting around a quaint little campfire on top of the hill.

Her dad never quite understood why his daughter couldn't stay put in one place. "You're like a roaming gypsy," he would tell her.

Wapa and Bailey also had their concerns about their friend's unsettling ways, but they knew Julie. She would still, on occasions, invite them to be a part of her fascinating, intriguing, and yet, sometimes, mysterious world.

It would be on a warm Saturday morning in 1989 that Julie made a visit to the farm. Her dad met her outside. He was all smiles as he greeted her.

"Jewels, I'm glad you're here. I have a surprise for you. Meet me at the barn in five minutes."

She thought for a moment. *What was this all about?*

Immediately, upon stepping inside the barn, Julie stopped in her tracks.

"Oh my. Oh my!" she stammered.

Standing before her in a slight ray of light was the most

beautiful horse Julie had ever seen. Finding herself at a loss for words, she could only stand and gaze.

Reaching the doorway, her dad asked, "Well, what do you think?"

At last, the words came gushing out of her mouth. "Whose horse is this? You know I would love to own a horse like him."

"Would you believe, I had this horse delivered yesterday, and I'm giving him to you? But you need to realize he's not broke, and I know you haven't ridden before and…"

"That's okay, really," Julie interrupted. "I'll find someone to break him, and I'll learn to ride." Thinking quickly on her feet, she added, "Perhaps my neighbor, Alex. By the way, did you know that a horse is an Indian's most prized possession? I'll feel the freedom of my ancestors every time I ride this beautiful horse. Thank you so much. This is the best gift in the whole wide world."

Suddenly, Julie turned around and gave her dad a bear hug. The surprise caught him off guard, nearly causing them both to fall to the ground.

"Could you show a little more excitement?" He laughed.

"Does he have a name?"

"That's your department, Jewels."

"I don't know. My first thought was Spook."

Julie walked over and slowly held out her hand: thus, allowing this new black-colored fox trotter to become acquainted with her scent. Seeing his contentment, she moved around feeling the strong muscles in his legs as well as stroking his flanks.

"He's simply gorgeous," Julie finally breathed approvingly. "Yes," she blurted out. "Because of his nature, I'm going to stick with that name."

"Then Spook it is," he agreed.

# CHAPTER 13

The following Saturday morning, Julie wasted little time in returning to the farm. She strolled into the barn. "Good morning."

Spook neighed gently and nudged her pocket for a treat. It was just beginning to burn off the light coating of frost as Julie led him out into the morning sun.

Noticing Spook's high energy level, she commented, "My, you're in a frisky mood this morning."

Spook stepped up his game and began to prance. The noise his hoofs made against the ground was a welcome sound. She had waited her entire life for a horse like him, and the whickers he shared made her happy.

Julie hesitated a moment, just long enough to rub his nose affectionately. Oh, how she already loved everything about this horse. There was no mistaking a bond was forming.

"Hi, my name is Blake," the words seemed to come from nowhere.

Startled, Julie looked around. "I'm so sorry. I didn't know anyone was within a mile. I'm Julie and this is my new horse, Spook."

"I like that name. I drove by your farm the day Spook was being unloaded. Seeing you outside this morning, I just had to stop. My passion has always been horses."

"Mine too. I mean, I have always loved them from a distance. Spook is actually my first. I can't ride him since he isn't broke." She saw a pleased look spread across the man's face.

"I would love to break him for you."

"You would?" She couldn't believe it. How could she turn him down? "Great!"

"As a matter of fact, I have a saddle in my vehicle. I have the time, so I can start right now if you want."

"Sounds like a good idea to me." She watched him retrieve the saddle. He was a strong man and placed the heavy leather load effortlessly onto Spook's back. She handed the rein to him.

Blake seemed to be a real cowboy knowing just what to do. He put one leg in the stirrup and, in one graceful motion, mounted Spook. The ride was on. Julie could only watch spellbound. Spook did have a wild spirit, but Blake had one of his own. This cowboy wasn't giving up. He rode Spook like a tornado, finally becoming one himself. At last, Spook quieted.

"Blake that was the most beautiful sight I have ever seen."

"Thank you. I would be honored to continue his training. If you like, you could ride my horse, Sebastian, while I get this one ready for you."

"I couldn't ask for more," she gushed.

Julie didn't know it at the time, but Blake was quite grateful for this opportunity. It was but a brief time later, he was stopping by the farm on a regular basis.

Blake was employed at a local warehouse in the city until midnight, and since Julie closed her business at 1:00 a.m., he would often take the hour difference to get the horses ready for their late night rides, many of them lasting until daybreak.

As Julie began to know Blake, she found he was his own

DOMINANCE

man with nothing to prove to anyone. She needed someone like him in her life. Being a religious man, Blake never failed to invite her to church. However, after learning how her faith was more centered on her Indian culture, he didn't insist.

"If you can't come to church, at least stop by my parents' house for Sunday lunch," he would say to her.

Julie soon learned their relationship, because they were from different paths, was one merely out of friendship of their love of riding. Although, she had really grown to like this tall, blue-eyed, tennis shoe, baseball cap-wearing cowboy that explored with her the full moon and dark nights.

On one particular Friday night, it was a full moon. Julie was beside herself to be on the back of Spook. They hadn't been riding for more than fifteen minutes when she pulled Spook's rein to a sudden halt.

"Did you hear that, Blake?" she whispered, while seeing his silhouette etched against the night sky.

Blake shook his head, but then he also heard a sudden flutter go past his ear. He spurred Sebastian through the thicket toward the noise.

Looking about, he remarked, "I think it was merely an owl."

In a composed voice, Julie added, "You're probably right. If I see an owl, hawk, or Eagle, I sense it's a message from the spiritual realm. I'm learning more and more about these animals of the night."

Little did Julie know the sound she heard was far more than the fluttering of an owl's wings. She still didn't fully realize or comprehend the complicated world she has been made a part of. However, right now, she was enjoying her nightly rides and that's all that mattered.

A short time later, Julie once again pulled slightly back on Spook's reins.

"Blake, look at those mounds over there. Ervin pointed

SHARON HOLIMAN

them out to me. It's an old Indian cemetery. Can't you just sense the calmness in this part of the woods?"

"There is a deaf-like silence here. I'll say that for sure."

"Blake, do you believe in spirits?"

"I guess so. I haven't had many personal experiences, how about you?"

"When I ride in the night, I feel a presence, like now, that I can't explain. It's as though someone is guiding and protecting me. As far as that goes, I've always felt welcome on this farm."

"Hmm. How interesting."

Looking around and seeing no one besides the two of them, he asked, "I appear to be the only other person here. You're not actually visualizing someone else are you?" Blake laughed at such a thought.

"You know what I mean. I'm talking about someone from the spiritual realm. I feel like I have a guardian of sorts out here."

"Well, right now I'm your guardian. Is that okay?"

Julie couldn't help but blush at his comment. "Fine with me," she agreed. They disappeared into the world where her ancestors had lived.

With moonlight or darkness, it didn't matter to them that this world didn't have people. The night had its own sound. Julie learned not to speak but to listen in order to get a better understanding of the spirit she believed had taken up residence.

While Blake and Julie rode in the stillness of the night, the horses did a repetitive step to their own beat. In this quietness, there was no need for them to be competitive. Once the reins are dropped, they are free to choose their own steps and path. The fox trotters knew the way home.

The following evening, while riding through an open pasture, Sebastian gave a slight buck and broke from a slow trot into a canter. Blake gave a loud war-whoop of delight as he sat tall in the saddle, moving with the rhythm of

70

Sebastian until they appeared to be one. Their grace and power meshed, and just before reaching the timberline, Blake began to slow Sebastian; thus, allowing Julie to easily catch up. His eyes sparkled with pleasure.

"We'll stop for a little while here to give the horses a breather." He swung his leg over Sebastian's broad back, sliding easily down.

"That was quite refreshing," Julie added as she dismounted.

A few minutes later, Julie's dark hair was again blowing in the wind, and her face was lit by moonlight; but before long, their nightly ride was over and Julie was securing Spook back in the barn.

She couldn't help but smile. She gave Spook a pat on the back. How much her life had changed since he had become a part of it. She knew without him, she wouldn't have this relationship with Blake, and she simply couldn't imagine what her life would be like without either one of them.

Each of Julie's nightly rides was a different experience and challenge. She could hardly wait for the next one. Since Blake had become familiar with all the nearby farmland, he would open gate after gate giving them vastness of freedom. They often built quaint little campfires that would dot the farmland, sending a small ray of light into the stillness of the night.

She remembered it was just a couple of nights ago that she had laughed herself silly at one of Blake's antics. "What do you think you're doing?" she asked, looking around and realizing they were in the midst of a field where cattle were usually fed. She could barely see through the moonlight a huge pile of hay.

Blake ran and thrust himself into the hay. "Come join me."

"I can scarcely see you. You're crazy you know that," she hollered just before she jumped into the midst of the hay. "I can't believe I'm doing this." She threw a big clump towards the sound of his voice.

Before she knew what happened, hay had been thrown everywhere. They were acting like a couple of kids. There was hay in her hair, her mouth, down her back, and all over her clothing. Julie laughed and laughed until her sides felt like they were going to split.

"You look like a scarecrow in someone's garden," she cried hysterically.

"I know another scarecrow standing right beside me," Blake told her while trying to keep a straight face.

He squeezed her hand, gave her an affectionate smile, and never uttered a word. What a fond memory. She wished more than ever she and Blake could find happiness together.

During the next few weeks, they had many more memorable adventures as their nightly rides began without any particular destination in mind. One night, she recalled Blake approaching a dangerous-looking hill.

"No! Don't," she had told him.

There was a small stand of cedar trees on both sides of them. Beyond was a sharp rising bluff. The front of which was harsh and desolate.

"That's far too steep to climb," she shouted.

"You just hide and watch me," Blake hollered back at her.

The size of the hill didn't matter to him. Blake had all the confidence in the world in Sebastian. So, ignoring Julie's plea, he dug Sebastian's hoofs right into the soil, and they continued to climb the hill.

*Thank goodness, he made it. I don't know what I would have done if Sebastian had lost his footing. I shudder to even think about the possibility,* she thought to herself.

"Okay, you've proven your point," she shouted. "Call me chicken if you want, but I'm not climbing that hill."

He replied over his shoulder, "All in good time, my dear

friend."

There was a devil-like glint in Blake's eyes that teased her unbearably. "You really scared me tonight, you know that? I just don't want anything bad to happen to you, that's all."

"I appreciate your concern." He looked over at the sunrise. "Julie it's breathtaking out here this morning. Our ride can't end now."

"I hear what you're saying. I love these rides, and I want to spend every spare minute I have out here. I even asked my dad about staying in his extra bedroom as the cabin isn't available. Slate is currently using it as a hunting lodge. He and a couple of his buddies use it from time to time. Since Slate and I divorced, I seldom use it. Too bad LJ had to bring drugs into our lives. Who knows, maybe things would have turned out differently. Although, we still do have a pretty good relationship for a divorced couple."

Her thoughts reflected to a few months back. "You know, I could have lost my life several months ago."

"What do you mean?" .

"I foiled a sting operation trying to protect that little cabin."

"I don't understand."

"I think LJ was responsible. It still upsets me every time I think about what went down that day."

"What?"

"I was out one afternoon hunting for mushrooms, when I smelled an unusual odor. As I neared my cabin, I found the smell to be coming from inside."

"Did you know what was happening?"

"I put two and two together once I saw an unidentified pickup beside my cabin. From the strong smell, I figured someone had built a meth lab inside. I knew I had to tell the authorities.

"Well, after I called and told them about my suspicion, they went out of their way to ignore me, or they just flat didn't believe me."

"Didn't they at least give you the benefit of the doubt?"

"No. I was so mad; I went back out to the cabin to get evidence with my camera. I was determined not to let LJ win this time. He'd taken enough from me." She cleared her throat. "The drug dealers must have heard me and came running out. They sped away, as though I had scared them off. After I stopped shaking, I went inside the cabin only to find destruction. Among the debris, I was surprised to find several firearms."

"Oh, Julie, you're a braver person than me."

"I know it wasn't very smart. After thinking about the whole thing, I believe I had a protector that day. There's no other explanation for me to be standing here talking with you."

"Did you give the guns to the authorities?"

"No. I decided I would keep them to compensate for the damage that had been done. I hoped the incident would merely fade away, but I was wrong. The following week at work someone handed me a note."

"Weren't you afraid by now? You had no one to go to for help?"

"Yes. The note indicated that if I valued my life, I should drop off the firearms per their instructions. Since the authorities didn't believe me, what other choice did I have? I was definitely scared for a few days. They actually could still carry out their threat. I almost panicked later at hearing a knock on my front door."

"Julie! The drug dealers didn't come back did they?"

"No. It was the authorities, and they were upset with me. I had apparently ruined many pain-staking hours of their work. They were on the verge of making several arrests at the time I alerted the druggies."

"The way I see it, the blame is all on them. They should have told you what they were doing. Surely, they didn't expect you to sit idly by and let them make meth on your farm."

"I know. Since then, however, I have basically walked away from the cabin."

"I'm sorry. The cabin meant so much to you."

Julie shrugged her shoulders. "It's been some time now. I try not to think about it."

Blake looked at his watch and noticed it was getting rather late. "I should be going. I'll return in a few hours."

"Okay. I'll be here, goodbye."

Those hours seemingly flew by and Blake was now more than ever anxious to experience his next intriguing adventure with Julie. That is as long as there wasn't a life-threatening incident lurking around the corner.

"Are you ready, Julie?" he asked. "If there's no objection, I would like to ride down by the river."

"I'm ready, bring it on." She smiled.

As they approached the water, Julie questioned, "What do you think would happen if I rode right into this river? I mean right down the middle, just Spook and me?"

"Nothing," Blake shifted in his saddle. "If the water gets too deep, Spook will float."

Then while leaning lazily on his saddle horn, he informed her that she should hold up her feet.

"Really, let me see?"

That was all it took. There in the moonlight, Julie and Spook went floating down the middle of the river.

"Come on in and join us," she hollered over her shoulder.

"Alright, here we come." Blake splashed into the river. "Yuk. Yuk."

"What's the matter? Are you afraid of a little water?" Julie teased.

"No, I'm not afraid of the water. I have my expensive boots on."

"It'll be okay, just hold your feet up. That's what you told me." Julie laughed at the sight of Blake trying desperately hard to avoid getting his boots wet.

Within twenty minutes of that moment and infamous swim, the couple left the river and resumed their nightly ride; and it wasn't until Julie noticed a slight glow in the east, which signified their ride was about over, that she spoke up.

"I suddenly feel like Cinderella, and the clock is nearing midnight. You know, Blake, I never want this relationship of ours to end. I'm riding on my favorite horse, in my favorite place, with my favorite horse lover."

"I know, and I feel the same way."

Then immediately, their eyes met as the darkness helped hide their secret. That was until the ignited sparks gave it away. Without warning, Spook reared up and Tonka barked causing a decisive break in their connection. Had they crossed some mysterious line?

"It's okay, Julie." Blake was quick to comfort her. "I think it was merely a shadow."

# CHAPTER 14

The following Saturday afternoon, after Blake arrived on a horse that he was training for a thirty-five mile endurance race, Spook suddenly reared up.

"Here, Julie, ride my horse. Maybe I can settle Spook down."

"I don't understand what's going on," Julie stammered as she handed over the reins. "Spook's never acted out like this before."

Anyway, whether something had aggravated or frightened Spook, Julie felt it would be an honor to sit up on Blake's Palomino. While still puzzled over Spook's action, Julie placed her foot into the Palomino's stirrup, but before her mount could be completed, he made a lunge forward causing her to cling on for dear life.

At seeing the forthcoming dirt road in front of her, panic set in. Only barely hanging on, the question in her mind was whether to let go or continue this ride. In the split second the Palomino reached the road's edge, Julie let go. Her body bolted like a human slingshot, landing her in the middle of the road.

As Blake ran to her side, he knew without a doubt she was severely injured. He immediately grabbed her into his arms, carried her to a nearby walnut tree, and tried to make her comfortable.

During those critical minutes of securing transportation, the image of Julie's bruised and injured body kept flashing throughout Blake's mind.

Returning to the tree, he found a stunned and dazed Julie. The hot sun had virtually dried her eyes shut from the gash in her forehead from her embedded sunglasses. Blake didn't realize the severity of her injuries until she tried to move. He reached down and gently picked her up.

"Oh what have I done?" he asked repeatedly with tears streaming down his face.

As he secured Julie into his truck seat, he looked blindly across the farm; fond memories of the two of them galloping across the field seemed so long ago.

The hospital was twenty-two miles away, and the ride to the emergency room seemed to Julie like the longest one of her life. The scent emanating from the chemicals and disinfectants made her sick to her stomach.

After barely being able to complete the paperwork, Julie was escorted to a room where the curtains parted, and she stared straight into the eyes of a short, round-faced man with curly gray hair and a stethoscope hanging from around his neck.

"Miss Julie, I presume." Julie slowly nodded her head.

After her examination was complete, Julie learned her right thumb had been bruised and jammed; she would need stitches to her forehead and above her left knee. Then last but not least, the exam also revealed that a couple of ribs, and her right leg were broken. Then, if that wasn't enough, the doctor conveyed that she would be on crutches for a surmountable period. Hearing the doctor outline Julie's injuries, Blake could hardly look her way. He felt so responsible for everything that had happened.

"That was quite an accident," her doctor finally spoke up.

"Yes it was," Julie said rather sharply. "I'm pretty

bummed out right now.

"I'm so sorry. I hope this doesn't affect how you feel about horses in the future."

"I'm sure I will always love them. Yet, riding them may be another story."

"Time has a way of healing," he said, while handing her several pages of written instructions. "Well, I wish you the best in your recovery. The nurse will see you out."

"Thank you." Julie clutched the instructions.

Being extremely careful not to bump her leg, the nurse escorted her to the main hospital entrance.

"Blake, did you comprehend all those instructions?"

He looked in her direction. "I hope so."

At that moment, Julie questioned what an awful sight she must be. Her clothing was bloodstained and torn. It was Blake who turned to give her a reassuring smile. He surely read her mind.

"You may be a little bruised, but you don't look half bad to me. I bet you feel worse than you look."

Julie wrinkled her nose, and they both managed to smile.

"Oh, it hurts," she said. "By the way, did you hear the doctor say it may be six months before I recover from this accident?"

"Try not to worry. I'll be your right hand, so to speak. And on that note, I'll be back in a jiffy with my truck to take you home."

After pulling alongside the front of the hospital, Blake immediately assisted her. Julie was relieved as she leaned her head back onto the front seat. After the hospital was well out of her view, she spoke up. "Well, I'm glad that part is behind me."

Seeing her squirming, Blake asked, "Are you sure you're alright?"

"I'm okay, just somewhat upset with the whole thing."

"I'm trying my best to get you home where you will be

more comfortable," he quickly added.

By the time Julie had reached her driveway, night had fallen. Blake turned off his headlights, and she became panicked. Every muscle in her injured body tightened. The realization of the accident hit home. She was going to be down for six months... at home... alone... helpless. Before Blake could open the door, Julie fought to regain her composure. *It's going to be okay.* She tried to convince herself of that. She started to stumble; Blake was there, his hand steady and comforting.

"Julie, again, I'm so, so sorry about today."

"Me, too, but it's not your fault. I have no idea what got into Spook to make him act so weird. An outburst like that just isn't in his nature. Without that weirdness from him, I wouldn't have been riding your horse."

Julie shook her head in disbelief. "I've tried all afternoon to make some sense out of it and I can't."

*The chief, looking on from his advantage point, would be the first to agree that his goal of getting rid of Blake had gotten way out of hand.*

As time passed, Julie became angrier and angrier with herself for being so virtually handicapped. If only she could go back to work at the club, but that was impossible right now. However, she was lucky to have a good, dependable manager overseeing it. In fact, Brody, her manager, was Slate's very best friend.

If she were perfectly honest, she would have to admit, she wished that were not the case. However, she respected Slate too much to have an open relationship with him.

Her mind traced back to one night her commitment to State was tested. Brody had driven his pickup up the hill near her observatory. To say his visit was a rare occasion was definitely an understatement. Brody merely tolerated and humored Julie over her love of the farm.

*Like anyone coming there, though, he was fair game as far as the chief was concerned.*

It would be soon after Brody's arrival that the sky became full of twinkling stars, and an inviting breeze calmly blew. However, it wasn't until the music playing from his stereo changed from a rock and roll beat to a romantic classic that, unexpectedly, Brody asked Julie to dance.

There under the magnificent, starlit sky their eyes locked into a flame of passion. Then without a single hint or warning, the once romantic melody abruptly came to a sudden standstill.

To this day, neither Julie nor Brody have ever brought up the mysterious, unexplainable happening on the top of the hill that night. And, even though, they can never be linked romantically, they have forever committed to an unbreakable, lifetime bond sealed between them on the night the music stopped.

Having nothing but time on her hands, Julie often reflected to the day of her accident, her pain, and her feeling of helplessness. Having reached her lowest point one rainy, dreary afternoon, she blurted out at Blake as he was leaving. "You know, I'm never riding again."

Immediately turning around, Blake asked, "Julie, have you really thought about this?"

Then seeing the serious look on her face, he sadly closed the door behind him.

It would be a few days later, Julie's frustration again overpowered her.

"It's all Blake's fault," she said, aloud to an empty house. "There! I finally verbalized my true feelings. It's my future on the line, not his. "

A knock on the door quickly brought her back to reality.

She looked out the window and saw Blake's truck in the driveway.

"Come in."

Blake opened the door and stepped inside. "Hi."

"Sell my horse!"

"Julie, you can't be serious?"

"I'm afraid I am. The price I paid was too high. Horse riding is no longer in my future. I just want to forget. I would rather ride my four-wheeler; after all, it's never thrown me."

Tears filled this proud cowboy's eyes. As he turned and crossed his arms over his chest, he sadly asked, "You mean forget me, too?"

Julie closed her eyes and rubbed the back of her neck. As she inhaled deeply, she confirmed, "Yes! You, too, just go away!"

At that moment, Julie did hold Blake responsible for her pain. She felt he was only losing a dream, while she was living a nightmare.

Blake returned home broken forever. He later sold Sebastian but not Spook. He knew if he did, one day Julie would regret it and resent him. He vowed never to take on the responsibility of hurting another person on horseback. Blake's days and nights of riding with Julie on the farm were now just a memory.

The two of them had spent many nights over the previous nine months roaming the hillsides on horseback, building campfires, and swimming the cool streams.

It was during Julie's final days of confinement, she would often find herself staring into the darkness yearning for that special time in her life. She would often remember them galloping on horseback across the open fields as she watched his eyes sparkle from the early morning sunlight.

"I was so obsessed by what I wanted, what I felt; I wasn't able to think about anyone else." She buried her face into her hands.

Julie often wrestled with the decision she made of sending Blake away. She had put such high stakes for her happiness into this farm, and now once again, it had brought her nothing but pain. So, what was the connection or pull that this farm held over her? Why did she keep returning repeatedly to this place? There were neither locks on the doors nor bars on the windows; but nonetheless, Julie often felt a prisoner.

## CHAPTER 15

It was a typical Friday night at the nightclub, when a piece of Julie's past walked in. Kail, a friend, from her old neighborhood had stopped by to see her.

"Won't Julie be surprised seeing me again after all this time," he murmured under his breath, while country music played in competition with the hum of conversation.

Finally, after not spotting Julie in the crowd, Kail approached the bar.

"Hi, Brody, I heard Julie owns this place. Isn't she here tonight?"

He responded in his own sharp way. "Julie's recovering from an accident."

"Was she seriously injured?"

"I think a broken leg is serious, don't you?"

"Oh, I'm really sorry to learn that." As he sat there thinking, his thoughts were soon transfixed to a much happier time in his life.

"If you speak with her, tell her I said hello."

"Sure thing. It could be days."

Even though, it would be several days before Julie's actual return, Kail wasn't ready to give up. He continually monitored her progress. It would be on her scheduled night back that he would arrive a bit early. *Will Julie recognize me after all these years?* He sat nervously picking at the label on his bottle of beer.

Being somewhat restless, Kail shifted his hips and pulled one foot up on the step of the bar stool. While raising his beer and taking a big swallow, he unintentionally sent a glance down to the other end of the bar. A nice middle-aged woman smiled back causing him to quickly shift his gaze. There was a time, he would have strolled over to her, offered to buy her a drink, and then sit next to her. However, tonight was different.

He dropped his foot back onto the floor, lifted his beer, and drank the rest. When he placed the bottle back on the bar, Julie was standing only a few feet away. The sight of her ignited an old spark. He hadn't seen her come into the nightclub nor had he noticed the noise from the crowd of well-wishers gathered near her. He had simply been oblivious to most of his surroundings, but once the crowd dissipated, he was able to acknowledge her presence.

"Hi Julie! It's been a long time, a very long time. Do you remember me?"

"Oh! My gosh yes," she gushed.

In a short amount of time, the couple was reminiscing about old times. With every stolen moment, they would recall more and more.

At one point, Kail reached into his shirt pocket and removed a small address book. "You've never been far from my mind. See, your name is still in my little black book. It even went to Vietnam and back with me."

"I can't believe you still carry that book." She smiled.

"Why not? You were an important part of my life."

He actually wanted to tell her why he came in tonight, but the distance in her eyes warned him she was not ready. So instead, he asked, "Whatever happened to us?"

"I guess we just went our separate ways," she managed to answer.

In addition, as their conversation resumed, Julie learned

that Kail was divorced after fifteen years of marriage and had indicated to her that he wasn't in any hurry to make another life-altering commitment, which was perfectly okay with her.

"By the way, I just want to thank you for coming to see me tonight. I've been really struggling since my accident."

"You're more than welcome. Besides that bad luck, what else has been going on in your life?"

"Well, a few years ago, I purchased a farm. Since then, I have gotten a divorce and lost a good friend. It's crazy. I actually believe these two events are somehow connected to the farm and probably would not have happened, if I had been living in the city."

"Hmm." Kail looked at her strangely. "I don't get it."

"That makes two of us. Anyway, my husband became mixed up in drugs while living in the country and even today, he can't give me an explanation. It's like he had no control over the situation. Then sometime later," she hesitated, "I met Blake. We both loved riding horses on my farm. One day, I had this horrible accident, and it cost my friendship with him."

"I'm still not able to do the math here." He scratched his head. "I get the fact that both incidents occurred at the farm, but they could have happened anywhere. What makes the farm responsible? I'm not good at charades. Help me out here. What's the common denominator?"

Julie groped for a believable explanation and realized there wasn't one. "Oh, I just merely think it's more than a coincidence. In my defense, I admit there's still a lot *I* don't understand."

And so it went until the morning's rays peeked in through the tiny window, which finally prompted them to say, "See you soon."

# CHAPTER 16

Julie and Kail had not only reunited after several years of separation but had learned to lean on each other as well. In doing so, it soon became evident to Kail how badly Julie missed the sights and smells of the country. In an attempt to fill her void, he made the decision to bring the country into her present world.

With a blueprint in hand, Kail began transforming Julie's front yard into a work of art. Among other things, he constructed several small flower boxes. Some were planted with wild flowers like those growing on her farm. He also installed a fishpond, gazebo, a small waterfall, and a fire pit in the hopes to brighten her spirit.

Julie was drawn to something the fire pit had to offer, but she soon learned an open fire in the city would not be tolerated. The smoke filled the city air and down the block it went, reflecting in every light it hit.

*How could one small fire excite the whole block,* Julie wondered as people began to gather. *Okay, that's not going to work,* she conceded. *Maybe just sitting in the swing and listening to the water cascade into the fishpond will be enough.* However, it wasn't. Therefore, Julie spent most of the next few evenings indoors.

Seeing the void in her eyes, Kail suggested they drive to

the farm. After all, he had never seen this mysterious place of hers.

"Sometimes, all it takes is time to destroy a bad memory," he told her. "Hasn't it been awhile since you've been there."

"You're right," Julie agreed. "I do believe timing is everything."

In the darkness of the next evening, Kail waited on the bottom step of the nightclub for Julie to get off work and before long, she joined him.

"According to the calendar, there's a full moon out tonight," she said excitedly, then looked over Kail's shoulder and caught a glimpse. It was as though she was seeing this wonder for the very first time.

"Take me to the place where you feel safe," he urged.

"No!" came Julie's first reaction.

Momentarily, she stood trembling with mixed emotions. Part of her wanted to run. Yet, part of her wanted to stay. The moonlight had triggered good memories, not bad ones.

"Okay," she blurted, "I've changed my mind."

"Great," he whispered, placing his arms around her waist as his mouth met hers with passion. There was no denying how his nearness and the unyielding presence of his strength offered the support she so badly needed. He held her close, submitting the sole protection of his arms.

"This feels so right," she whispered.

"Well, then," he managed to say, "I have a full tank of gas, and I'm ready to see your farm."

"You'll fall in love with it, everyone does."

Within moments, the couple was on their way and just before the farm came into view, Julie took hold of Kail's arm. "I'm a little nervous about this."

"It's okay." He slowed his truck and shut off the whine of the engine. "Anytime you want to turn back, you just say the word."

"No. No. Although, I don't want to wake my dad. I've

been concerned about him lately."

"How so?"

"Well, among other things, he's been sleeping far too much. Some days, he tells me he doesn't get up until around 1:00 o'clock, and that's not like him at all. I'll just direct you on how to get to the other side of the river. When it's a normal hour, we can come back. You know, when it's daylight, then I can really show you around."

"We can come back anytime, you just give the word." Kail stopped his truck again further down the road.

They got out and went to the front of the vehicle where he crossed his arms over his chest and leaned against the hood of his truck. By now, the moon was shining straight down on them. It was like one shooting star after another was trying to fall right into their pockets.

"Oh, how I've missed all this." She turned toward him and smiled. He was opening his baseball jacket and inviting her to step into his embrace. Before long his arms and jacket were wrapped securely around her.

It felt so good to be held by him, to feel the warmth and strength of his arms firm and tight around her. It was enough now for Julie to know, she hadn't pushed him away again. The past was melting away and only the future was present.

Nevertheless, how could she dismiss the previous tragedies? Her marriage and friendship with Blake had been destroyed on this farm. What if something awful like that happened to Kail?"

From the turmoil going on inside her, Julie wasn't sure about him being out here tonight, and she didn't want to jeopardize this rekindled relationship in any form or fashion.

Kail, then seeing the moon reflecting a blank look, questioned, "Hey, a penny for your thoughts."

"Hmm," Julie not wanting to put a damper on the mood quickly rebounded, "I was just thinking, there's no other place in the whole wide world I would rather be right now."

"Me either."

They stood in each other's embrace for what seemed only seconds but in reality were several minutes, before they decided to leave the country and return to the city.

After that magical night, Julie looked forward to every chance to see Kail with a sense of eagerness. How often their eyes met in amusement over some silly little thing. She was falling for him again, and there wasn't a thing she could do about it.

*However, she wasn't the only one in charge. The chief knew she was yet to fully understand this farm of hers.*

# CHAPTER 17

Julie knew for some time now her farmhouse was well overdue for a face-lift, and she felt somewhat disappointed at her dad for not having stayed on top of the repairs. She also had specific concerns regarding his irrational sleeping habits and temporary memory loss. In addition, it saddened her to see how his hair had gone from salt and pepper to pure white and how his once broad shoulders had a slight stoop to them.

While pulling into the farm driveway, throwing up dust and gravel, Julie spotted her dad in the backyard. Rolling her window down, she hollered, "Hi Dad, how are you?"

Walking over to her pickup, he responded, "I'm fine."

"Can I come inside and visit with you for a minute? We need to talk."

"Can't we talk right here, I'm rather busy?"

"I would rather go inside and sit down at the table," Julie insisted.

"I don't think that's necessary." His voice was harsh.

Seeing Julie was relentless, her dad hurriedly walked to the backdoor and stepped onto the porch. He slung the screen so hard, it nearly struck Julie in the face.

"Dad, what are you doing?" she asked, trying to dodge the screen.

Entering the kitchen, Julie threw up her hands, totally unprepared for what she was faced with. "I can't believe this. Dad, what's going on?"

There she stood looking head on at a kitchen sink with stack after stack of dirty dishes. In the corner of the room, trash was piled to the ceiling. She could hardly see the table for all the newspapers. Picking up one of them, she lashed out, "This is over three months old."

"What do you mean, Jewels?" he asked, rather confused at her outburst.

"It isn't healthy to live like this," she quickly pointed out.

Then, while navigating through a narrow pathway, shaking her head in disbelief, she mumbled, "I knew I needed to do repairs, but this is ridiculous."

Finally, in the bathroom, she stepped on a weak board. It creaked and nearly gave way. Utter frustration took over, and not knowing exactly how to defuse the situation, she threw up her hands once again, and walked out the backdoor trying to stay in control.

With little hesitation, she climbed inside her pickup and backed out of the driveway. Tears streamed down her face, and her heart was plagued with pain. Was the farm affecting him? Was whatever the entity had in store ruining her father's mind and health?

At that moment, Julie realized she didn't know the man inside, and her greatest fear was that she had lost the relationship she had fought, so hard to regain. *What kind of a bond could we have now?* She aimlessly drove down the lonely country road back to the city.

Pulling her pickup into the garage, Julie sat powerlessly for several minutes going over the similarities to the other tragedies on her farm. Here she was, yet again, running back to the city with tears streaming down her face.

She pounded her fist against the steering wheel. "How do I go on from here?"

She desperately wanted someone to magically make all this unhappiness disappear.

The following morning, she called Kail. He could only sit and listen to her unfold her latest experience.

"Julie, I'm here to help you in any way I possibly can."

"I hate it. I hate to have to do it, but my dad needs to be removed from the farm. I have given it some thought, and I'm going to write him a letter."

"You mean like an eviction notice?"

"Something like that, I guess." She shook her head wondering if her dad was becoming a victim much like the others.

"Kail, the man living on my farm isn't my dad anymore." There are five acres with a small trailer on it for sale a couple of miles up the road. Maybe I can convince my dad to move, and hopefully someday, he will realize it was for his own good."

"What can I do to help you?"

"Right at this moment, just support me in this endeavor?"

# CHAPTER 18

After sleeping on it, Julie concluded, she really needed to confront her dad in person. She ultimately dismissed the eviction notice idea, but would he slam the door in her face? She hoped not, she still loved him.

Rounding the last curve on the country road, Julie saw Tonka in the driveway looking anxious. She opened her door and gave him a pat behind the ear. "Hi boy, how's the mood on the farm this morning?"

"I thought I heard someone," a voice came from behind her.

"Oh, hello, Dad. Are you up for a talk?"

"I would like that, Jewels. I don't understand what's happening with me."

"I believe you. I've returned today to discuss a proposition with you. Do you remember seeing a 'For Sale' sign on the property up the road?"

"Yes, I saw the sign."

"Well, I spoke with the owner," she began, "he's leaving a completely furnished trailer on five acres. I think you should consider buying it. You must know the farm has become far too much for you to handle."

"Maybe you're right."

She was relieved he agreed. "Fair enough," she said,

realizing her headache was dissipating and a good feeling about their relationship was replacing it. Once they had finalized their conversation, Julie gave her dad a big hug. She was happy everything had gone so well.

She walked over to her vehicle and started the engine. "Thanks." She waved goodbye.

The following morning, Julie called Kail. "Good news. I'm ready to get the farm repairs started."

"I take it all went well?"

"Yes they did. Things couldn't be better right now."

Then on the following Saturday afternoon, when the sun was descending behind the treetops, Kail nailed the last shingle onto the farmhouse roof. Gone were the dips and the missing shingles Julie had to constantly look at each time she made a visit.

"Kail, you are so talented," she said, seeing him climb off the ladder.

"Enough with the compliments," he teased, passionately wrapping his muscular arms around her.

*Although, not everyone embraced his passionate moment. For you see, the chief, who was now standing only a few feet away, could only hang his head and show his disapproval.*

"I think the roof looks pretty sharp," Julie exclaimed. "How will I ever be able to repay you?"

"You just did." He pulled her even closer. "If we lived out here, just think how much more work could be accomplished."

The comment caught Julie off guard. She hesitated for a moment before answering. "It's not a 4-star resort. Although, I'm sure you're right. I can see where you're losing a lot of time traveling back and forth."

Julie was pleased that shortly after that conversation; they packed a few personal belongings and moved into the farmhouse. She was glad to be in the country again.

Kail snickered under his breath. He couldn't believe there was actually a place to hang his clothes. "Julie is your nickname still appropriate."

"Kail! Don't go there. You might find your things outside in your truck. Anyway, it's a girl thing to like to buy clothes. Are you the one who stuck that nickname on me, Flea Market Fanny?"

"I don't think it was me." He smiled. "I'm not taking credit for it."

Julie was happy as a lark to be back on the farm and in spite of her fears and apprehensions, her life appeared to be heading in the right direction.

# CHAPTER 19

One day in late fall, Kail approached Julie. "Oh, Miss Julie, do you know the snow will soon be falling, and you have a very skimpy woodpile?"

Her good friend, Brody, offered to cut her wood, but she had him working on inventory at the club. "Yes. I do." She laughed. "It happens about this time every year. With my job in the city, I haven't had time to address it."

"I think tomorrow would be a good day to remedy that situation. I spotted several downed trees yesterday, an excellent source for your winter's supply. Plus, it would open up some of your blocked trails.

With that thought in mind, Kail and Julie woke up around 6:00 a.m. the following morning. Julie had her usual chocolate cake. Kail opted for a bagel and cream cheese. They knew it wasn't a very heardy breakfast for a couple who planned to spend their entire morning in the woods, but it was what they were hungry for.

"Well, how do you feel?" Julie put her juice glass in the sink. "Are you ready for your day of wood chopping?"

"Yep. As ready as I will ever be."

"Well, as soon as I grab a couple bottles of water, I'll be ready to join you."

"What kept you so long?" he asked, finally seeing her

come out the backdoor. "Did you have to go to the spring for the water?"

"No, I had to bake the bread for our sandwiches. I thought we might get hungry later," she said sarcastically.

"I'm heading on up in my truck. Let's get this show on the road."

Approaching the hill on her four-wheeler, Julie saw Kail waiting for her.

He shook his head. "Man you're as slow as molasses."

She ignored the comment. "I think it's time to show you something, hop on."

Kail did as instructed and after heading down one of her trails and veering to the right, Julie brought the four-wheeler to a stop. "There it is. See the area over there where the two big trees are leaning over to form an archway? That's where the seven fork trees meet. See, they appear to form a natural entrance. I never showed you before. I just didn't think you would understand."

Curiosity got the best of him. "A natural entrance to what?" He got off of the vehicle.

"To the sacred ground. This area was revealed to me on my first vision quest, which is an Indian's personal spiritual search in case you want to know."

"You really play on all that Indian mumbo jumbo don't you? Well, I've heard and seen it all. This farm has you believing all sorts of nonsense."

"I know you don't understand but before my horse accident, I went on a quest. Madelyn has lived out here for a very long time, so I told her about the quest, and she brought me right to this very spot. I'm convinced this place is for real. Madelyn is a horse whisperer, and she has a sixth since about the spiritual world, I guess you'd say."

Looking down at his watch, he grumbled. "Whatever! The day is getting away from us. We have wasted a good half hour and nothing's been accomplished."

So, jumping back on her vehicle, he strongly urged Julie

to start it up. "Enough of this nonsense, let's get out of here! You have spent far too much time alone on this farm."

Julie mumbled to herself. *Bringing him here was definitely a mistake.*

However, before long they had made up for lost time. The back of Kail's truck was filled with freshly cut wood.

"My, that looks good," Julie commented. "It was a very good and smart suggestion on your part. By the way, thanks for opening up my trails."

"You're welcome, and we do make a good team. That is, once you get started. While I finish loading these last few pieces of wood, how about you ride down and pick up my spare chain? I left it on the workbench in the garage. I may need it before we finish."

"I can do that."

"Bring back more water," he hollered as she descended the hill.

"Okay, anything else you need?"

"There is just one more thing. Don't lay out anything for dinner. I want to take you out to eat tonight and maybe to a movie. That is, if it's okay with you."

"That sounds great to me, if we have the energy after all this wood cutting."

"What are you talking about? I thought you were Wonder Woman, a woman of steel."

"Don't you worry about me, I can keep up with you any day of the week," she said, laughing and at the same time releasing some of her previous anger at him. Lately, he seemed to be able to push her buttons at every turn. She was a bit tired, but she wasn't going to let on. What he didn't know wouldn't hurt him.

Before long she had returned with his items and soon discovered he was anxiously waiting for her.

"Just a minute, don't turn it off, I want to show you something. Drive over to your so-called sacred ground."

With a suspicious look on her face, she asked, "Why?"

He positioned himself behind her and repeated, "Just drive back over there where you showed me earlier."

Nearing the sacred ground, Julie cried out, "Oh no, Kail! What have you done?"

With one side of his mouth quirked in a cynical smirk, he glared. "That old tree was just in the way. It should have been cut down a long time ago."

Julie dug her nails into her palms. Kail had ruined everything. "I can't believe you did that. You had no right to cut it down! You are so thoughtless, especially after I told you how important this whole area is to me. It was sacred!"

"Sacred? You don't think I believe in all that farm nonsense, do you?" His laugh was evil. "You're foolish if you do."

"Kail, it's not funny!" Her fury was overwhelming. Tears threatened to spill onto her cheeks and every muscle in her body ached, knotted with tension. "I absolutely see no humor in this at all." She placed her hands on her hips. If he thought she was foolish, well... "You know what? If you think my believing in my heritage, the culture of my ancestors is so ridiculous, then perhaps you should find someone else."

"Whatever. You know you don't mean that. Besides, there's still work to be done, and it isn't getting done by itself."

At that moment, she did mean it, but no matter how mad she was at Kail, the tree was gone forever and his leaving would not bring it back. She closed her eyes, took a deep breath and willed herself to calm.

Returning to the worksite, as one might suspect, there was little conversation going on between the two of them.

"Hey, be careful where you throw that piece of wood." Kail jumped out of the way as a small log barely missed his head.

"Don't worry. If I was aiming at you, believe you me, you would know it." She hoped he got the message that she still wasn't happy.

"About another ten minutes, we should be heading down the hill. I can almost taste those hush puppies." He was trying very hard to disseminate the tension between them. "Do you think you need to call Big Joe's and make reservations for tonight?"

"It would probably be a good idea." Although, she really wasn't in the mood to go now, her stomach was growling. She definitely didn't want to cook. "Also, let's not unload the wood tonight. It can wait until tomorrow. I'm getting hungry now."

"What did you say? I can't hear over the roar of this truck."

Julie rode beside him. The truck motor and the small engine of the four-wheeler were loud, and as they got closer to the house, she heard a shrill sound. "Is that the telephone ringing?"

"I thought the ringing was in my ear," Kail responded.

Julie quickly jumped off the four-wheeler and raced inside. Breathing erratically into the phone, she answered, "Hello."

"Hi, how are you doing?" Bailey's familiar voice asked.

"Oh, I'm alright."

"You don't sound it."

"Is it that obvious?"

"I'd say so."

"I'm so mad, I could spit nails. I've been working on an attitude adjustment this afternoon."

"Whose attitude?"

"Mine! It's all Kail's fault."

"What happened? What's wrong? You sound ready to explode."

"What's wrong? You should be asking me what's right. That would only take a second to answer." She dropped down onto the couch with a sigh. "Kail ruined the sacred ground."

"How did he do that?"

Brushing a weary hand across her eyes, Julie replied, "He cut down one of the leaning trees to the main entrance of the sacred ground."

"I'm so sorry. What reason did he give?"

"He doesn't believe there's something supernatural or whatever it is out here, and now I'm afraid for him. He doesn't comprehend what he's done."

*Julie was right in having concern for Kail's safety. Now, only a short distance away, a surmountable amount of anger was festering itself inside the chief. How dare Kail be so defiant. The words repeatedly clouded the chief's mind.*

"What are you going to do now? Is there anything I can do?"

"I don't know. I don't know what anyone can do. I just cannot let it consume me." Julie inhaled deeply. "I know I still want Kail in my life. He's in the shower right now, so I can't talk long. He's taking me out for dinner and a movie."

"I won't keep you. I just want to borrow your angel food cake pan. My brother-in-law's birthday is next week, and I'm baking his cake."

"Not a problem. We can drop the pan by your house on our way to the movie."

"Thanks. I hope everything works out. Goodbye."

After hanging up, Julie stopped by the doorway and watched Kail button the last one on his shirt. *Why can't he be compassionate? I thought he understood how important this farm has become in my life. I have witnessed first-hand the destruction and devastation to the lives of those who are important to me. Not a day goes by that I don't feel a presence around me emanating from this farm. How can I convey that to Kail? How can I keep him safe?*

## CHAPTER 20

Julie reflected with fond memories her night out with Kail. Overall, it had been a delightful evening and a few good days came along later, as well. However, there were those times Julie would just as soon forget. Particularly, the ones Kail used to isolate himself from her.

It was as if their night on the town had been a farewell party. The magic that had been in their relationship had now faded away. Kail was no longer the warm funny, charismatic person she had grown to love. She feared the worst.

"Good morning." Julie greeted him. "Are you ready for your breakfast?"

"I've already eaten." He walked toward the backdoor.

"What's your plan for today?"

"If you must know, I'm going to cut firewood."

"I'll be up shortly to help."

"That won't be necessary." His tongue was sharp.

"Alright, I'll fix you a nice lunch. Maybe this afternoon then," she raised her voice over the slamming of the kitchen door.

Sometime later, while looking at her watch, Julie began to get concerned. As she picked up her keys, she heard the sound of his truck coming down the hill. She breathed,

"Thank goodness he's okay." Upon glancing toward his direction, she commented, "You had me worried. You didn't go over to the sacred ground, did you?"

Kail gave her a stern look. It was as though he stared right through her, beyond her at something else entirely. Without speaking a word, he walked over and placed his splitting maul against the wall. After seating himself at the table, Julie noticed a strange glaze in his eyes.

"You and your disgusting Indian beliefs are a bunch of bull," he muttered.

"I don't appreciate that comment, Kail. You're scaring me."

Kail suddenly pushed his chair back from the table, stood up, and walked over to the coffee pot. After returning, he sat starry-eyed for hours, alternating between drinking coffee and staring out the window.

Julie glanced in his direction. In the pit of her stomach, she had a sinking sensation. She couldn't help but notice the slight quiver in his right cheek. Who was this person, and what had happened on top of the hill?

By the time the wee hours approached, Julie was exhausted. Her eyes were burning, but she didn't dare close them. Realizing something needed to be done, she asked of him, "What's going on? I can't fix what's broken, if you don't talk to me."

Getting no response for her efforts and out of sheer desperation, Julie decided to call Wapa. "Please, please answer," she whispered under her breath. Once hearing his voice, she breathed a sigh of relief.

"What's the problem, Julie?"

"I've been up for hours pacing the floor." Then raising the level of intensity, she needed him to understand, "I can't go to bed, and I'm afraid to leave my house."

Being disturbed by her comment, Wapa asked, "Are you afraid for your safety?"

"No! No! Kail is just sitting at the table drinking coffee

and staring out the window."

"You're this distraught over Kail, who's just sitting and looking out the window? Am I missing something? Julie, I don't see the problem."

"You don't understand! He's been this way for over twelve hours, and he has communicated very little with me in those hours. I have known this man since I was six years old. He has never acted like this before." It was time to tell him what Kail had done. "Wapa, yesterday, he cut down one of the bent, leaning trees at the entrance of the sacred ground. Today, he may have cut down the other. I'm not sure. But this behavior is bizarre."

"Get out of there! Get out of there, now! I don't know what's happening, and it will take me thirty minutes to get there. Go over to Madelyn's house or lock yourself in your pickup until I can get there."

"Okay, but please hurry."

She returned to the kitchen just in time to see Kail's chair go crashing against the wall. Her blood suddenly ran cold. A quick glance in his direction revealed there was a burning anger on his strong face. A brief lowering of his eyelids disguised the animosity lurking in the depths of his darkened eyes.

As seconds passed, Kail raised an accusing finger in her direction. With a powerful surge of emotion, he broke the silence and demanded, "I want money! Give it to me now!"

This man was foreign to her. She bit down on her lip determined to not let him get into her head. She glared back and winced at the bitterness in his voice, while trying to keep any sign of fear off her face. "You haven't spoken a word to me in hours. When you do finally break your silence, you ask for money. Are you robbing me?"

He shrugged his shoulders. "It's for my labor. I don't work for free you know."

Julie tried to reorganize her thoughts. His eyes locked with hers, and she saw anger spark, enough to make her cringe. Why didn't she do what Wapa told her to? She should leave but couldn't bring herself to do so.

Kail picked up the chair off the floor and sat back at the table. She studied him while trying to find the man she once knew. Now, she could find nothing familiar in this stranger's hard face. She looked away, annoyed with him on so many levels and afraid of him at the same time.

He lifted an eyebrow, his voice was calloused and indifferent. "If you don't want to pay me, I guess I will just take stuff." He looked around. "Something to compensate me for all I've done."

He pushed his chair out of the way before slowly and deliberately walking into Julie's bedroom. His face was blank and his eyes ice-cold. Julie held her breath. The silence felt heavy as she followed him to the nearby nightstand holding a nineteen inch portable television.

"This is a start," he muttered. He took a pocket knife out and cut the cord. He growled, leaned over to scowl at her and quickly picked up the TV.

While going out the backdoor, he lost his footing and stumbled down the steps. Julie rushed to the door in time to see him pick himself up and throw the TV into the back of his truck. He walked back into the house to an end table where he removed her barometer which measured the pull of gravity by drawing pictures in the sand.

From the look on his face, she pretty well knew he was going to destroy one of her favorite things. "No, Kail! Please don't!"

Ignoring her plea, he broke it apart causing sand to go everywhere. Continuing his destruction, she felt powerless to intervene. As he headed for the garage, she cringed. "Oh no! Not my stained glass tools."

Finally, the destructive spree ended, and Julie heard the sound of tires throwing gravel against the side of the farmhouse. Kail had either damaged or taken everything that wasn't nailed down. She didn't get in his way for fear he would physically hurt her in some way.

The echo of his footsteps now had an eerie effect on her mind. It reminded her of how alone she was. For just a fleeting moment, she allowed herself to remember the many fun times they shared, but the memories were painful. Tears stung her eyes.

"How could he do this to me?" She studied the devastation then sat on the couch and allowed the pain of everything that had happened the last couple of days to soak in. Her heart was broken. Kail was a highly educated, intelligent engineer. What happened to him? What did she do to deserve this?"

All at once, the backdoor burst open. She raised her gaze to meet Wapa's.

"What in the world happened?"

Still in shock and dismay, Julie managed to ask, "Can you put my life back together?"

Looking around, shaking his head, Wapa promised, "I'll certainly do my best." He put his arm around her. "Whew. What a mess!"

Julie leaned on him for a minute before pulling away. She choked back her sobs.

"Wapa, I know the farm's responsible. Kail cut down one of the sacred trees and now he's paying the price. My world is spinning out of control. Please make it stop."

"I'll be right back." He walked to the medicine cabinet.

Julie hollered in his direction, "Bandages won't fix my problem. First, it was Slate, then Blake, and now Kail. In addition, don't forget about my dad."

Returning with some aspirin and still amazed by all the destruction, Wapa said, "I don't have it all figured out either." He handed her the medicine. "These are for your headache. Where do you keep your broom?"

"It's in the utility closet down the hall. How did you know I have a headache?"

"I just know. This house looks like a bomb exploded in

it."

"Kail was acting like a mad man. My large Indian picture that always hung over the fireplace is over there in pieces, and here is a part of a lamp that was standing in the corner."

Wapa kept sweeping the debris. "It is hard for me to conceive that anyone in his right mind would do this."

Julie gave a sigh of exhaustion, wiped away the tears still streaming down her face and continued to pick up the remnants of her past. "Kail seemed delighted to go around in a circle throwing things on the floor. And the sand, he had a ball with it. There will be residue here for a very long time."

After considerable sweeping, Wapa stated, "That was quite a chore, but I think I got most of it. I could sure use a cup of coffee about now."

"That's a good idea. I could use one myself. It won't take long."

After they finished an entire pot of the hot liquid, Julie confirmed her headache was better. She placed her hand on Wapa's arm. "Thanks for coming."

"Anytime. I am, however, disappointed that you didn't take my advice and leave."

"I should have, I know, but I wasn't afraid for my life, just my things."

He smiled. "Julie, I have a thought."

"Okay. I'm open for suggestions."

"You have been up for many hours. You need rest. Why don't you try to get some sleep? Tonight, when the moon and stars come out, let's go up on the hill and build a campfire. We can continue our conversation there. Together we'll figure this out."

She had to admit, she was exhausted. "I would like that."

After a few hours of rest, she did feel better and once Wapa returned, they retreated to the little campsite where he removed sage from his medicine bag and preformed a ceremony cleansing the air of evil spirits. Even though there were still a lot of unanswered questions, Julie was feeling a form of peace.

Hours later, with the noisy night sounds rather subdued, the two were still sitting around the fire enjoying the cracking sounds and before either one of them realized it, they could see a glimmer of light approaching.

"This time of morning is so breathtaking. Kail and I spent so much time right here. Wapa, what went wrong?"

"I've been giving that a lot of thought." He shook his head. "I really feel you should give my friend, Night Hawk, a call. Having been a shaman for over twenty-five years, he acts as a go-between the physical and spiritual realms. I believe he can help you. That is, if anyone can."

"I'm sure you're right," Julie acknowledged. "I thought I could handle any and every thing."

"For some unknown reason you've been chosen to endure this journey. It seems like you have been offered a challenge. I'm surprised I haven't met with some ill-fate myself."

"You're kidding. You're a hollow bone."

Wapa nodded and in response repeated, "I still think Night Hawk might be your best bet."

"Maybe so." She reached over and gave him a hug.

"Wait a minute. Keep those arms off me. Let's not take any chances here. But seriously, it's about time you get an understanding of what's happening."

"I know you're right." He was right, but she wasn't sure she was ready to talk to Night Hawk. Maybe, she would just put it off until she could get herself together better.

*A short distance across the field, the chief stood patiently watching his plan unfold minute by minute. Yet, at the same time, Julie struggled for that single thread, or piece of knowledge to hold her unraveling life together.*

As the little campfire reduced itself to a glow of embers, Wapa stood. "I'll escort you down the hill. You, my friend, need to get some rest."

"Thanks again for all your support." She gave him a goodbye hug. "Be careful going home."

Julie then walked around the corner of her house to check on her guineas. *Everything looks secure,* she thought to herself. Then memories of Kail flashed into her mind. Thoughts and emotions were going round and round like a top spinning out of control. It would be several hours, with her mind racing ninety to nothing, before she could accept the fact that he was actually gone. Although, he had physically removed every reminder of himself, his spirit lingered in everything he had touched.

If she looked long and hard enough in her mind's eye, she could still see him standing on top of the ladder repairing her roof, and if she closed her eyes and listened intently, she was certain she could hear his familiar laugh. Nevertheless, when she opened them again and looked eagerly and longingly at his side of the bed, he was gone.

The next thing Julie consciously remembered was Madelyn's rooster alerting everyone that a new day was approaching. She tried to remove the sheet that had her bound up like a mummy. Holding her head, she mumbled, "I feel terrible."

Her eyes flickered with flashbacks of yesterday's events. She hadn't expected that kind of treatment from Kail. If she were honest with herself, she would admit that nothing about Kail turned like she had expected. She closed her eyes and deeply inhaled to calm her nerves. *Why should I stay on this farm?* She suddenly questioned herself. *There's nothing left out here for me.*

As Julie began to pace restlessly around the house, her stomach tied in knots. With a multitude of thoughts racing through her head, she subconsciously packed a few things and put them into the back of her pickup. After closing the tailgate, she sat behind the wheel and hesitantly drove to Madelyn's driveway.

"Good morning, Madelyn."

"No need to explain. How long this time?"

"What was the clue that gave it away?" Julie sheepishly questioned.

"I think it was the dust I'm still trying to get out of my house after Kail went barreling down the road in such a hurry."

"Oh! You noticed that, did you?"

"I'm sorry, Julie, I really liked him. Do you expect him to return?"

"No. He's out of my life for good."

"Well, just don't worry about your farm, I'll keep an eye on it."

"You're a lifeline. How will I ever repay you?"

"Over the years you've done plenty. Don't forget you took care of my greenhouse and my horses while I was away on business."

Julie gave her neighbor a hug. "I still owe you."

Backing out of Madelyn's driveway and driving slowly down the lonely country road toward the city, Julie sadly reflected on how her life had been like a rollercoaster, and Madelyn had witnessed much of it over the last few years.

She lived in the city, then the country, then the city again. There was someone special in her life and then there wasn't. Somehow, she needed to shake this feeling and gain control. It seemed like the only answer to her complicated life.

Therefore, that's just what she did. Trips to the farm were now only out of necessity. She hoped Tonka and Spook would understand and not forget her. At this point, she had to do what was best for her. However, she wasn't always known for making the best of choices.

For instance, asking Blake to sell Spook after her

accident. He knew her so well. She would have really regretted such a decision.

However, she was confident this time. It wasn't as if she would never return to the farm, it just wasn't going to be very often.

All Julie really wanted was to share the farm with someone who had the ability to make her laugh and someone who, not only enjoyed the farm, but would also embrace her and her Indian culture. Was that asking too much?

*No, not as far as the chief was concerned. That is as long as it's him we're talking about.*

## CHAPTER 21

One early morning and out of the blue, Julie received an unexpected call from her older sister Carol; a rather quiet and laid-back individual, slender built with long, straight black hair and French-like characteristics.

Due to her job with the telephone company, Carol had lived out of state for the past ten years. Therefore, her contact with Julie had been reduced to mere letter writing, much in the same way they had done previously, that is, when they were young. During her normal days off work and vacation periods, she often returned to her family in the city.

"Hi. It's Carol," the voice on the other end of the line said.

"Well, good morning. This is a nice surprise. Are you in on vacation?"

"Just for the weekend, I'll be returning to Kansas City Sunday night. In the meantime, I want to invite you to a rod run. We'll celebrate your 43$^{rd}$ birthday. I'll even bake a cake."

"It does sound rather tempting since I've been staying pretty close to the house lately. Will Tommy be driving the Essex?"

"Yes. I know you will have a good time. Please say

you'll come."

With little hesitation, Julie accepted the invitation. "You talked me into it."

"Great. See you around 10:00 o'clock tomorrow."

The following morning, Julie woke up with a bit of excitement. She was actually glad Carol had called. Maybe it was time to do something different. She had lately been rather isolated.

After putting her breakfast dishes in the sink, Julie bent down to tie her tennis shoe. She soon heard the rumble of the Essex rolling down the street. *There's no mistaking that sound.* She hurriedly grabbed her house key and went outside.

"Good morning, Tommy. The Essex looks like you stayed up all night polishing it, but I know you didn't. That red 'Candy Apple' paint really sparkles in the sunlight."

"Good morning, sis," Tommy quickly echoed.

"I'll have you know that's a three minute special you're looking at."

"Right! I've never known you to do anything in three minutes."

"Get in this street rod and quit being mouthy. Carol, are you going to let your sis talk to me like that? I can see right now it's going to be one of those days."

"You got that right, bring it on." Julie laughed and acknowledged Carol's presence with a hug around her shoulders.

"Well, if we're all ready," Tommy said, "I'll back out of here, and we'll be on our way."

"Ready from the backseat and ready from the front seat," came comments.

Approaching Smith Park, Julie could hear 50's music blaring. Everywhere she looked; there were roadsters, coupes, T-buckets, and sedans.

"This looks like it's going to be a fun day. I'm just sorry I don't have my own street rod. Tommy, maybe you can keep an eye out for one."

"I can do that, sis. What make and model?"

"I don't know. Ask me again at the end of the day. I'll have a better idea then."

Carol spoke up, "After we get registered, I will introduce you to our club members. You already know some of them."

"Oh, I do recognize Jon and Tina standing over there. I haven't seen them in ages."

"See, I told you there would be people here you would know."

Shortly, Carol was saying, "Hi everyone. Glad to see all of you. For those of you who don't know, this is my sister Julie. I dragged her out of her house today to be with us."

The rodders were all friendly and made a point to include Julie in their conversation. Then out of the corner of her eye, Julie noticed a quiet young man sitting by himself.

"Who's that over there with the curly black hair?" she questioned.

"That's Shawn. He's a very shy young man and he's single."

"He's a cutie with that sweet smile," Julie acknowledged.

Before long, and mostly through Julie's storytelling, she had Shawn virtually wrapped around her little finger. His eyes were fixed solely on her, occasionally interrupting her with a question but mostly content to leave the stage to her.

"Shawn, I'm sorry. I get a bit carried away sometimes."

Of course, she made a point to shy away from all the mystery surrounding the farm.

"No, don't apologize," he was quick to say. "I get why you feel that way. I'm just a city boy who would love to live in the country. I could listen to you talk all day."

While the two sat enjoying the sunshine and each other's company, Julie learned how really shy, timid, and sheltered a life Shawn had led. *He reminds me a little of myself,* she thought silently, *kind of an oddity in this world.*

As their conversation progressed, the minutes seemed to fly by.

"Julie," Carol said, "sorry for the interruption, but the fan belt toss is about to begin. If we want to participate, we need to get in line."

"Okay, I'll be right there."

"Hey, Shawn, come and join us," Julie coaxed. "Seems like we're going to get in line for a game."

Shawn beamed at her invitation. He wasn't used to anyone paying attention to him.

After tossing the belts, Julie and he walked away with one each to their credit. Coming up next were both the spark plug change and the creeper race. After the race was over, Shawn turned to her, his smile spread from ear to ear.

"Julie, congratulations, you did really well on your creeper. Those guys, still standing in line, are going to have to work really hard to beat your time. I'm glad you came today. I'm having, so much fun."

"I am too, but these physical activities are making me hungry. Why don't we go over to where they're barbecuing?"

"I'm in," Shawn said.

After securing their meal, Shawn and Julie enjoyed talking and listening to the 50's music that still filled the entire park. She had heard Roll Over Beethoven, Blue Swede Shoes and Long Tall Sally among many other of her favorites.

"Once we finish our food, we don't want to forget to vote for our favorite street rod. I even asked Tommy this morning," she continued, "to be on the lookout for a good deal on a street rod for me."

"Great," came his response.

The couple was soon walking through the park looking at all the street rods before selecting their favorite. Julie was busy making a mental list for herself as well.

"I can't express how glad I am you came today." His voice was rather timid. "It's been such a fun afternoon."

"I've also enjoyed myself. By the way, I was just thinking. It has been a long time since I've been to my farm. Would you like to come for a visit tomorrow?"

"I would like that very much. About what time are we talking?"

"Meet me at my house around two o'clock. Call and I'll give you directions."

Hearing the music stop, Shawn checked his watch. "Oh, it's four o'clock. They're ready to announce the winners."

"Hi," they heard a voice say over a microphone. "My name is Max, and I'm the club president for those of you who don't know me. On behalf of our club, we hope you enjoyed spending your day with us."

"I know I did," Shawn whispered.

Minutes later, Ronnie, the vice president in charge of the day's event could be heard over the blare of music letting the street rodders know to come back next year and to have a safe trip home.

There was a hint of sadness in Shawn's voice. "Well, the event is over. I'm so sorry you lost the creeper race, but as I said before, you did really well. I thought you would have it in the bag."

"That's okay. Maybe next time. I had fun trying."

"Me, too. I've never enjoyed myself more, and thanks again for tomorrow's invitation."

"You're welcome. I will see you then. Goodnight." She handed him a card with her phone number on it.

Climbing into the back seat of the Essex, Julie expressed her feelings about Shawn. "We had such a good time. He appears to be a really nice guy."

"Yes." Carol looked over her shoulder. "I've known him and his family around two years now. It always seemed Shawn had difficulty making friends. Somehow, you managed to break that barrier today. How did you do that?"

"I don't know. There were so many things we had in common. Anyway, he just seemed to want to talk. However, I did notice he appeared to be a rather fragile individual. Have you noticed that about him?"

"Yes. He's so sweet, but he does give the impression he needs to be guarded much like you would your favorite China."

"Right away I had a connection with him even though he is younger," Julie quickly added. "Plus, much like me, he's a little different in his thinking. I just hope I'm not making a mistake inviting him to the farm."

"I agree," Carol expressed. "Shawn deserves the opportunity to spend a nice day without any complications."

"I'll call and let you know how it goes."

"Please do," Carol insisted, realizing the situation could have consequences but hoping for the best.

"Well, here we are." Tommy brought the Essex to a complete stop. "If you want to continue this conversation, you'll have to call your sis at the house."

"Okay, just one more thing"

"Make it quick," Tommy snapped in his usual cool manner.

"I just want to thank you both for everything."

"You're more than welcome, "Carol said. "You and Shawn have fun tomorrow and try not to worry."

"Goodnight, sis," Tommy bellowed. "Thanks for going with us."

As Julie walked to the front door, she reflected on the day's events. *I had a fantastic time. Everyone was so friendly, especially Shawn, and I'm looking forward to an even better day tomorrow.*

## CHAPTER 22

With only minutes to spare before Shawn's arrival, Julie dressed in a pair of cut-off jeans, a sleeveless blouse, and her favorite sandals. Then at precisely 2:00 o'clock, she heard a decisive knock.

"Hi Shawn. Are you ready to view the farm off the back of a four-wheeler?"

Answering with a tone of excitement, "I'm ready as I'll ever be."

"Then climb into my pickup, and we'll get started. It's not far at all." She thought of Brody and how he loved to ride the four-wheeler. Although, being the workaholic he was, he never had or took the time. She felt like he wasn't a romantic soul mate, but a soul mate nonetheless. Their friendship ran deep. Shawn's voice took her from her thoughts.

"I had fun yesterday."

"I really enjoyed it myself. I'm so glad for having had Carol's invitation to the park. Otherwise, we may have never met."

"I was actually thinking the same thing."

Within fifteen minutes of watching the countryside go by, Shawn pointed out, "I would loved to have grown up on a small farm like that one over there. I really do love animals. In the city, my family has an aquarium with black Mollies and gold fish. Plus, we all share Sara, our family calico cat. She will just sit for hours mesmerized by the fish."

"Well, maybe I can introduce you to some new animals out here."

Shortly after that conversation, she pulled her keys out of the ignition. "Here we are. Sit tight and I'll be right back with my four-wheeler."

Before Julie was out of earshot, Shawn spoke up, "It's beautiful out here. I can already see why you love it so much."

"You know, I get that same reaction from everyone who comes here. However, don't let it deceive you. There is a mystifying aura that can't be seen by the naked eye. It quickly engulfs and manipulates."

"How's that?"

Stopping in her tracks, Julie turned toward Shawn and responded rather cautiously, "This can be a mysterious, yet beautiful place at the same time, and I'm looking forward to a spectacular sunset this evening."

At that very moment, confirming her words of accuracy, Julie began to feel the beginnings of a warm caress she still didn't fully understand.

*"It's only me."*

Shortly she returned with her four-wheeler. "Are you ready for the grand tour?"

"I'm ready."

Briefly, Julie was stopping on top of her hill. It was a beautiful flat pasture and with woods lying beyond. "This field covers approximately fifteen acres," she pointed out. "Every year, I cut my hay from here. Then to the right is my observatory. Climbing up those steps, the countryside seems to open up and invite you in."

"Wow! Can we spend some time here?"

"Late this afternoon, when the sun begins to descend is the best time. Right now, we'll cross this pasture and go down by the river. It's not my land, but the owner allows me to use it as a means to get there. Most of the farmers work with each other out here."

They made their way to the destination Julie wanted. Pulling her four-wheeler to a stop, she hopped off and spread a blanket on the ground. "I love to watch the water trickle over these rocks. Occasionally, I've been known to toss a little message bottle into the stream."

"You wouldn't happen to have a bottle with you?" he asked, hoping for a yes response.

"Of course, I'll be right back." She was always prepared just in case she had the notion to throw a message in the river. She grabbed the small bottle stowed in the picnic basket she'd put together and carried on the four-wheeler, along with a pen and piece of paper for Shawn to write on.

Being anxious, Shawn continued, "Any idea what I should write?"

Julie shrugged. "Just let your imagination go wild. That's what I do."

Upon completion of his note, Shawn tossed the little bottle into the stream and watched it float out of sight. He then returned to the blanket thinking aloud. "It would be so neat to get a reply. I'm jealous of you having this little oasis all to yourself. I can't wait to come here again."

Julie moved close to him and placed her hand on his shoulder, making his cheeks flush. "You're welcome anytime."

"I wouldn't have missed this experience for the world," barely left Shawn's lips. All at once, the dense undergrowth behind them began to rustle

"What was that?"

She noticed the startled look on his face. "I don't know for sure. It probably wasn't anything of importance. I'll go look." Going over to the bush, a rabbit jumped out and fled. "Just as I thought, it was a rabbit." Then pointing Shawn in a southwardly direction, Julie changed the subject. "See the highest point over there? It actually looks down on my farm. That's the best place, except my observatory, for viewing sunsets. I think we should go over there, and I'll show you around."

Julie and Shawn crossed the pasture before continuing along a path that took them parallel with the fence. All at once, she pulled to a stop. "Shawn, look over there," she whispered while pointing.

Shawn followed the direction of her hand. Less than a hundred yards from them stood a buck and doe wandering through the clearing, searching for their dinner. The buck lifted his head, caught their scent, and bounded gracefully away. Shawn sighed and let out his breath, not realizing he had been holding it.

"See the approaching hill? I need you to hang on. The ride may be a little bumpy as this area was recently cleared of small timber."

While they jostled and rolled over the uneven ground, Shawn hung on for dear life. "What do you mean a little bumpy? Don't you have any shocks on this thing?"

"There's nothing wrong with my shocks, just hang on. We're almost there," she hollered back.

"Thank goodness for that. I hope you have a better exit plan." Once she stopped, he climbed off rubbing his backside. "How about I drive us back?"

She laughed and glanced over the land. "Shawn, look around you. Have you ever seen anything so beautiful?" They were encircled by another large pasture, which was also surrounded by tall timber.

"This is amazing," he said, while looking in awe. "The sun and the moon are in view at the same time. I've never witnessed anything quite like this before."

"You're experiencing what's called the in-between."

"I don't know what it's called, but I feel I'm caught up in a time warp."

They hiked for a time, then spotting a nearby log just before reaching the timber, Julie suggested they sit and talk. "I never get tired of this place. I surely love it over here. If it was my land, I would have built my observatory right over there on that spot."

"I see what you're saying. Just remember, though, I still want to climb the one on your property before this night ends."

"Right," she smiled. "Next thing on the agenda."

Julie was greatly enjoying her visit with Shawn. The more she listened, the more she could see the similar traits they shared. She had finally found someone who also met the out-of-the-box criteria, and it was somewhat refreshing to say the least.

Time passed quickly with the sharing of their individual experiences and before they knew it, the night shadows began to descend around them.

"Maybe we should walk back to the four-wheeler," Julie spoke up. "If it gets much darker, it won't be visible to us."

"I see what you mean. It's but a mere silhouette now sitting out there all by its self. Oh, but wait before we go, I want to tell you this one joke."

"Cool. Could you make it a fitting one? I don't know," she hesitated, "one that encompasses two people stranded at midnight in a dense forest with Bigfoot on the loose."

Shawn apologized, "I'm afraid I don't know a joke about Bigfoot."

"That's okay, I don't know one either. I was just trying to get a little rise out of you."

"Holy Toledo!" Shawn burst out. "Where did that sudden darkness come from? Julie, how did you do that? I can't see anything. In fact, I can't see my hands in front of my face."

"I didn't do anything," she quickly assured him.

Her words offered little comfort or support. Then a light, almost like a spotlight flashed on and off, blinding them with its piercing beam. Was it in the distance or right in front of them? It was hard to tell.

"What's going on?"

"I don't know," she stammered, while staring into the darkness, waiting to see what would happen next. "That light kind of reminded me of the spook light in nearby Joplin. It dates back to the 'Trail of Tears'. You know, back in the 1830's. Some people feel it is the ghosts of two young Native American lovers looking for each other. Anyway," she continued, "if you've never seen it, the light quickly appears from nowhere, causing the hair on your arm to stand up."

"That's enough information, Julie." He rubbed his arms. "That's what it does all right."

Suddenly, the light flashed on again and slowly began to encompass them before going out. It was huge, not like a flashlight, more like a beacon. No human could hold something that big. What was it?

"Seriously, Shawn, I think we need to make a run for it. We're like a pair of sitting ducks out here on this log. Follow me into the timber."

As the two ran the remaining way across the field in the dead of darkness, a horrific wind came out of nowhere making it almost impossible to run against its force.

"Julie! What's happening? Please, tell whoever is doing this to stop!"

"I wish I could," she shouted over the roar of the wind.

Finally, at the brink of exhaustion, they reached the timberline. For the next several minutes, Shawn and Julie sat on the ground and stared at each other without any sign of emotion. There was neither a leaf stirring nor a sound emanating from anywhere and darkness, total darkness.

Once Julie restored a form of sanity, she was able to verbalize, "I'm so sorry, Shawn. I shouldn't have brought you on this property."

Julie's mind flashed with a thought she'd been busted for trespassing on her neighbor's land. As if Shawn had the ability to read her mind, he whispered, "Julie, what's this about?"

"To be honest," Julie stopped in mid-sentence, "I don't have a clue."

"No clue?" he questioned in a stronger voice.

"At first, I really thought it was my biker neighbor. He's a very obnoxious person. He has nothing to do with his neighbors. This kind of behavior wouldn't be beneath him. However, the projection of that weird light circling us tonight came from an unknown source."

"I think I would have felt better knowing it was from your obnoxious neighbor."

Julie looked over at him. "We can't stay here forever. It's been awhile since we saw the illumination. Maybe the drama is over. Let's run over to the next field. If the light does come back, there are cattle over there we can use as shields. It will not be able to penetrate through them. If we try running into the open field, we'll be fair game, so to speak."

"Could we think up a better plan? You do remember I'm from the city. What about just heading back to the four-wheeler?"

"Have you forgotten it is in a large open area and we would be a target for a long while? It's either the cows or the open field, your call?"

"Okay, if my legs will stay under me."

"Then let's get off our butts and get out of here."

No sooner had Shawn and Julie reached the security of the cows, the light once again flashed on and appeared like it was searching for them. It began on the left side of the field and worked its way to the right, then every once in a while; it hesitated as though it had found its target.

This was definitely something she'd never experienced.

"Is this ever going to stop?" she wanted to scream.

She felt dizzy, bewildered, and definitely confused as to why everything bizarre seemed to happen to the men she cared about?" Had she indeed made a mistake by bringing Shawn to the farm? Then a cold, icy-like chill made its way down the middle of her spine. She had answered her own question. Bringing Shawn here was a terrible mistake. While attempting to clear her mind of such thoughts, she heard a loud snorting sound coming from behind them.

Realizing they were in real danger of being trampled, she grabbed Shawn's hand. "Let's get out of here. This wasn't a good plan after all."

Hoping to out run the bull, Julie and Shawn left the pasture they'd ventured to and in the total darkness, frantically traced their steps back through the woods and into the open field where they, at last, reached the four-wheeler. Julie nervously placed her key into the ignition. Suddenly, a stark illumination, of the taunting beam, glanced off them once more.

"You have got to be kidding me," Julie mumbled. Her heart raced. She somehow knew that whatever this thing was, it seemed to be from...out of this world.

Then the glow danced around them playfully, antagonizing them before it began to narrow itself until it eventually went completely out. Julie's mouth went dry. She felt she had been defeated. Then to make matters worse, she turned the key in the ignition and there was not a sound coming from the engine.

"Do something, Julie," Shawn persisted. "We need to get off this hill. I'm feeling sick."

"Shawn, keep it together just another minute. I'm going to get this engine started if it's the last thing I do."

"It might be the last thing. Have you considered that option?" he said, in a panicked voice.

"Stay with me, Shawn, just a while longer."

"Try the key one more time, please. It has to start."

Upon hearing the sputter of the motor, he breathed a sigh. "Oh, thank you. Thank you. We're moving. Let's get out of here."

While racing off the hill, Julie hollered over her shoulder. "Hold on." Then immediately she screamed. "No! No!" She pulled to a stop.

There in the stillness of the night, they were blinded with the brightness focused again straight at them.

"Shawn," Julie tried to whisper, "watch the angle of the light. It's starting to turn away from us. There in the distance you can see a dim glow of the city lights. There is hope yet." With the light having changed directions, Julie once again began her descent off the hillside. "No!" she shouted again. Apparently something electrical had happened and they no longer had headlights.

"What in the world is going to happen next?" Shawn tried to make sense out of tonight, but couldn't. "We're surely going to die trampled to death by cows or by a light of unknown origin."

Somewhat, having regained her composure, Julie said with conviction, "I'm not staying here a second longer. We're going to escape this hill, lights or no lights."

"Oh my! Oh my! How much further do we have to go?"

Julie quickly let Shawn know she was trying to concentrate on getting them out of their predicament. She gritted her teeth, just a few more seconds to safety. That was all she needed, just a few more seconds. Julie then placed a death grip on the handlebars and squinted. She was trying desperately to maneuver through the darkness and the timber stubble to end this drama once and forever.

"I don't think it's much further now, Shawn. I can feel the gravel on the road, and I can barely make out the outline of my house in the distance." Only seconds later, she confirmed. "I think we're actually going to make it. Yes, we're clear now."

Julie nervously pulled the into her yard. "Shawn are you

still with me? Are you okay?"

Prying his body off the four-wheeler and looking rather pale, he answered, "Ask me later, once I'm back in the city." Immediately, he added, "Excuse me, I have to sit down. My knees want to buckle underneath me."

"It's the wrath of the farm. You're another one of its victims, and I'm so, so sorry."

"Are we talking some kind of voodoo here? I don't want to be a party to anything like that."

"Maybe on the way back to town, I will enlighten you a little. Even though it will be hard for you to comprehend."

"Whoopee! I don't know if I can handle any more enlightenment tonight."

"I know and I realize that now, Shawn. Go ahead and get into the pickup."

Having secured the four-wheeler, Julie headed down the dusty gravel road toward the city.

"Oh! No! Shawn! My headlights just went out, but I'm not stopping until we reach the graveyard. Keep your fingers crossed. This phenomenon isn't over yet."

By now, Shawn just about had all he could take. He threw up his hands. "The graveyard! How handy."

Finally, having reached their destination, Julie's nerves were taut.

She pulled on the light switch a few times with no results. She then stepped outside and lifted the hood. After checking a few of the intertwined wires, Julie shook her head in disgust, closing the hood. "Well, that was a lost cause," she mumbled under her breath, then got back into the vehicle.

"How did it go?" Shawn anxiously asked.

"True to form, I've learned to expect the unexpected out here. My life has been plagued with bizarre happenings since I've owned this farm. My goal, right now, is to get us back to the city."

"Mine too. I share that same goal."

"Oh!" Julie gasped. Her body suddenly tense.

Here they sat encased, yet again, by another spotlight.

"I've had it." Julie didn't know how much more she could take tonight. She slowly turned her head toward the light, nearly jumping out of her skin at the sound of a sudden knock.

Roll your window down, came a request. Julie hesitated before responding. Upon the second knock, she slowly began to lower the glass.

"Sorry if I scared you," she could hear coming through the tiny opening. While trying to find some composure within herself, she said, "It's my headlights, they won't work."

"Just follow close behind my patrol car, and I'll assist you to the nearest gas station."

Julie let out a sigh of relief. "Thank you."

"Shawn, it's going to be okay. After we arrive, I will call my friend, Wapa. He's never going to believe this one."

"I don't either." Shawn breathed in and out noisily. "Will this night ever end?"

Within minutes, they pulled onto the parking lot and not too soon for either one of them. Stepping quickly out of her pickup, Julie thanked the patrolman and went inside to call her friend.

"Do you know the gas station on Division next to the blue water tower?"

"Yes."

"Well, the farm has singled out another victim tonight. I'll explain later. That is, once I feel in control and my mind's not exhausted."

"I'm on my way. Hang tight. It will be around midnight."

Back in the pickup, Julie tried to explain. "I really thought my neighbor was having a little fun tonight at our expense but there's no way a human could have pulled that off. Not out there in the wilderness on the top of the hill. Right now, I'm confused and I feel victimized. I keep running back to the city each time something happens, and then the farm draws me right back into its clutches.

She glanced in his direction. "You will probably want to forget this night ever happened, and I don't blame you."

"I feel exhausted. I can't put the fear I felt into perspective. I'll just be glad to get home where life is normal."

"Shawn, I totally agree with you. I can't begin to explain where that light came from."

At seeing Wapa pull onto the lot, Julie quickly opened her door. "You're such a dear friend," she hollered in his direction. "I've dragged you out here at midnight, and you don't even know why. I'm so relieved to see you." She threw her arms around him.

"I'm sure it's just another episode in your journey."

Joining them, Shawn said, "This is an episode I can't wait to come to an end."

Inside Wapa's vehicle, several minutes passed with little conversation. Finally, he pulled into Julie's driveway. "Well, I've brought you both back to civilization as we know it."

"Not a minute too soon." Shawn's voice still held fear.

Turning toward him, Julie asked, "Shawn, can I follow you home? You look a little green around the gills to me."

"No! I'll make it on my own."

"I would feel better if I followed you." Julie tried to encourage her gesture.

"I just need to clear my head."

"Again, I'm sorry."

"Julie, is it wise to let him drive home alone?" Wapa questioned.

"I tried to talk him out of it. What else can I do?"

"Just be sure to follow up with him tomorrow. He doesn't look good to me."

"I will and thank you so much. You really saved us tonight."

"My pleasure." He smiled.

Long after Shawn and Wapa had left, Julie sat down at her kitchen table. Her blood felt it had hardened in her veins. Pure willpower had kept her on her feet tonight. In a two-hour period, Julie relived the night's events over a thousand times in her mind. Still, she couldn't make any sense out of them.

While staring grimly through the darkness at her bedroom ceiling, she finally went to sleep. Around 3:00 a.m., she restlessly lay on her side. With her covers twisted beneath her, her tape recording mind played the same scene over and over. The vivid memories refused to go away along with hundreds of thoughts that raced across her brain with no actual word spoken.

The following morning, a series of ringing sounds caused Julie to sit straight up. Swinging her legs off the bed and wincing at their unaccustomed stiffness, she was finally able to stand. Her sleep-drowned brain finally registered to the familiar sound as she picked up the receiver.

"Is this Julie? I'm Shawn's mom," she heard a voice say. "Can you tell me what happened last night?"

"What's wrong?" In a semi-conscious state of mind, Julie asked, "Is Shawn alright?"

There was a slight hesitation and a crack in the woman's voice. "No! He's not. Shawn wrecked his car early this morning. He's been taken down for x-rays."

"Oh! No!" Julie burst out crying. "You can't be serious. Tell me he's going to be okay. I shouldn't have let him drive home."

"We're waiting for the doctor. We should know something later on today. As far as we know now, there are no broken bones but until they've completed all the tests, we don't know."

"Oh! I'm so sorry. I feel responsible. He went with me yesterday to my farm. His tests have to come back negative," she pleaded.

"I appreciate your concern. I was just hoping you could shed some light on what happened last night. I will call you later with the results of the tests and x-rays."

While trembling visibly, Julie turned away from the phone and stared bleakly out the window. The morning's rays had just begun to shine in on this May morning, so beautiful and peaceful.

Julie simply stood there motionless drinking in the warmth as her eyes brimmed with tears of sadness. She desperately tried to will herself into thinking happier thoughts. Still, nothing could distract her overwhelming feeling of liability.

"He's an innocent victim," she shouted repeatedly. "What has he done to deserve this? Is this never going to stop, this destroying of lives?"

Unable to wait any longer, Julie called the hospital to check on Shawn's progress. She was told he was improving somewhat. After that, daily calls were made to monitor his condition. When he was finally released to go home, Julie would often call his mom. One day, she was surprised when Shawn actually answered the phone.

"Shawn, it's so good to hear your voice."

"I guess you know I've been under psychiatric care?"

"Yes. Your mom told me," Julie sadly responded.

"I can't come back to your farm. You know that, don't you?"

"Yes. I wish I had answers for you."

Just before hanging up the phone, she heard, "Me, too."

No one should ever have to go through what Shawn had. "Why?" Julie cried out in misery. "Why did Shawn have this happen to him?"

Julie's whole being was ravished in heartache and disbelief for Shawn and his injuries. How could she explain what happened to him, she still didn't fully understand herself. For long moments, she would sit in total silence and shut her eyes against the pain.

Occasionally, she would turn on the radio and hum along with the music. Then there were those times she would just sit in her recliner, reflecting on how quickly her life seemed to change. She told herself it wasn't going to be easy, but someday she hoped to be able to put this horrible tragedy behind her. She didn't know if she would ever be able to return to the farm. She felt the price Shawn paid for going there had been far, too high.

In the following weeks, Julie poured her energy into her work, family, and friends; although, there wasn't anyone around her who actually understood or fully comprehended what she was going through.

*I do and perhaps in time you will.*

# CHAPTER 23

It had been over a year since Shawn's accident, and Julie had visited the farm only a few times since then. For now, she was content to just live a quiet life in the city. One thing she was very thankful for were her farm neighbors who were caring for her animals. Without them, she didn't know what she'd do.

She kept in contact with her dad via the telephone. His memory had improved somewhat after moving from the farm, and she was grateful. Her concern now was more centered on his diabetes.

In addition, there was one visitor who always put a smile on her face, Slate, her protector. He often checked in to see how she was doing. Many times after hunting wildlife or searching for Morels, he would stop by to give her an update on the farm. It hadn't been very long ago he had brought her barbecue.

He told her he rather enjoyed sitting under the gazebo, while the water cascaded into her fishpond. However, what he really missed was spending time on top of the hill around a cozy little campfire with her. He hoped she would soon change her mind and return to the farm. In the meantime, he was merely okay with this arrangement.

This overcast Friday morning in 1995, Julie was

relaxing and enjoying the fresh smell of rain coming in through her open door. All of a sudden, a bright flash of lightning followed by a loud clap of thunder and a cracking sound pierced the moment. The house shook all the way to the foundation.

"What the heck?" She jumped up off the couch knowing lightning had hit something and that something, she felt, was her home. Unable to find any sign of damage, but still concerned, Julie called the emergency number posted on her refrigerator.

"What is your emergency?"

"Hello," her voice trembled as she spoke. "I think my house was just struck by lightning. I have checked both inside and out, and I don't see any sign of smoke."

In a short amount of time, Julie heard sirens in the distance and noticed her neighbors had come out to see what the commotion was all about.

Seconds later, a fire marshal and a fire truck pulled into her driveway. Rushing up to them, she said emotionally, "I'm so, so glad you're here."

"It's all in a day's work." The fire marshal scurried toward her house. Then made his way back to where she was standing after his inspection.

"Good news, your house looks fine. Therefore, I'm sending the fire truck back to the station. I would, however, like to take a look at your attic."

"Right this way." Julie directed him into her garage.

As the fire marshal attempted to pull down the ladder, he stopped in midstream. "Oh! This isn't good. I just got a whiff of smoke."

Immediately following his comment, the extra oxygen sent blazing flames down the opening. Without hesitating, the fire marshal called for backup.

"No!" She couldn't believe this was happening! Why? Why?

Within moments, she heard the piercing sirens again. As

they intensified, she was shocked to see four fire trucks this time. Then the most helpless feeling washed over her body at several long flat-water hoses being dragged across her yard.

Changing her focus, she watched a fireman remove an axe. Continuing to monitor each step and stride he made up the ladder, she shut her eyes and put her hand over her ears to fight against the devastating, chopping sound he made.

Watching her house being destroyed minute by minute had made Julie's knees want to buckle. Less than an hour before, she had been sitting quietly in her living room unaware of the tragedy that was about to unfold.

Then while shifting her attention from the chaos and mayhem going on in her mind, she heard a lady's voice.

"Excuse me. I'm a reporter from the Springfield News Leader. I'm assuming this is your house. May I have a moment of your time?"

"Yes," Julie managed to say. She didn't know what to do. "I guess so. Yes."

"I'm writing a feature for tomorrow," the reporter informed. "Your house will be the cover story. It's highly unusual for lightning to strike without a thunder storm, just light rain."

"I know. I don't know what to think either. I wouldn't have been as surprised if it had happened out in the country."

"How's that?" the reporter questioned.

"I was just thinking out loud. I'm pretty upset right now."

Julie really didn't want to go into detail with the reporter about her life on the farm and why she was now living in the city, or why this house was where she lived when a catastrophe struck at the farm.

"I can surely see you have good reason for being upset," the reporter acknowledged. "I'm really sorry to have to leave you standing here like this, but I must be going in order to meet my deadline."

"I understand," Julie managed to murmur.

A few minutes later, her thoughts shifted back to the interview with the reporter.

*I'm not quite sure what I told her. Had anything I said made any sense? Oh well, I can read all about it later.*

"Excuse me, please!"

Julie recognized Kim's voice. She was the neighbor from across the street and she sounded frantic. Had her house been hit, too?

"Could someone call an ambulance? It's my husband!"

The fire marshal approached the distraught woman. "What's wrong, ma'am?"

"I came out to see what was going on, and I noticed my husband lying in a daze on the porch. He was doing some work outside, and I think the lightning must have struck him somehow. Please, hurry and call an ambulance!"

*Is there no end to this?*

It was but a matter of time until Julie heard an ambulance siren. She knew its destination. Moments later Chris was on his way to the hospital with Kim following behind. It was determined the electricity from the lightning strike to her home had traveled and somehow entered the end of the tape measure Chris was using and apparently electrocuted him. Thankfully, it wasn't fatal, but it was still serious.

Noticing how unsettling this had been for Julie, one of the firefighter's said, "He'll be fine. He just needs to be checked out."

At last, the firefighters were rewinding their hoses, and most of the commotion had settled down. "May I look inside?" Julie asked the fire marshal as he approached.

"Your house is structurally sound, and the fire is out. That's the good news. However, I can't really prepare you for what you will see inside."

"I've stood by this afternoon and watched this unfold," she commented. "I tried to watch it outside the box, trying to stay disconnected somehow. I'm ready to view the damage."

Walking through the backdoor entrance, she stopped. She was met with smoke residue and water everywhere. The walls, in places, appeared like black ink had been spilled on them.

"Follow me into the laundry room." The fire marshal motioned. "I want to show you something."

"Okay."

"I surmise the lightning bolt hit the power extension," he pointed out. "Then it ran down the guttering into your bedroom. From there it jumped into here. See it welded your washer and dryer together before exiting your open doorway. You were really lucky today."

"Looking at all this mess, I don't feel very lucky. In fact, besides the mess, it's kind of hard to breathe in here." Julie gave a slight cough.

"Have you seen enough?"

"No, I might as well see the rest."

"Okay, but you know you can't stay here?"

"I'll just grab a few salvageable items and leave. I cannot let this fire destroy my life, nor will I let it force me back to the farm."

Hearing the determination in Julie's voice, the fire marshal turned and walked down the hallway in the direction of Julie's bedroom. Being aware of the hazardous debris on the floor, he advised, "Watch where you walk."

With every step, her heart broke a little more at the devastation. It reminded her of Kail's destruction of the farmhouse only worse. She wondered why she kept putting off talking to Wapa's friend Night Hawk. Entering the bedroom, he stopped so fast, she almost ran into him.

"What the...!"

"What's the matter?" She stepped up beside him.

Shocked, she stood gazing into a mass of transparent gray matter. Something she'd never seen before.

"This is odd." The fire marshal looked taken aback. "This is definitely not smoke residue. It looks like, and I know this sounds off the wall, but somewhat like an...entity was burnt here."

An entity? For a moment, she stood speechless. "This is the kind of unexplained phenomenal happenings, I continually deal with on my farm." She realized, she'd said that as a matter of fact.

As the substance dissipated, the fire marshal looked bewildered. "You've seen this before?"

"Not exactly," she tried to explain. "I know this sounds crazy, but it's as though the farm I own or something that exists there, doesn't want me to live in the city?"

The fire marshal shook his head not knowing how to respond to the information Julie had shared with him. He surely thought she had inhaled far too much smoke or at best was traumatized over the destruction of her house. Although, he would have to admit he himself was still visibly shaken.

"I can't explain what I just saw in there." He turned toward her. "I need to call the office. Be careful in here. We don't want any more mishaps."

"I appreciate all you did today. I will be ready to leave shortly."

Julie stepped outside into the night air and was met with a slight mist of rain. While backing out of her driveway, she stopped at the edge of the street, rolled her window down, and viewed her house through the mist. Her neighbors had long retreated, and the traffic in the street had subsided, leaving her virtually alone again, her life in shambles.

Feeling helpless, Julie waved goodbye to the fire marshal, rolled up her window, and slowly drove down her street in search of a motel; a nice quiet dry place to sit and gather her thoughts. At last, she spotted a lit vacancy. Upon securing room key #23 and releasing a much-needed sigh, she entered the tiny lonely room.

After having survived all the previous drama and a restless night, Julie slowly climbed out of bed the next morning. She stepped over to the small window and looked outside at her surroundings. Despite last night's late rainstorm, only drizzle fell from the low gray clouds that remained.

Standing there meditating and watching raindrops fill a dip in the pavement, Julie wished she were watching from the comfort of her own home. Then conscious to the fact she was only prolonging the inevitable, she slowly walked away. She leaned back on the bed and rested her eyes. The silence in the room was deafening, almost unbearable.

Hoping to drown out some of the silence, Julie fluffed up her pillow and walked to the small, brown television that sat on an old-fashioned table. Then having watched it until she felt brain-dead, she more than welcomed Monday morning with open arms.

Today was going to be a meeting of the minds, one between her insurance agent, the contractor, and herself.

After nearly a week of negotiations, Julie was given the green light for Brian to begin the process of putting her life back together, which at best would take a few weeks.

Finally, Julie received the call she had been waiting for. She would soon be moving out of the motel and back into her house.

She pulled into her driveway and caught a glimpse of a 'For Rent' sign in the next-door neighbor's yard. Apparently, during her absence, the previous renter had moved. Surprised but hopeful nevertheless, Julie secretly wished for a single, good-looking cowboy to move in.

Realizing she was probably wishing in vain, she quickly parked her pickup and went inside to check on Brian's progress. Being pleased with his work, she returned to the motel and called Wapa to tell him the news.

"Isn't it wonderful?" she asked, hearing Wapa's voice on the other end. "I never thought I would be this excited to move back into a house in the city. Maybe life here isn't so bad after all, only one more week."

"I can't believe what I'm hearing," Wapa responded. "Haven't you had an urge lately to see your farm?"

"No, maybe sometime soon, though. I've really missed Tonka and Spook, and I need to check on my dad. Although, I know he's doing okay or my brother Jarrett would have gotten in touch with me, since he now lives in a doublewide on Dad's five acres."

"Well, let me know if you want someone to ride with you to make a farm visit."

"I will," Julie promised.

# CHAPTER 24

Julie was ecstatic to be back in her house and her life was returning to some form of normalcy. She had already replaced her damaged TV, washing machine, and dryer. What was still missing was a refrigerator scheduled to arrive Monday afternoon.

Sitting there in her living room, channel surfing, Julie came across the Oprah show. The word Prince Charming caught her attention. *What does Oprah mean?* One should never leave their home wearing sweats if one wants to meet Prince Charming.

She chuckled to herself. "What does the Oprah show know about sweats anyway? I personally know how comfortable they are, and I have my favorite pair on right now. See." She pointed to her dark blue ones as if it was possible for Oprah to actually see them. Oh, great, now she was talking to the TV.

Still chuckling, Julie's eyes were drawn to a nearby clock. Noticing the time and hoping to receive an important letter in today's mail, she turned off the TV and walked outside. While in route to her mailbox, she just couldn't let go of the sweat-pant comment.

After sorting through her mail and finding her important letter, she nearly made it back to the front door, when she heard a friendly hello from across the fence. She glanced up to see a man. Without taking time to focus on his face, and being embarrassed about her sweats, Julie could only murmur a weak reply before scurrying inside.

*Oh, darn.* She peeked out the window, hoping to actually see who belonged to the voice. *Darn it, darn that show for making me feel so bad about my appearance.*

What was it about the encounter that she found so intriguing?

Being upset with herself, she walked to the Styrofoam cooler to get a Pepsi. Suddenly, she had an idea. While wasting little time, she immediately rushed into her bedroom, changed into a low cut top, a pair of blue jeans, and a splash of her favorite Musk perfume.

"Alright, I'm ready as I will ever be." She marched out the front door like a woman on a mission, embracing a thirty-two ounce plastic mug.

Seconds later as she neared the neighbor's house, her confidence level began to diminish. Should she continue to pursue this charade or simply retreat? Then thinking now wasn't the time to give up, she nervously climbed up the two steps and knocked on the front door. Her light tap soon brought a sexy 6' 2" frame to the doorway. Unable to speak, she could only stand there and stare.

"Can I help you?"

"I'm your neighbor, Julie," she finally managed to stutter. "I live on the other side of the fence. Can I have? I mean, can I borrow some ice?" She displayed her mug.

Smiling in her direction, the neighbor stepped aside and invited her in.

"You're original. I like that. By the way, my name is Drew."

"It's nice to meet you." She extended her hand.

"Is my neighbor married? The way you avoided me, I thought you must be."

"No. No." Julie quickly recovered. "It's really quite

funny. Do you ever watch the Oprah show?"

"As a rule I don't, but I know who she is."

"Well, I was watching her show, all comfortable, in my favorite sweats," Julie began, "when I learned men aren't interested in women who wear them. I still had that on my mind. Therefore, I couldn't get back into my house fast enough."

"I love it." A proud smile crossed his face. "You know, I can't tell you what you were wearing."

"Really! I'm glad to hear that even if you are just amusing me." She couldn't take her eyes off his handsome face.

"Here, give me your mug. Would you like a Pepsi with your ice?"

"Yes, that would be nice. I won't have a refrigerator until Monday due to the lightning damage. You know my house was nearly destroyed?"

"When I moved in, I saw a carpenter over there." He handed back her mug, then quickly added, "How about coming over tomorrow night for a cookout? That's the least I can do for my neighbor in distress."

"Under the circumstances, I accept your offer. What can I bring?"

"Just your mug and it's okay if you want to wear your sweats." He smiled, and she was again mesmerized by his perfect features.

"I'll consider that. What time should I arrive?"

"Just open your window, I'm sure you'll be able to smell the charcoal," he teased.

Julie chuckled to herself as she went out the door. *"Well, he does have a good sense of humor."*

# CHAPTER 25

Mr. Casanova, alias the neighbor, who seemed comfortable whether on his Harley or in a business suit, had definitely struck a chord with Julie. Every time she saw him, she was reminded of his strong jaw line, the way his right eyebrow seemed to be higher than the left. How could she forget how much his nearness affected her? Yet, she had reservations about allowing this new man to be a part of her chaotic life.

One night while lying in bed, she quietly opened the door and invited thoughts of Drew to dance and play in her mind. It had been a long time since she had met anyone special. Drew was a lot of fun, and they seemed to have connected with each other. He didn't need to know her past, not right now anyway.

The following Saturday morning, Julie was busy in the kitchen. Out of the blue, she heard a knock at the front door. She walked into the living room and noticed Drew looking through the screen at her.

"Hey, Julie." His smile warmed her heart and made her feel good. "Have you ever been on the back of a Harley?"

"Most definitely."

She walked to the open door and peered out at him. "I was in my own little world. I had no idea you were anywhere around."

"Oh, that's okay. You know, you should keep your door locked. You don't know who might just walk in. Anyway, how about we take a ride? We can stop later for a burger."

"I'd like that."

Just the thought of riding behind Drew made her giddy. She tried to calm the butterflies forming in the pit of her stomach.

"But I don't have a helmet."

"I bet I can find one."

Her stomach growled. She didn't realize how hungry she was. "May I suggest we stop by Taylor's Drive-in for the burger? It's my second favorite place."

"You're the boss," he teased. "Meet me in my front yard in fifteen minutes. I'll have you a helmet."

"Okay."

Julie could barely contain her emotions as she watched Drew walk across the yard. She couldn't wait to climb on the back of that Harley and wrap her arms around his gorgeous body.

She jumped up and down. How did he do this to her? He made her feel young again.

"Oh, I can hear him revving up the engine. I need to stop this jumping and get over there."

After locking the door, Julie hurried to the Harley and picked up the purple helmet he had waiting for her.

"A very nice helmet and a very nice day for a ride!" she hollered over the rumble, then immediately snapped her fingers. "Wait a minute. I forgot something." She jumped off the Harley.

"There's not a lot of room for excessive baggage," Drew said, to her backside.

Upon returning, she commented, "I forgot my sunglasses. Do you like them?"

"Yes. They're cool looking. Are you sure we're ready now?" he jokingly asked.

"Yes. I am."

As Drew eased onto the city street," he said, over his shoulder. "Hold on for your life."

In quick time, the Harley was headed down Route 66 to Paris Springs Junction. Eventually, he pulled over and stopped beside a creek where they skipped a few rocks, then off to a small park near the edge of the city.

"Oh, it's been years since I've been in a swing like this," Julie gushed.

Once her swinging motion slowed down, she dragged her feet to a complete stop.

"There's something I need to tell you." Inhaling deeply, she looked in Drew's direction.

"Okay, I'm sure I can handle anything you care to share with me."

"Well then, here goes. First of all, do I look Indian to you?"

"Take off your sunglasses. I need to see your eyes. Hmm, I never thought about it, but you have some similar traits, especially your high cheekbones. Is that a bad thing?"

"No, it's not that." She sighed. "Not many people know my great, great grandfather was a Cherokee Chief. In saying that, perhaps my life would have been better if I had been allowed to grow up on an Indian reservation."

"Whew. That's not where I thought this conversation was going."

After thinking for a moment, the curiosity got the best of him. "Have you ever participated in Indian rituals?"

"Yes and I have a very good friend who is a hollow bone."

"What's that? I've never heard that term before."

She had to think of how to put this so he would understand. "Okay, it's kind of like...well, say you find an old bone in the woods and it's hollow in the middle, then it's probably because insects or animals have cleaned it out.

It appears to be immaculate and the inside is totally smooth."

"Okay."

"A Native American hollow bone is kind of like that. They are totally cleaned out. As a hollow bone, you have no ego, no concerns, no pride nor doubts. All you have is humility. Spirits can come straight to you and straight through you."

"Really, that's pretty cool. I would like to meet him."

"That can be arranged. Now, I have one more thing."

"Alright, let's hear it."

She then started to explain about owning a farm.

"That's it?" Drew sounded somewhat deflated. "You own a farm?"

"Not just any farm." Julie laughed at seeing the expression on Drew's face. "It's not your typical farm. It's a little more complicated than that."

Then not knowing just how to share her complex life with this new man, she hurriedly changed the subject. "How about I save this topic for later? I'm really getting hungry."

"Okay with me." Drew quickly stood. "I'm pumped and hungry at the same time. Just note, though, you're not off the hook."

Within a few minutes, they had made their way back to the city limits. Shortly, Julie tapped him on the shoulder and directed him to pull over.

"Why are we stopping?" He looked puzzled. "There's no food here on this empty lot."

"I know, but there used to be." Julie climbed off the Harley. "This is actually an historical site. This corner was once the home of Red's Giant Hamburg. Red's was the first fast-food restaurant with a drive-thru window. I used to come here a lot when I was young."

Julie then walked over to where Red's fifteen-foot-tall black, cross-shaped misspelled sign once stood and tried to explain how the sign would have been too tall to fit under the utility wires if the "ER" letters hadn't been left off hamburger.

"How odd, didn't he ever correct it?"

"No." She walked back to the Harley. "It read Giant Hamburg until the day it came down. It did make for good conversation, though." She laughed.

"Okay, I'm ready to go to Taylor's."

Within twenty minutes, Drew and Julie were seated in a booth near the back of the room. Looking around at its unique furnishings, Drew commented, "This restaurant is really old-fashion looking."

"Yes, it's timeless and did you notice they also have a drive-thru window? By the way, both of my favorite restaurants opened in 1947, a year before I was born. But as you saw today, Red's is only history now having served his last hamburger in 1984."

"Oh, our order is coming." Julie saw and recognized their waitress.

While enjoying the golden brown, crinkled-cut fries, she commented, "They're not as good as Red's, but they're not bad. Oh, darn it." She spotted a drop of catsup on her blouse. Being embarrassed, she immediately dipped a portion of her napkin into her water glass in an attempt to remove the stain. "Look how nervous you made me. I'm not usually this clumsy."

"Think nothing of it. I'm just glad it wasn't me."

Julie then saw Drew hesitate for a moment and knew he was about to bring up the previous subject matter. She really wished he would forget about it. What if all this talk immediately drives him away?

"Wasn't there something you wanted to share with me?"

"Darn it! Yes, but it's hard to talk about. Well," she squirmed as she propped her elbow upon the table trying to cover her recent wet spot. "My farm, at times, appears to destroy my happiness and redirects my life for a surmountable amount of time. Whew, I finally got that out." She breathed a sigh of relief.

"Well," Drew drummed the table with his fingers, if that's the case, why don't you sell the farm and walk away."

"In theory, it sounds like the right thing to do. Believe me; I have tried on more than one occasion."

"Tell me more." He smiled in her direction. "I'm somewhat intrigued."

"Somewhat, really? What if I told you I believe there's a spirit living out there? Would that information change things?"

"Not at all. Why should it?" Drew sat back against the booth. "Have you ever seen this spirit with your own eyes?"

"Hmm. No, not exactly, but for years, I have believed in spirits." She knew she had his full attention. "Well, for example, one day after my sixth birthday," she began.

"Your sixth birthday?" He laughed. "You mean your $16^{th}$ or your $26^{th}$?"

"No! My life is very complicated and has been since I was born. I was six years old, not sixteen, twenty-six or thirty-six. Anyway, I accidentally fell into my aunt's spring. She had sent my cousin and me to fill her water bucket. The wooden makeshift opening to her spring was old and weak looking. Once, I bent my knee down on the board it gave way. I fell in headfirst. Immediately, I felt a gentle hand turn my body around inside the small opening. Without that intervention, I would have drowned."

"And now you think it was your spirit, so to speak, who saved you that day? Is that what you're saying?"

Heat rushed to her face. "I guess so. It would explain a lot. Now, take the incident regarding the farm that happened just before my $30^{th}$ birthday." Here she was again trying to explain her crazy life.

"I suppose this is the farm we're talking about?"

"Yes. When I'm there," Julie hesitated. She couldn't believe she was telling Drew all this, but it was too late to turn back now. "Often I sense a presence, a warm reassuring feeling throughout my body." Then shaking her head, "I'm sure none of this makes any sense to you. Anyway," she said, in a second attempt of clarity, "haven't you ever encountered or experienced an unexplainable phenomenon in your life? Perhaps, as simple as seeing someone out the corner of your eye but when you turn your head to get a better look, there's no one there or when you get an eerie, creepy feeling that someone is watching you but there's not."

She looked toward Drew. "Would you classify that merely as having an active imagination or is there something more to it?"

"In response to your question," Drew cleared his throat, "I believe you believe and maybe someday you will let me see this farm for myself. Then I can make up my own mind. Right now, I just don't see how my life could be affected in any form or fashion by a spirit." Being somewhat revved up by this topic, he ended by saying, "No sir. No spirit, either good or bad, could ever control my life and that is a fact."

Julie could bring up the story about the oval shaped mirror covered in rose petals that fell and splintered into a million slivers or the time her dishes unexpectedly fell off the shelves in her kitchen or how her music box played a song without any assistance from her, or any of the other weird things that had happened to her over the years, but maybe there would be a better time and place for that. Drew had probably heard enough for one night. She didn't want to completely overwhelm him. After a while, he would probably think she was making up a story just to get his reaction.

*As usual, the chief isn't far from earshot and would like*

152

*nothing more than the opportunity to debate and take this subject matter to a higher level. Maybe even to the point of letting Drew experience firsthand a phenomenon initiated from another realm, one with his name written all over it.*

"Nevertheless," Drew continued, "you know I've enjoyed this day immensely. I wouldn't have missed it for the world. Thank you for recommending Taylor's, and maybe we can come here again sometime."

"I would like that very much." She couldn't keep from smiling. "And I'll be sure to bring a bib the next time."

A short time later, Drew was pulling into his driveway. "I'll walk you home and say goodnight." He climbed off the Harley.

Approaching Julie's front door, he hesitated before saying, "Thanks again for today, and especially for sharing a piece of your personal life with me. It was quite fascinating to say the least."

"It was my pleasure." She smiled. "Even though, I realize you are somewhat a skeptic."

"Well, maybe just a little skeptical." He took the key from her hand and placed it into the lock, lifted her chin, and forced her eyes to meet his.

"Yes. No. Yes," she barely whispered as she savored the sensational feeling of his lips pressed against hers.

## CHAPTER 26

The visit to Taylor's had been a pivotal turning point in this new relationship. Drew now often stops by and spends several hours sitting with Julie under the gazebo with the night air being rich in the scent of wild flowers. His visits often allow them to get a better understanding of each other and many times during their conversation, Julie gets re-occurring butterflies in her stomach.

"I love watching the moon and stars. I have spent many hours sitting outside around a campfire," Julie confessed one evening, while her fingers slowly crept into the warmth of Drew's palm.

It was a simple gesture perhaps, although this was the first time she had reached out to him.

Slowly, Drew began to interlace their fingers together. He gently rubbed his face against her knuckles, causing a warm and fuzzy feeling. The experience didn't hold a candle, though, to the melting feeling that happened next. Drew stopped the swing, brought her close, and kissed her passionately. It was as if this one kiss opened a door deep down inside her and part of her had been set free.

"I know by far this is the best night ever." She breathed heavily.

The following morning, Julie reeled with anxiety from

the tender moment Drew had given her that mind-altering kiss. Hesitating for a just moment at the sink, she couldn't help hold back a small smile beginning to cross her lips. Shortly thereafter, her phone rang.

"It will all work out, take care of yourself. I can cover your shift today, myself. Thanks for calling."

The call had been from one of Julie's employees, and this meant a very long, grueling day was evident for her. She couldn't wait to put this one behind her.

Finally, with her shift complete, Julie walked through the living room, laid her mail on the desk and checked her answering machine.

"Hi," the familiar voice began, "I would like to take you out for a nice dinner tomorrow night. I will pick you up at six o'clock."

*I'll be waiting with bells on.* She smiled at this invitation from Drew.

The following morning, Julie woke up with a smile on her face, still brimming with excitement over the message from the night before. Around 4:30 p.m., she decided to make strides to get ready for her pending dinner date. She didn't know where Drew would be taking her, but it really didn't matter. From the message, it sounded like tonight would be extra special.

After six o'clock came and went, Julie walked to the window and looked toward his house. He should be getting home anytime. If he were going to be late, he would have called her; she rationalized, then sat down and turned on her television. It seemed like every five minutes she was up looking out the window or standing alone in the living room surveying her surroundings.

Finally, she sank down onto the couch only to bounce to her feet again. Walking to the stereo, she selected her favorite Elvis album and without hesitation began to sway to the rhythm, her wayward thoughts wondering what it would be like to be held close in Drew's arms once more.

However, by eight o'clock, tears were trickling down her cheeks and her eyes swept unseeingly over the bits and pieces of the furniture she had collected after her fire.

Julie simply couldn't stop thinking about Drew. He was so handsome, and when her eyes met his, she felt helpless. She wanted, right now, to glide into the circle of his arms and stay there to feel his breath on her ear as he whispered assurances.

It was 8:30 p.m. when Julie's phone began ringing. She moved forward without thinking, collided with the sharp edge of the end table, uttering a sharp cry of pain.

"Hello," the voice said on the other end. "Are you ready for dinner?"

"Our date was for six o'clock. In case you hadn't noticed, it's now 8:30 p.m." She placed the phone back in the cradle.

Julie was hurt and disappointed at the same time. She had never been stood up before and tonight angered her. But what if there was a slight possibility that something happened out of Drew's control? She hadn't even let him defend himself.

Being thoroughly irritated with herself and the whole situation, she tried to read but to no avail. At last, she gave up and went to her loft bedroom. Hesitating on the top step, she wondered what had really happened.

After falling into an exhausted sleep, within the hour she was awake. She longed for the comfort of Drew's arms, and the reassurance of his voice. She stared helplessly into the darkness. Her thoughts focused on his face dancing in her mind's eye. She turned on her side after thumping the pillow into a more comfortable shape.

It was after six o'clock in the morning as Julie awoke from her shallow, anxious sleep, convinced she had heard a noise. Her eyes felt heavy, as though she hadn't slept at all. She lay still for a moment, her heart pounded like a hammer in her chest.

The sound she heard appeared to be coming from, of all places, her window. "I must be mistaken. My window is on the second level." The suspense was too much to ignore any longer, so she quietly got out of bed and went to investigate. To her surprise, there was a long stemmed white rose brushing against it.

"What the heck, you're crazy!"

There standing on a sixteen-foot ladder was Drew with the rose clutched between his teeth. She was fully aware of its early traditional 'true love' meaning. How thoughtful he was this morning. She beamed at his effort.

"That's so sweet, but you're not out of the woods yet." She shook her finger at him.

"Wait! I can explain everything."

"Okay, then climb down off the ladder." He soon joined her at the kitchen table, while giving her both the rose and a kiss. "Well," he began, "since he hadn't had an opportunity yet to rectify the situation he had apparently caused. "I was on a job site yesterday, in the middle of nowhere, and everything that could go wrong did. We just couldn't go off and leave everything in a mess," he paused before continuing. "There was no way to call and let you know."

Julie couldn't stay mad at a man who could always make her laugh. He complemented her life and made it whole. She was infatuated with him. Still holding his white rose, she stood up and placed it into a bud vase.

"I was really mad at you. I thought you stood me up. I realize now, I was wrong. I apologize."

"Apology accepted. Now that we have that bit of controversy settled," he said, giving her a gentle kiss. "Next issue on the docket, are you about ready to meet my parents? I know my dad will immediately fall in love with you. He owns a business in my hometown, and mom works there sometimes. She basically keeps the bills straight."

"Do you think your mom will like me?"

The question caught him off guard. He needed to choose

his next words wisely. "Well, now my mom may be a different story. I'm not really sure."

"What do you mean, you're not sure?" She saw the awkward look on his face.

"For one thing, my mom is very religious, and she's always selecting someone at church for me to date. I keep telling her, I don't need help with my dating skills."

He then stopped briefly before proceeding, "I have tried to talk with mom about you, but after I told her you owned a nightclub, she went ballistic. It didn't seem to matter that you don't drink. She thinks, you're too worldly for me, I guess. She wants me to marry a Christian woman."

"Maybe, we should put off meeting your parents for a while. Suppose neither one of them likes me?"

Drew's dark eyebrows lifted. "My parents will believe I took one look and fell head over heels in love with you."

Still having skepticism over his comment, Julie sighed, "I wish I had your confidence."

The discussion regarding Drew's mom was one of several. However, the day finally arrived for Julie to meet her. A meeting she was dreading, to say the least, and rightfully so for his mom did give her the cold shoulder. On the other hand, she was a hit with his dad.

"That's mom's problem. She cannot stop me from having you in my life." He then confessed, "Julie, I'm growing very fond of you. Once the time is right, we'll be together forever."

"I hope you're right." She held back unshed tears. "I've grown very fond of you, too. I just don't want to come between you and your mom."

Julie knew firsthand how lonely one feels without the love of their mother, and she didn't want that for Drew.

"I say we've spent enough time on this subject." Drew pulled her into his embrace and held her for a long time.

It had been weeks and Julie's mind was finally clear from the thought of his mom, but the issue of going out to the farm kept coming up.

One night, Drew again brought up the subject of wanting to go there. Could Julie have both Drew and the farm? In her heart, she was afraid something might happen to him in a like manner to that of Shawn. Was she just being paranoid?

Eventually, Drew was winning her over. Each day they talked more and more about moving. Drew's rental lease was coming due, and it would be a perfect time for him to move to the farm. Julie loved and hated the farm at the same time. She had vowed to never return because of Shawn's accident, but that was before she met Drew.

Maybe she had just overreacted. Could she find it in her heart to allow Drew the opportunity he wanted so much? She knew he would grow fond of her mysterious 125-acre farm with its Indian mounds perched high on the hill.

Drew's eyes would light up every time he talked about the possibility of moving out of the city. Julie knew she couldn't resist his plea forever. She was in love with him. One day, against her better judgment, she caved. Perhaps Drew and she could live out their lives on the farm.

"Okay, if that's what you really want." Julie gave him a hug.

The preparations were soon set in motion for the big day, and Drew was so excited he could not sit still. He was like a little boy with a new toy.

Looking at all the boxes ready to be loaded into her pickup, Julie said aloud, "Looks like I may have to move out a few things to make room for yours. Then again, I'm willing to do that." She threw her arms around him. "I'm so happy at this very moment."

"Me, too. I live in the hope and belief we will build our dream together for the rest of our lives. I love you more today than yesterday, but not as much as tomorrow."

Hearing those words, Julie simply melted into his arms and let the excitement overwhelm her. She could hardly contain herself. She knew she wanted to begin a new chapter in her life with him.

"Oh, by the way, what did Bailey have to say after you told her you were moving back to the farm?"

"Her views are the same. She says I have the revolving door syndrome. My dad calls it the roaming gypsy syndrome."

"Well, I call it the moving syndrome, and I'm anxious to get started," Drew said excitedly.

"I agree with that analogy. I know you will like living on the farm. It's so peaceful there. Not at all like it is in the city. There's no comparison."

Only minutes later, Julie pointed out the window. "Look in that direction. See the fencerow over there? My property begins on this side of it."

"Yes, I see it. How many acres did you say you own?"

"All together 125, there are eighty acres here and forty-five more that lie further down the road by the river. I will show you that property some other time."

"What do you plan to do with all this land?"

"For a long time, I've been making various trails that zigzag throughout the woods. I get my bulldozer out and push, pull, and drag the debris to open up new trails from time to time. However," she took a breath, "hard winters have wreaked havoc with many of them and they look pretty pitiful about now."

She sighed. "Sometimes, I even have to bring my chainsaw into the woods to cut up trees that fall and block the trails. I enjoy it. It's good therapy for me. I would eventually like to see these trails turned into a retreat for handicapped children. At least, that's one of my passions. Maybe you could help me fulfill this dream."

"Maybe I can." He smiled.

Julie caught a sparkle in his eye she had never seen

before.

He stepped out of the pickup and looked around. "Julie, it's everything you said it was and more. I love it already. I feel you made the right decision moving back here."

"I hope so." She grabbed a box from the back of her pickup. "Follow me and we'll get this stuff put away. I can't wait to take you to the top of the hill."

"I am anxious to see your observatory. You've talked so much about it. By the way, do you think we can build a campfire and stay up there for a while?"

"I think so and once the fire is just right, we can roast wieners and watch the stars come out."

*Of course, as one might expect, the chief's eyes beamed at the actual sight of Julie. However, seeing Drew was another matter. The chief gave him a dark, sinister look.*

They soon were on top of the hill. "Wow! It's awesome here." Drew's face beamed. "Those colors in the sky are breathtaking. I wish I had thought to bring my camera. Julie, why didn't you say, Drew grab your camera?"

"I'm sorry. Tomorrow night I'll say, Drew grab your camera."

"Okay. Smarty pants." He pretended to be miffed. "Don't get smart with me."

"Well then, if you will lend me a hand, we'll get the fire going. There's plenty of wood over there in that pile, and the sticks for the hot dogs are by the picnic table."

"Looks like you've done this before," he chuckled.

"Many more times than I can count, and I never get tired of coming up here. This is my sanctuary, my little piece of heaven. This is where I find peace of mind. My friends know, if they can't reach me by telephone, they can find me right here."

## CHAPTER 27

Julie and Drew were soon embracing a new lifestyle, including moonlit nights, the stars, the campfires, and the Indian rituals.

"Julie," Drew said one evening by the campfire. "We should get married."

"I confess. I have imagined what it would be like to be married again." Julie fondly stroked his hand.

"Then what's the problem?"

"Oh, just the same old thing, I can't seem to get close to your mom. I'm not the daughter-in-law, she had in mind."

Drew reached over with his hand, and touched Julie's cheek. It was an affectionate gesture bringing color racing to her face. "It doesn't matter what my mother wants, it's what I want that counts."

"You're right, of course, but let's give her a little more time and see what happens. We have the rest of our life to get married."

"I'm not giving up." He gave her a sensual kiss that left her breathless.

From that moment, they sat quietly by the campfire waiting until the last of the embers faded before retreating.

The following morning during breakfast, Julie approached Drew. "I need to go into town and take inventory. How about coming with me? It's been several days since you've been away from the farm. An outing would do you good."

"You're probably right. I have about thirty minutes of work left on the well house. If you can wait until I finish, I'll go with you."

"Good. While I'm waiting, I'll rinse my pickup off. I sure hope it rains soon. I'd like this dust to settle."

Having connected her garden hose and spraying water everywhere, Julie heard a familiar voice.

"Washing your pickup, I see."

"Oh. Hi, Alex. Yes. Dust is really a problem this time of the year. I should really park behind the house."

"It's sure good to see you living out here again?"

"Thanks. I'm glad to be back. You and Madelyn made my return possible. I can never thank you enough."

"You're welcome. I hope to see you riding again soon."

"I miss that time in my life very much, but since my accident I'm afraid to get back on a horse, maybe someday."

"Hope so for your sake. Well, you both take care now."

"We will." Julie waved goodbye."

"I heard talking." Drew acknowledged as he climbed into the pickup. "Was that Alex?"

"Yes. He just stopped to say hi. I know both he and Madelyn are glad every day that I've moved back to the neighborhood. They don't want me to ever move back to the city and neither do I."

*Me either expressed the chief.*

## CHAPTER 28

It had been nearly a year since Drew moved to the farm, and he had completed many projects Julie couldn't have possibly done by herself. Although, by concentrating solely on them, he wasn't able to help her financially. Therefore, after a while it became a sore spot. Occasionally, Julie would bring up the subject matter of him quitting his construction job.

"How would I have time to find another job? You keep me busy around here," came Drew's usual reply.

"I just thought you might keep your eye open in case something opens up."

"I can do that," he nonchalantly confirmed again and again. That irritating response was merely to avoid the issue of getting a real job.

As expected, this rift was definitely playing a part in their relationship. At one time, he eagerly met her at the door with a kiss, always anxious to share his day's activities with her. Now, he just seemed to go out of his way to ignore her. What was really happening to the couple who once seemed to have a bright future together?

Before things got too far out of control or blew up in her face, Julie decided to discuss the situation more thoroughly.

"I...I want to talk about us," she said, one evening at her

wits end. Drew looked up from his position on the couch with a puzzled frown.

"However, before I begin," she paused, "can I get you something to drink?"

"A beer sounds great, but I'll get it." He quickly disappeared to the kitchen. "What can I get for you?" he hollered back.

"Wine, please."

Drew should have been able to sense the seriousness of this talk as Julie seldom drank wine. However, tonight she felt it would help her out in the nerve department.

Julie slipped off her shoes and pulled her feet up under her, looking up only when Drew returned with their drinks.

Taking a sip before she began, she managed a slight smile. "Thank you."

Julie's fingers nervously twirled the stem of the wine glass before sitting it down on the end table. She embraced a nearby throw pillow to her chest, offering her only temporary comfort.

"There's so much to say." Her voice cracked with emotion. "I don't really know where to begin."

Julie couldn't help but remember when she and Drew were alone together, with no thoughts of past, future, or the outside world, things seemed perfect between them. Then life in the real world isn't always like that.

"Drew, I don't know what's happened to us." Julie's breath strangled in her throat as she fought the mad pounding of her heart.

"I don't understand it all myself. Should I leave?"

"No, I really don't want you to but something needs to change. I miss our old life."

Julie could no longer hold back the tears. "Why do things have to change? In the beginning, we were so happy. I love you too much to ever let you go."

"You're stuck with me for life," Drew added, brushing away tears. "Julie, try this on for size," he suddenly interjected as if the thought had just occurred to him. "Why don't I talk with my dad about working for him? I could save for our future. In the meantime, maybe I can shake whatever is draining my energy."

Reluctantly, Julie leaned back on the couch, shut her eyes, and thought for a second. Not being able to come up with any other idea or solution, she agreed with Drew's temporary separation concept and the promise of financial security.

The following morning, with last night's thought still ringing in his head, Drew called his dad and made the necessary arrangements in an attempt to potentially set what was wrong in their relationship on the road to recovery.

The morning of Drew's departure arrived all too soon for Julie. In the back of her mind, she wasn't completely convinced this was the right scenario for them, but it was too late to back out now. The stage had been set.

Before turning over the key in his Harley, Drew leaned over and gave Julie one last kiss.

"I love you. I will call from my parents' house."

The words cut deeply through her heart, and Julie fought to get control of herself. She knew this separation would have complications and possibly her life with Drew would never be the same.

"Goodbye." She waved. Sadness engulfed her.

Soon the sound of Drew's Harley grew fainter and fainter until Julie could hear not a fraction more of the sound she loved. She stood for several more moments, gazing at the magnificent countryside around her but noticed not a single leaf of it.

*It was just as well Julie couldn't cast her eyes upon the chief. She would have been deeply offended to see the slight grin spreading across his face.*

*What was this chief up to now? Had he set a plan into*

*motion or was this just merely nature taking its course? He answered the soundless question in his mind.*

That afternoon Julie lay silently on her bed, trying to shut out the memory of the Harley leaving her driveway, only to recall the sound of Drew's voice.

She then threw her legs over the side of the bed and got up. She stepped outside and called for Tonka.

"Hi, boy." She gave him a treat from her pocket.

He wagged his tail and let out a bark. Julie bent down and wrapped her arms around him.

"I know you miss Drew. So do I." She sobbed and stroked Tonka's back.

Gathering herself, she wiped away the tears. "How about taking a walk? Would you like that?"

Julie placed her hands into her jacket pockets as she walked down the gravel road with Tonka close by her side. Near a bend in the road, she stopped and looked back at the lonely little farmhouse.

All at once, her shoulders drooped. She felt a dark cloud encase her entire body. About now, Tonka nudged the right side of her leg. She tried to smile as she reached down and scratched behind his ear. He again gave her a slight wag of his tail for reassurance.

"It's going to be okay, Tonka. I hope so anyway."

Suddenly, the thought crept into her mind of how much longer she would have this faithful companion. He had been with her since her journey began on the farm. For the first time, she noticed the white hair in his muzzle and it saddened her.

Walking back to the house, Julie looked up at the gold horizon, a sign that dawn was approaching. She glanced in Tonka's direction. "Such a pretty sky, don't you think?"

Moments later, she entered the bleak kitchen and strolled to the sink. Her face grew serious as she filled a glass with water. She took a big swallow before walking to the refrigerator. She opened and closed the door. The thought of food made her sick.

Repeatedly, Julie looked at her watch. She wandered from room to room, unable to settle. She felt cold inside yet she couldn't bring herself to make coffee. There was a long pause while she waited to hear Drew's footsteps taking him from room to room. Hearing none and close to exhaustion, she finally went to bed. Once nestled under her big feather-filled quilt, her thoughts again returned to Drew.

Several hours later, Julie set aside the covers and got out of bed. The pillow beside her was cold. With a long sigh, she brushed the hair from around her face, her body riddled from exhaustion. Finding herself at the window, she pushed the curtain aside and stared. It was a beautiful night outside, but in her bedroom was a heavy, dark cloud hanging over her heart and a deadly silence in her mind.

After waking up the following morning, she still dealt with the aftermath of Drew's decision. She couldn't stop blaming herself for what happened. She should have never allowed their relationship to get so far out of hand. It was then that Julie understood how alone she really was. Yesterday's trials inundated her mind. Life goes on. There were choices to make and chances to take. Of course, there would be those times she would yearn for that special someone to talk with and that special someone just happened to be Drew.

Mid-afternoon the following week, Julie backed her pickup out of the driveway and headed toward the city. Shortly, she was knocking on Bailey's front door.

"Julie, what a nice surprise." Bailey embraced her friend. "I was thinking about you only this morning. Please tell me everything. I know you have a story. I've never known you without one."

"Well," Julie began, "I came in to do a little shopping and to return your book. I know you thought I had probably lost it."

"No. I knew it would show up eventually. By the way, how are you and Drew?"

"I don't know," she quickly responded. "He has moved back to his hometown to work for his dad. I'm waiting for him to call."

"What? I thought you were going to get married right away."

"Drew has changed. He doesn't appear to be very healthy to me. Bailey, I'm really scared and worried. I haven't slept very much since he left. I don't know what to do." She paused. "I believe there's a connection between his health and the farm."

"If you want to go check on him, let me know. I will go with you."

"Thanks, I'll consider that."

"I mean anytime. Oh, thanks for returning my book. I'm reading a mystery right now. If you want, I will save it for you."

"Thanks. I will pick it up the next time I'm in the city." Julie gave Bailey a goodbye hug before walking out the door.

Within forty-five minutes, Julie had turned into her driveway and there was Tonka waiting for her.

"Hi, boy." She gave him a treat before going inside to put her groceries away.

She was feeling a hollow emptiness that absorbed her spirit. However, hearing the nearby phone ring, she dropped everything and rushed to pick up the receiver.

"Please let that be Drew," she said, under her breath.

Her heart immediately skipped a beat. It was so good to hear that voice again. She'd missed him so much.

Being a little disheartened, she quickly let him know. "I was beginning to worry. I thought you forgot my number."

"My beautiful Julie, as the cold winds blow outside, I'm warmed by the thought of you. I pray for your peace of mind as I work toward my own. I focus on the positive aspects which will strengthen and grow each of us to become an unstoppable force together."

"That's beautiful, Drew. Is that how you really feel?" Julie gushed at the sound of his voice.

"Yes. You know I always tell you how beautiful you are, and someday we're going to be married."

"I want that very much." Her voice quivered tearfully.

"It's been busy here. I haven't worked this hard in a long time. Mom's been fixing dinner every night for dad and me. Before I leave the house in the morning, she wants to know what I want to eat. That part has been really great, but I've missed you."

"I've missed you, too."

"After I got away from your farm and had time to allow it all to soak in, I believe that life is composed of far more than what the natural eye can see. I've come to terms that the spirit on your farm made me ill. It took me a long time to admit that. Julie, I'm going to fight back the best way I know how, in my own way and on my own terms. However, right now I need to get strong. I need to get back to my old self. You know I love you, and I want the best for both of us."

"I love you, too. Get better soon." Her voice cracked. Somehow, she knew in her heart things would never be the same between them.

As the days turned into weeks, Drew did become stronger. Nevertheless, there was no mention of him returning to the farm. He did talk a lot about riding his Harley around his hometown, and the word soon got back to Julie about the young women who enjoyed the company of the handsome man who rode the Harley.

The urge to be wild and free seemed to creep back into Drew's life. It wasn't long before Julie began to feel their relationship was being put on the back burner. For some time, she knew Drew was taking country music dance lessons. He told her that a woman in his Sunday school class offered to give him the lessons, and he didn't feel right turning her down. In fact, Drew tried to convince her the dance lessons would only strengthen their relationship. Julie begged to differ because he was never interested in dancing before.

However, she was trying to keep an open mind, and with New Year's Eve just around the corner, it would be a perfect time for him to show her his new dance moves. As the time approached, Julie became excited. Maybe 1999 would be their year.

"Hi honey." It was Drew on the phone. "I'm so sorry. Something came up, and I won't be able to see you. I know we were going to bring in the New Year together, but I promise I will make it up to you."

Trying to choke back her disappointment, she held onto her emotions. "Sometimes things happen out of our control. When will I see you again?"

"I don't know. I'll call you later. Bye."

A cold shiver exploded throughout her body. Anguish throbbed inside her mind like a great, dark bruise. It was impossible to conceal her misery. Therefore, being unable to control her trembling body, she cried out in anger. "I can't lose him this way." But her mind told her she wouldn't force him to love her if he didn't want to.

As time passed, there was little communication between them, and Julie screamed at the twinge of pain that tied her heart in knots. Not being able to sleep, she was often crazed by images of Drew, tortured by memories of their time together. Was she going to lose him?

Her heart told her she wasn't letting him go so easily, but her pride said she wouldn't chase him and beg for his love. Why, why wouldn't she allow herself to fight harder for something she wanted more than anything? Was it her or the farm that stifled her will?

She had nearly given up hope. The incoming call startled her.

"Hi." Drew began with a slight hesitation in his voice.

"Drew where have you been? I have so many questions. I've doubted our relationship."

"I know, honey. So many things have happened. I've been trying to find a way to tell you, but there's no easy way. I couldn't just write you a letter, not after all we've been through."

"What are you saying? You owe me the truth," she cried.

"Bear with me. This isn't going to be easy." He cleared his throat. "As you know, I went to church for some form of stability in my life, and I began feeling good for the first time in a very long time. Then the unthinkable happened." Drew paused for a moment and then blurted out, "I fell in love or least I thought I did."

With those words still ringing in her ear, she interrupted, "Tell me it isn't the dance instructor?"

"Yes," he hurriedly spit out. "We've been married for a month."

"What! You are not serious?"

"Julie, I'm so sorry. I can't get you off my mind. Please don't hang up, please. I've already filed for divorce, and I'm so sorry I screwed up everything for us."

Julie stood in absolute shock. She couldn't believe this conversation was happening. The color drained from her face as the receiver fell to the floor. The intense longing she'd felt earlier ravished her entire body. Tears stained her face but her willpower prevented her from breaking down. She hurriedly walked into the bathroom and stepped into a steamy, sweltering shower.

The memory of the Drew she'd loved filled her heart with pain. She stood for the longest time allowing the hot water to pulsate over her entire body.

In sudden horror, she questioned herself. *What's*

*happening*? Something---or someone---was in the shower with her. A pair of familiar arms had clasped themselves around her waist. The intense feeling was real, both pleasant and perplexing. Part of her wanted to pull away but her pain hurt so badly. She found herself succumbing to the initial comfort of the arms but only for a moment. What was happening? Confused, she closed her eyes and let the warm water wash away the amorous happening. Suddenly, she gasped for air. A blast of ice-cold water hurriedly sent her scrambling out. She grabbed a nearby towel, only pausing momentarily to catch a glimpse of her reflection in the mirror. She looked like death warmed over.

Wrapped in the comfort of her towel, she made her way to the living room. Still lying on the floor was the receiver. She picked it up to end the irritating sound, dropping into the nearby recliner.

In an attempt to stop the pounding, suffocating sensation going on in her head, she leaned back and shut her eyes. She desperately hoped and wished for some kind of clarity, understanding, or resolution. Not only to what had happened with Drew, but also what had just transpired in her shower.

For the next few days, Julie constantly looked out her living room window searching for solutions. At best, she hoped to hear the familiar sound of the Harley coming down the lonely country road.

## CHAPTER 29

April flowers were in full bloom, and the countryside looked like a beautiful work of art, but Julie's nagging feeling of indecision and insecurity still lingered. She climbed out of bed with the grim determination to shake all negative thoughts from her mind.

She stepped outside. The sky above immediately caught her attention with its pale blue canvas and elegant white clouds. Before long, Julie found herself climbing the steps to her observatory.

As her eyes scanned across the countryside, she became troubled. *Oh, how quickly things seemed to change.* The previous dream-like clouds were starting to roll in an angry motion.

Without hesitation, she quickly descended the steps and returned to the security of the farmhouse with a lonely and abandoned feeling. She picked up the receiver and dialed Bailey.

"Did I call you at a bad time?"

"Not at all, how are you doing this morning?"

"You mean besides feeling lonely and sorry for myself. I'm just overwhelmed I guess, and the pending storm doesn't help matters either."

"I hesitate to bring this up again, but have you thought

about selling out and moving back to the city?"

"How odd you ask me that this morning. Last week, I was looking around in the barn, and I came across the old 'For Sale' sign. Well, it was all I could do not to place it right back in the front yard. I've never really felt that way before."

Bailey was surprised at this response. "Well are you?"

"I don't know. Since then, I've been pondering a crazy idea like moving back to the city and hiring a handyman to live out here, some middle-aged man that has nothing to prove. I'm through trying to find someone to share my life with."

*The chief listened intently. If it were conceivably possible for Julie to see him, she would notice the steady stream of steam bellowing out of his nostrils about now. Pounding his fists against the old Oak, he verbalized. "This farm can function perfectly well without a handyman."*

Bailey was surprised by Julie's comment. "Do you have someone in mind?"

"No, not at all."

"I guess you could run an ad in the newspaper?"

"Why not, I don't know why that idea hadn't already crossed my mind. Thanks."

Taking Bailey's suggestion seriously, Julie decided to call Wapa and see what he thought about the whole idea.

"Good morning. I'm thinking about making another transition in my life," she blurted into the mouthpiece.

"What are we talking about here?" Wapa heard determination coming from his friend.

"I'm pretty serious about moving back to the city. Maybe I can re-direct my life with the help of a handyman. He can live on the farm and take care of everything for me, like an over-all fixer-upper."

"Sounds like you have given this some thought. My

advice would be to make sure he has good references."

"That's easy enough. Thanks, Wapa." While Julie placed the telephone back in its cradle, she gazed out the window at the still dark, angry clouds. After the damage to her house in the city, storms made her very uneasy. Finally, she sat down in the recliner, propped up her feet, turned out the lights, and hoped for the rhythm of the falling rain to lull her into contentment.

Suddenly, a sound from outside startled her. She quickly rose up and rubbed the back of her neck where the hair stood up. She listened intently, but heard nothing else and concluded it must have been the wind. Realizing she would be placing an ad tomorrow, she sat back down with pen and paper in hand and composed what she wanted to say.

Much to her surprise, she woke up the next morning to a bright, sunny day. Staying in bed was only putting off the inevitable. Before long, she had showered, ate breakfast, packed her suitcase, and just before walking out the front door, picked up her ad, verified its contents, and called it in.

"WANTED: Middle-aged handyman who would love the serenity of living in the country in exchange for farm chores.

The next morning, Julie received her first call in answer to her ad.

"Hi. My name is Chase. Are you the party looking for a handyman?"

"Yes," Julie responded.

"I know your ad was for someone middle-aged. Would you consider someone younger? I work hard."

"Actually, you woke me up, but in answer to your question, I really had in mind someone older. So, I can't say because I don't know. You're the first one to call."

"Thank you." He hung up the phone.

She had other calls that day, but the younger man stayed in her mind. She took notes on all of the callers, and then recalled she hadn't gotten a number on Chase.

Julie answered her ringing telephone many times on day two. About the sixth ring, she heard a slightly familiar voice.

"Hi again, this is Chase. Have you changed your mind about hiring a younger man?"

"No, I haven't. Not yet, at least."

"I really would like this opportunity. You wouldn't be sorry, just give me a chance," he pleaded.

"I kind of had my mind locked into hiring someone with farm experience. Do you have any?"

"No, not really," he confessed.

She felt herself weakening, but stood her ground. "Then I'm sorry."

The following morning, Julie was in a deep sleep. Her telephone jingled its way into her dream. She hurried to pick up the receiver, if only to silence the annoying sound. "Julie speaking," she mumbled.

"Good morning to you," the male voice happily replied.

"No. Tell me it's not you again." Julie ran her hand through her hair. It was actually kind of nice to hear his voice. "This is the third morning you've called and woke me up."

"You can call my landlord, and you can call my employer. I know I can do the job. You just have to let me prove it to you."

Reluctantly, she pulled open a nearby desk drawer and removed a pad and pen. "Okay. Give me their numbers and yours. Then I'll make up my mind."

"Fair enough." He relayed to her what she needed. "You won't regret it. You have a great day now."

Later that afternoon, Julie called her friend, Wapa.

"How are things going?" he immediately asked. "Have you found a handyman, yet?"

"That's why I'm calling. My first call about the ad was from a young man."

"I thought you were looking for someone middle aged."

"I am but this young man has called me three days in a row. I called his references like you suggested. His landlord said he was neat as a pin and appeared to be a hard worker. Listen to this from his employer and I quote: 'Chase is extremely neat, and I have never seen an employee work so hard.' Doesn't that sound great? What do I do now?"

"It's your call."

"I guess I will think about it for a while. Oh, guess what else is new? Alex has a horse for sale. It's a beautiful Chestnut-colored Morgan."

"Will this new horse be delivered soon?"

"How did you know?" she asked, puzzled by his comment.

"Have you forgotten who you are dealing with?"

"Oh yeah, I do tend to forget sometimes. The name of the horse is Phantom. You know from Phantom of the Opera."

"Right, a little more mystery is just what you need in your life."

"I do have a concern."

"Yes and what's that?"

"He walks on three hoofs. I hope it isn't a mistake buying him."

"Remember, you have a horse whisperer across the road at your disposal."

"True. Thanks for reminding me."

"Anytime, my friend. Oh, Julie, don't get so involved with the handyman and Phantom that you forget about the vision quest coming up."

"There's not one chance in one thousand that I will forget. I've been looking forward to having that peace of mind again. However, I must admit, I haven't prepared myself mentally, and I know that I must overcome these earthly wants and desires to fully receive this vision."

"Well, hopefully the quest will take you to the point of realizing what you can go through and still come out in a good way with your heart and mind clear, and your body able to function."

"I can hope anyway."

"Take care, my friend. I trust you will make the right decision regarding your handyman."

Pressing the button to hang up, she kept the receiver in her hand. She thought of Night Hawk. Why had she put off talking to him? Wapa was right, he could probably help her and tell her what was and is happening with the goings on at the farm. However, now wasn't the time to think about that. She had other things at hand.

She let off the phone button and at the sound of a dial tone called Chase. "Hi, this is Julie. Would you like to have a look around the farm tomorrow?"

"Yes. Most definitely."

"Fine, I will pick you up around ten o'clock."

"Thank you so much. Oh, ah, does this mean I'm hired?"

"We will talk about that later." She took down his information and anticipated meeting this young, persistent man.

The next morning, she drove right to his apartment, as though she had been there before. Waiting on the sidewalk was a nice-looking young man approximately 5'7". *He has to be fifteen years my junior,* Julie thought to herself. *Oh well, it's too late to turn back now.*

She pulled up beside him. "Good morning. You must be Chase?"

"Yes, and you're, Julie?"

"That's me." She smiled at his eagerness.

"I've been watching for you. I'm excited about seeing the farm." He climbed, into the passenger seat.

During their drive, Julie took the liberty to inform Chase

what would be expected of him, and he in turn had a few questions of his own.

"See it didn't take that long," Julie said, seeing her driveway just ahead. "I'm going to go on and drive up the hill. You can look down over the farm from there."

"I love it already. I know I can do all the chores you spoke of. I want this opportunity, and I want it bad. I can cook, push a vacuum, and feed your animals."

"Great," Julie responded. "I'm going to let you familiarize yourself with everything. In the meantime, I need to go across the road to visit one of my neighbors. I won't be gone long."

"That's okay. Take your time."

As she parked in Madelyn's driveway, she spotted her working in the garden. "Hi, everything looks great."

"Thank you. I've already had lettuce, tomatoes, and green beans. I'll give you some for your dinner."

"That would be great. By the way, I'm getting a handyman to live out here. That's what I'm doing today."

"Does this mean you're moving back to the city permanently?"

"Yes. My life is a mess again, but this time I'm not leaving you and Alex feeling responsible. I probably shouldn't have, especially since I'm moving back to the city, but I bought a horse from Alex to give Spook some company. There is some concern about his right foot. Do you think I could consult with you if there is a problem I can't handle?"

"Sure thing, call me anytime."

"By the way, the potential handyman's name is Chase."

"Don't worry about anything out here. I will keep you updated on both the new horse and the handyman."

Madelyn handed Julie a sack of vegetables. "Add these to your dinner."

"Thank you, I will." She gave Madelyn a goodbye hug.

Returning to her farm, Julie spent the next few minutes

showing Chase the ins and outs of farm life, and on the way back to the city, she discussed her dream for its future.

In response, Chase commented, "I know your concerns and rightfully so, but I promise you I can do the job."

"I'll make my decision and give you my answer in a few days."

"And I'll look forward to your call." Chase smiled back at her.

The next couple of days Julie struggled with her decision. After considerable pacing, she sat down at the kitchen table and dialed Bailey.

"Good afternoon. Do you have a minute?"

"Sure. You caught me at a good time. I'm taking a break from kitchen duty."

"Well," Julie began, "I met with the young man with impeccable references."

"Were you impressed with him?"

"Gosh, he's so young."

"Are you having second thoughts about hiring him?"

"Yes, I'm really struggling right now. I took him to the farm and showed him around. Nevertheless, I keep asking myself why a middle-aged man with some actual farm experience hadn't answered my ad."

"I wish I could be of more help. I guess you will have to just trust your gut feeling."

"You know, Wapa and I are getting ready for our vision quest, so I need to make a decision. I very much need to calm down in order to prepare my mind, body, and spirit."

"Is there any reason except this young man's age that causes you to doubt his ability?"

"No, it's mostly his age. What the heck, I'm going to call him and let him know he has the job. Thanks Bailey for letting me sound off."

"You're welcome. Enjoy your quest."

"Thanks again, Bailey."

Immediately, after ending her conversation, Julie dialed Chase. "Hi, this is Julie."

"Oh hello, have you made your decision? I hope it's me."

"That's why I called. I have made my decision. After much deliberation, I'm going to give you a chance to prove yourself."

"You won't be sorry."

A few days later, Julie felt the timing was right, so she once again called Chase.

"Good morning. Are you ready to make the big move to the country?"

"Yes. I'm packed and ready."

*The chief couldn't believe the words coming out of Julie's mouth. She was really going through with this charade. This action seemed like anything but a workable solution.*

Julie was surprised to find Chase had everything neatly packed in boxes when she arrived. She could see that moving him to the farm wouldn't be much work at all.

"You travel lightly." She made the comment while loading the last box into her pickup.

"Yes. I don't like clutter."

"Once we arrive, you might want to ignore what you see." She laughed. "I have two nicknames, where most people go through life with only one. My first is *Miss Chocoholic.*"

"And the second one is?" he questioned. "I'm waiting."

"My second nickname is *Flea Market Fanny.*" She couldn't help chuckling as she looked at the neatness of his belongings.

"Then I'm here just in time to save you." He laughed.

On the short drive to the farm, Julie and Chase talked non-stop.

"Look," she said, "we're already here. I will show you to your room and while you're putting your things away, I'll help by bringing in the remainder of your boxes."

Julie was in the bed of her pickup when Tonka began to bark. She looked up. "Oh! Hi Alex."

"Surprise," he blurted out, "I've brought you something. Should I put him in your barn?"

She walked over and gave Phantom a welcome pat. "Yes, by all means. By the way, did you know I'm getting a handyman?"

"Yes. I was talking with Madelyn the other day, and she said something about it."

"I moved back to the city again. I guess that comes as no surprise to you. However, the handyman will be responsible for the chores this time. I wanted to give you and Madelyn a much-needed rest. The handyman is moving in today. That's why you caught me here."

"I'll miss you, but you have to do what's right for you. Thanks again for buying Phantom."

"You're welcome. I think."

"I'm on my way into the city. Can I get you anything?"

"No thanks. I'm heading that way myself. That is, after I get Phantom and the handyman settled in. I'll be back tomorrow, though. Chase was actually the first man to answer my ad. He called me every morning checking on the job. The only thing is he's a little bit younger than I wanted. I had hoped for an older man."

"Well, good luck. I'll stop by later and see how things are going."

"I appreciate that. Thank you." She could only hope the lack of her presence on the farm would stop any happenings toward Chase.

Julie barely had time to be acquainted with the new handyman and Phantom before her scheduled trip with Wapa. She woke way before dawn on this day. Opening the front door, her eyes caught a glimpse of a slight glow in the east.

"It's going to be a beautiful day for a trip. I just know it. I'm ready to let go of my old life. I very much need this vision to strengthen my heart and mind, while changing my perception of the world."

"Well, good morning." Wapa climbed the steps to the front door. "You appeared to be a million miles away."

"Hmm. I guess I was."

"If we're going to get there before sunrise, we had better be going."

"Let me lock up first."

"I'm excited to see my old friend, Ocacona. Thanks to his generosity, we will be using his teepee."

"I appreciate him doing this for us. Does Ocacona have a meaning?"

"It means, White Owl."

"That's beautiful." She took a deep breath and couldn't help but smile. It felt as though some weight had been lifted off her chest. "You know I feel rather carefree this morning."

"It's definitely good, my friend, to see a smile on your face."

"I guess my mind is relieved now that Chase is handling the chores at the farm. I can see so much potential." As she closed the door and leaned back in the seat, she gave a sigh of relief

Wapa glanced at his watch. "We've actually made pretty good time this morning. We should be there in another fifteen minutes."

"Wonderful," came her lazy reply. It seemed she had closed her eyes for not more than five minutes, when she felt a nudge on her shoulder. She barely heard Wapa.

"We've arrived."

Julie shook her head and blinked her eyes open to wake up. "I can't believe we're here already."

The two wasted no time in climbing out of the car. Right away Wapa spotted his friend. They barely had time for introductions when they were taken to be purified in a sweat lodge. Julie knew that once they stepped inside his teepee, there would be no more communication between them until the ceremony was over.

After purification, they entered the teepee and the three sat around a little campfire. It would be kept burning the entire time and had been made ready for them from apple shavings, sage, and seven different kinds of wood. The fire, itself, represented the fire of life that would carry their prayers to heaven. Occasionally, through the glow, they could see a silhouette of each other.

Early on, the trio smudged sage and smoked the sacred pipe in order to get rid of the bad spirits. Throughout the following hours, while they prayed, Julie and Wapa were aware of the beating sound of the drum emanating from inside, and during the following hours, they ate red grapes and drank water as their nourishment.

In order to begin the vision process, one must pray in a good way. The spirits, coming as sparks of light, give directions. Their purpose is to tell you what it is you are seeking and what you need to do to become active in your own life.

A few hours into the ceremony, Julie had her first vision. She saw herself walking into a familiar green pasture and coming in her direction was a stunning horse. She noticed he was limping. "Phantom is that you?"

He looked so sad and vulnerable. Her heart broke for him and his pain. His big brown eyes focused on her and words whispered in her mind...*Help me.* Before she could react, he turned and limped away.

"Is that really you, Phantom?" She reached out. "Wait, don't go." The horse never looked back, and the vision slowly faded into darkness.

In a short time, a bright glow replaced the darkness, and

now the pasture was an Indian camp. *What happened to Phantom? Is he somewhere in this camp? What does this all mean?*

While trying to sort through the mayhem going on in her mind, Julie spotted the most beautiful and perfect young Indian maiden. She was being led into a secluded cave against her will. Julie looked on in disbelief. Why would the chief of this tribe allow this?

A few minutes later, the chief arrived at the cave's entrance. His voice was low and powerful. He spoke to the warrior standing guard. "I want her kept here, untouched by human hands."

No, this is wrong. Please, someone help her. Julie desperately tried to talk. Why wouldn't her words come out?

The young maiden began to moan, while she sat with her back to the rock wall, rocking back and forth and swaying from side to side. Julie saw the pain in her eyes mounting. The maiden surely wished to die. Who was this young woman and why could she feel her pain and sorrow with such intensity?

Julie looked on with empathy, her own heart breaking. Sadness, so much sadness, she had to help this woman.

Then, her vision started to fade. *I can't leave now, my vision isn't complete."* Slowly she was drawn back into reality. As they sat quietly for a few minutes, letting the visions sink in, no one spoke.

Ocacona handed them a soft cloth, and they wiped the sage from their face. The fire had now died into embers, the three stood. Ocacona escorted them back to the sweat lodge. There they sang sacred songs, prayed, and shared their visions with a medicine person whose job it was to provide spiritual guidance and interpretation for each of them individually.

Julie was anxious to find out what the man thought lay behind her vision. She sat cross-legged in front of this wise old soul and recounted what she'd experienced.

"Very interesting." he pondered his thought for a few moments. "I reflect that the maiden is you."

"Me?"

"In some way, you think you are being restricted from living your life. There is a spirit you feel that surrounds you. I believe there is some truth in this secret deception."

Was he confirming her suspicions? Did that mean the farm possibly held the spirit of a chief from another realm?

Her mind was in a whirl. How could he know these things? She hadn't shared any of what had transpired on the farm. "Are you saying I'm being held captive like the maiden?"

"I am saying there is a property from which you have the evidence you need. You will have to decide if it is truth."

Wow! Overall, it's been quite a quest," she confirmed, shaking her head. "Thank you. Your insight and wisdom has given me plenty to think about in the next few days."

"Now that your vision is complete, do you feel ready to participate in the big feast, it's part of your quest, you know?"

"I am anxious for a cup of coffee. However, I don't know about the food, but maybe I can eat something." Julie soon found each bite of food felt heavy in her stomach.

"I kind of feel the same way," Wapa said, after pushing his chair back from the table and standing to his feet.

Following a quest experience, a person begins to assemble all the knowledge they have been given. Even, if one doesn't believe in this process, a quest can still be used to bring focus and clarity into that person's life.

Alone in a teepee with no distractions, one comes face to face with their self and gets to know who they are and who they are not. With the noise of daily life removed, one is more able to hear the whisperings of their soul, which remind them why they came here in this life.

The event was over much too soon for Julie. She still had questions and concerns, but she said her goodbyes and walked to the car waiting for Wapa to join her.

Once on the road, Julie's eyelids became heavy. No matter how hard she fought it, her head began to wobble, much like one of those bobble headed dolls. She was so sleepy.

"If you keep that motion going, you're going to break your neck."

"I'm sorry. I can't help it. I'm relaxed, exhilarated, tired and the caffeine has me awake all at the same time."

Wapa laughed. "You would be more comfortable if you leaned your seat back a little. The lever is there on the right side. Go ahead and take a nap."

"Thanks." She reached for the handle.

After about a thirty minute nap, Julie woke up rubbing her eyes. "Please forgive me. I haven't been much company on the way home."

"I'm a little tired myself. Do you have a big day planned for tomorrow?"

"I need to call and see if my nightclub is still operating. No, I'm just kidding. I left Brody in charge. Probably, after getting some rest, I will gorge on a big chocolate bar and eventually call Chase. I'm kind of anxious and apprehensive at the same time to see how he has made it so far. How about you, what are your plans?"

"Well, I need to go through my mail, check my telephone messages, and keep my appointments. By the way, speaking of keep, you will keep me updated?"

"Most definitely. However, I have concluded it's meant for me to live my life as a single woman. There are worse things, you know."

"Just because you hired Chase doesn't mean you don't need someone special in your life."

"A person, with a normal life would agree, but my life is anything but normal."

"It unquestionably doesn't fall within the realm of reality, but that's what I like about you. You make my life interesting to say the least."

"I'm glad you see it that way." She smiled. "Thanks again, Wapa for everything."

"You're welcome. Keep me in the loop."

It had been a good trip. Nevertheless, Julie was ready to retreat to her bedroom. In fact, it was mid-morning the next day before her feet finally made it to the floor. After she finished eating, it was time to call Chase.

She picked up the receiver, sat down at her table, and dialed the number. In only two rings, she heard Chase's voice.

"Hello."

"Hi, Chase, it's Julie."

"Oh hi, how was your trip?"

"Great, thanks. How are things going with you?"

"Couldn't be better."

That was music to her ears. "No strange happenings?"

"None that I'm aware of. Stop worrying, I've got everything under control."

"Okay, I'll try. You let me know if you need anything. "

"Will do. I gotta go now. Have chores to do for the lady I work for."

"I'm sure she appreciates it." Julie smiled. Chase was a good young man. They said their goodbyes, and she hung up satisfied things were indeed okay.

*Only a few feet away, up on the hill to be exact, a discernible look of disapproval was spread across the chief's face. He would have to figure out what to do about this situation.*

## CHAPTER 30

Julie glanced around the property and liked what she saw. The transition for Chase had gone well, and she was definitely pleased with her decision of hiring him.

Upon entering the barn, Julie gave Spook a pat on the back before she shifted her attention to Phantom. She groomed the beautiful horse before rubbing a crystal up and down his leg. *This treatment may not help, but it can't hurt either.* It was something her horse-whispering friend Madelyn would do.

Phantom looked relaxed by the whole ordeal, but she was still concerned about him. Surely, there was something she could do to help his bad leg. She put her grooming tools away and started out of the barn. With a slight pause, one hand resting on the barn door, she peered back at her horses. She loved them both. The next moment something wet was licking at her hand.

"What is it Tonka? Are you feeling left out this morning?" She reached down and scratched behind his ear, his eyes closed in contentment. "Boy, I'm really concerned about Phantom. I'm thinking about calling Madelyn. She was such a big help in curing your snakebite last year. I'm sure that with her insight on spiritual matters, she can help Phantom, too. What do you say we go inside and give her a call?"

The dog happily followed her into the house. She picked a treat out of the bag and gave it to her trusty friend. It wasn't long before she had Madelyn on the other end of the line.

"Hey, how are you this morning?"

"I'm doing fine. I've been merely working around here in the greenhouse."

"I bet your plants have really grown since I saw them last. Hey, I have a question about Phantom. I mentioned the problem with his right hoof to you the other day."

"Yes, I remember. How can I help?"

"Remember, I told you I was going on a vision quest?"

"I do."

"Well, oddly enough, Phantom was part of my vision. At least, I believe he was."

"How so?"

"I saw a horse limping much in the same way he does. In fact, the green pasture looked similar to my own. Could that have been possible?"

Without any hesitation on her part, Madelyn responded, "Spiritually, it sounds to me like you should take Phantom to the sacred ground. I wouldn't do it once but take him on three separate occasions. On the third trip, he should follow you back walking on all fours."

"That sounds simple enough, my friend. I hope you're right." Her heart would soar in thanks to The Great Spirit if that were all it took to help the horse. "Thank you. You're always there for me."

"Not a problem. You know that."

Julie hung up and saw Chase come into the room. "Guess what, Madelyn believes Phantom will walk normal one day."

"Really, are you buying into that? I thought the vet told you it was hopeless."

"I'm not putting him down. I have to at least try

everything I can to help him before even considering such." She had no intention of letting him deter her from her decision.

She mentally prepared herself for the trip up the hill with the horse. "Phantom." She placed her hand on his back, patted gently, then put the bridle in place. "Are you up for a jaunt to the sacred ground?"

Phantom gave her a slight nudge making her think he knew something was about to take place. "Alright then." She took the rein and led him out.

It was a beautiful early spring day. The temperature was around seventy-two degrees. The weatherman had given a rain-free forecast. However, she knew the Missouri weather could change in a flash.

As she walked across the yard, she heard the repetitive clogging of three footsteps. It saddened her but maybe today would be his first on the road to recovery.

Upon crossing the creek, she looked over and noticed her golden stalks of wheat glistening in the sunlight. She was grateful for the bountiful amount. Before long, Phantom decided to rear up, pull the rein out of her hand, and head back toward the creek.

What had happened that frightened him? She simply wanted to cry as she followed Phantom and watched him limp back toward the farm buildings. It was a very long, disappointing walk back to the farmhouse.

After securing Phantom back into the barn, she sat down on the porch steps. Unable to figure out what happened, she let her thoughts wander. She removed her shoes and wiggled her toes in the newly mowed grass. Her mind was a million miles away. She snapped back to the present at the sound of the handyman's voice.

"I see you're back, how did it go?"

Chase seemed not to really care, but asked the question out of politeness. "Well, I enjoyed the walk, but something spooked Phantom, or he thought it was way too long of a way to trek on three legs. He got away and came straight back to the barn."

"So, he's still walking on three hoofs. How much faith are you putting into your neighbor, the so-called horse whisperer anyway? Honestly, maybe the vet was right."

"Chase, I've witnessed firsthand Madelyn's horse whispering and healing powers. I feel she even saved Tonka's life. I have total faith in her, she's phenomenal."

"Right! I'll believe it, once I see it."

Worry laced its way up Julie's spine. Was Chase changing already or was he just having a bad day? *Great Spirit please let it be a bad day.*

*While Chase's words got lost in the wind, the chief was busy contemplating a few chosen words of his own or maybe even something stronger would be appropriate. Perhaps sending him on his way, in much the same manner as those before him, would be fitting.*

# CHAPTER 31

This particular May morning was cold, wet, and windy. Unlike the last time she'd visited the farm, but Julie rose thinking of going to the country. She not only wanted to take Phantom to the sacred ground, but she had another agenda as well. So, from the comfort of her recliner, she dialed Chase.

"Good morning," she said happily. "How are things?"

"Everything is under control. Will you be coming today? I'll fix you a nice lunch and detail your pickup. Please say you'll come."

"Well, actually I had planned on it, but the more I think about the weather, I'm not so sure."

"But the sun is shining here."

"Really, don't you see dark clouds in the horizon?"

"None."

"Well, I was kind of excited about taking Phantom back to the sacred ground. This will be his second trip, you know; and, of course, I always look forward to having lunch with you."

"How about getting a clean vehicle?"

"Yes that, too. You do such fantastic work." She knew how much he liked compliments. Therefore, she decided to ignore her weather concerns. "I have a few last minute details to address, then I guess I'll head that way."

Within the hour, Julie had her ducks in a row and was ready to head to the farm. As she traveled, she saw through her rearview mirror, clouds slowly lifting away and a speck of sunlight peeking through. By the time she actually pulled into her driveway, the weather was pleasant.

Opening the backdoor of the farmhouse, she was met with a rich, tantalizing aroma. "Oh my, it smells so good in here. I'm glad I didn't let the gloomy weather in the city stop me from coming."

"I'm definitely glad you didn't." Chase teasingly walked over and closed his arms around her, pulling her body flush against his.

In a natural response, Julie's arms slid comfortably around his neck. For just a moment, she took comfort in the strength and security of his embrace; although, for an instant, she wondered if this was wrong.

*In a brief amount of time, their relationship had taken on new meaning, and it wasn't setting particularly well with the chief.*

"Thanks for coming," Chase whispered in her ear.

"You're more than welcome." She blushed. Why would this young man make her feel giddy like a schoolgirl? "I surely wasn't expecting to receive this kind of reception."

"Really, I feel its way overdue. I've played this moment over and over in my mind. I could stand here forever with my arms around you but our lunch would soon go through a cremation process."

"We can't let that happen." Julie smiled as she dropped her arms from around his neck.

"What would you like to drink?"

"Iced tea, if you have it."

He walked to the refrigerator to obtain the pitcher of amber liquid. "Oh, before I forget it, you have some mail that came this morning. If you want, I can put it in your pickup, when I do the detailing."

"That would be great."

"Are you ready to eat? I have the table ready for us."

"I'm famished and it smells so good. Yes, is the answer."

Chase served the wonderful meal of salad, pork chops, mashed potatoes, green beans and for desert, ice cream. They sat in companionable silence and ate their meal. Julie felt comfortable at the domestication of it all.

After finishing off the last of her iced tea, she gave a big yawn. "I could just about take a nap."

"Well, go for it." Chase began to clear the table.

"No," she said, while helping him with the dishes. "I should check on Phantom. He's more important than a nap."

"Suit yourself. I'll get to work on your vehicle."

"Thanks," she said heading out the backdoor. Walking into the barn, Julie acknowledged both horses but her focus was mainly directed toward Phantom. "It's time for your walk." She placed the halter over his head and led him out the barn door. "We need to get you walking on all fours."

Phantom merely blinked his eyes and turned his head away. "Ignoring me isn't the right answer. Remember your job today is to enter the sacred ground."

The two of them walked along the path. As they neared the sacred area, Julie was feeling confident. However, without notice, Phantom jerked away and headed back toward the barn.

"What's wrong with you?" she shouted in frustration. What could be causing this, it didn't make sense. Alone, once again, she headed back to the farmhouse.

"I see Phantom beat you back to the barn, again. Maybe you need one of these to calm your nerves." He held a beer out toward her.

"I don't think so. I have one more shot at it. Hopefully,

the third time will be the charm."

"I think you may need many shots. It looks like a lost cause to me."

His sarcasm was beginning to irk her. "I won't give up. Not just yet."

## CHAPTER 32

By August, Chase was definitely settled in, and this unassuming handyman's status had become much more on this unpredictable farm.

"Hello, Chase," Julie echoed through the telephone. "This is a heads-up call. I'll be out tomorrow."

"Great. What would my lady like for lunch?"

"Just surprise me."

"What brings you out this way? Me?"

She chuckled at his playful tone. "Maybe, but truthfully I want and need to take Phantom to the sacred ground for the third and final time. By the way, how's he doing?"

"Phantom's doing great. I walked him a little bit today, and Spook walked with us, too. Tonka stayed behind in the yard and guarded the farm."

"Great. Thank you so much. I really appreciate all you do for me. See you tomorrow."

"Goodbye. See you soon."

The following day, Chase met Julie outside. Barely having time to step out of her pickup, he grabbed her and gave her a gentle but passionate kiss.

"I know you want to get with Phantom as soon as possible, so," he whispered. "I have lunch ready and waiting."

"Thank you." She found herself enjoying his embrace much more than she should.

Julie couldn't hide the truth from herself any longer. Her feelings for Chase were too strong and intense to deny. She was falling in love with him. He was falling in love with her.

*The image of Julie's affection with the man didn't set well. The chief would have to put his plan in motion soon. He refused to let her love another. She should know that by now.*

After having enjoyed her lunch, a flushed Julie walked outside and went into the barn. Anticipation of the horse's reaction had her worried. However, she knew Phantom's future was in her hands, and she hoped she hadn't been too neglectful in this third pursuit.

"Hey boy, you have a big job ahead of you today. Wouldn't you like to gallop across the field with your head held high and your mane flowing in the wind like your ancestors? Come on then," she coaxed, placing the halter over his head.

Soon she and Phantom were walking out of the barn on this all-important day. After walking across the barnyard to begin this final journey, Phantom stopped and hesitated for a second. She gasped, fearing he was about to pull away again but was pleased when he didn't.

After walking across the top of the hill, Julie crooned softly, "This is the furthest you have come so far, you know." She hesitated for a moment while she rubbed his nose for reassurance. "I'm so proud of you today."

She had placed such high hopes this beautiful horse would be able to walk normal, and she had bragged so much to Chase. How could she face him if she failed? Perhaps that's the reason she had put off this final trip for so long. She would have a very hard time admitting defeat to him, and still remembering his affection during lunch, she did not want to jeopardize their relationship in any way.

"Phantom, it's all up to you now." She stroked his mane and laid her cheek against his head. She then tried to get him to walk. It seemed he didn't want to budge. He stood, as though frozen in time, almost statuesque.

She nudged him once again. "Please move." She prodded to no avail. Nothing she tried seemed to work.

Distraught, she finally gave up all hope. What was wrong with him? Why wouldn't he move? Was something on the sacred ground holding him back? She wondered if Phantom would ever be normal.

Flooded with mixed emotion, after failure on her third attempt, she helplessly walked away and headed across the field by herself. She definitely felt like she had failed everyone around her, especially Phantom. Why had she put so much faith into healing him anyway? The vet couldn't heal him, so why did she think she could.

With her mind clouded in thought, Julie barely heard the sound coming from behind her. She hesitated briefly and listened. Was she hearing correctly? She glanced over her right shoulder, then turned away pretending she had neither seen nor heard anything.

She began to walk again and then slowed her pace to listen for the familiar sound. There it was. It was a beautiful clopping noise, and as Phantom came closer, it was like magic to her ears. There was not the usual three-step gait. Julie was actually hearing four hooves hit the ground. She could barely hold back the smile that made its way across her face. When she reached the farmhouse, Phantom was standing right beside her. She had to blink back tears of joy.

"Chase," Julie hollered, "Come quick."

The man ran out of the barn. "What's wrong?"

She pointed to the horse. "Look!" Chase shook his head. "This is where I eat crow?"

Trying to control her emotions but wanting to scream at the top of her lungs, she emphasized, "I told you so!" She couldn't believe only moments ago, she was so willing to think that taking Phantom to the sacred ground had failed. A good talk with herself about her faith was in store. "Just wait 'til I call Madelyn! She's going to be as excited as I am."

She turned toward the house and saw Alex turning into the drive, perfect timing.

"I can't believe my eyes," he said as he stepped out of his truck. "Phantom is actually standing on all fours. I don't know what you did, but I don't think I would have believed it if I hadn't seen it firsthand."

"I can't believe it myself, but I give the credit to Madelyn. She told me to take him to the sacred ground three times. Today was the third." Julie patted Phantom on the back. "This is wonderful."

"How about half and half credit," Alex replied. "I believe both of you played a big part in all this."

"Thanks, works for me. Now I have to go call her and tell her the good news!"

*And not to be left out of this happy occasion, from his Oak tree position, the stern-faced Chief couldn't hold back his smile either. He was so proud to call her Cherokee and maybe someday he could find a way to personally enlighten her about this unpredictable farm of hers.*

## CHAPTER 33

Weeks had passed since that joyous day on the farm. Looking at Phantom now, Julie marveled at his recovery. However, something new had recently developed. Her attention was no longer directed toward Phantom but in a more disconcerting direction to her handyman. He would do something special for her and then expect a compliment. Julie saw signs of disappointment in his eyes, if she didn't say it in just the right way.

Chase would give her a list of things he'd done since her last visit, not just the big things, but also every little thing. If she didn't praise him for his accomplishments, he would brood and get upset. He had become verbally abusive over it at times, and his actions had frightened her somewhat. Maybe this visit would be different. At least she hoped so.

Looking in the direction of the backyard, Julie saw Tonka coming across the field wagging his tail. She immediately dismissed Chase's idiosyncrasies and focused her attention on her dog. She feared his rabbit chasing days were about over. He had recently developed a limp from the increasing arthritic condition in his right hip. Nevertheless, today he seemed better and was eager to walk by her side. Once the pair reached the barn door, Julie stood in the doorway alternating her attention between

Spook and Phantom.

For a brief conscious moment, her mind fixated on the past. She couldn't help but yearn for her nightly rides with Blake. However, she realized that wasn't an option so she placed a halter on each horse then led each one out to the backyard.

How good she felt walking them in the fresh air with Tonka coming slowly behind. She longed to live out here again, but it just didn't feel right for her to do so, maybe someday.

She shook her head and looked toward the top of the hill. She secretly hoped for a form or sign of encouragement or confirmation this could happen. Then shrugging her shoulders, she walked the horses into the pasture. After standing there for a few moments watching them gallop across the field, she turned and spotted Chase in the front yard. Thinking he would join her, she walked to the porch swing and sat down.

However, instead of sitting beside her, Chase chose to pace. His shoulders stooped, his hands were jammed in the pockets of his jeans. Julie opened her mouth to disapprove of his behavior but seeing the warning sign on his face, thought better of it. What was this about? They hadn't even spoken to each other, yet.

After studying the rigid line of his jaw, she searched for a clue as to what she had done to upset him. Finally, she reached out and grabbed his arm. Immediately, the muscles of his forearms stretched taut. "Chase, what's going on? Aren't you glad to see me?"

He glared at her with his stiff jaw closing with a snap. She quickly looked away and tried to think of something that would calm him down. He had never physically touched her, but she feared he would. She decided to stand firm, knowing this would be another time she wouldn't stay long. "Well, I'm glad to see you. You know I think hiring you was the best thing I ever did. Do you have your list handy? I know it must be a mile long by the looks of things around here."

Hearing these words of praise, Chase began to relax the muscles in his arms and a slight smile began in the corners of his mouth. Taking two ungainly steps, he stopped with a frozen smile on his face and pulled a piece of paper out of his pocket. "Here it is. I was hoping you'd ask for it."

She knew she'd said the right thing. "Oh, my goodness this is wonderful. You're too good to me, Chase. Look at all the things you've done. And with perfection, I might say."

He sat down beside her. "Thank you. It's nice to be appreciated."

Placing her hand to his cheek, she said, "You know I appreciate everything you do."

"Sometimes, I don't feel that way."

Oh, no, it was about to start again, she could feel it. Why did he have to be this way? All she wanted was to make him better. Let their relationship grow. Chase stood up and shoved his hands back in his pockets, his brooding look returned. Before things got any worse, she decided to leave. "I'd better be going now."

Julie put her right foot down to stop her swinging. She had certainly been frightened by his behavior this afternoon. Although, she knew that deep down he was a good person, and he truly cared for her. She could change him in time. Yes, it would only take time.

"If I upset you, I'm sorry." Julie looked up into his eyes. "I always seem to say the wrong thing at the wrong time."

"No," Chase interrupted. "You have nothing to be sorry for. It's me. Sometimes I don't understand it myself. If you want to get back to the city before dark, you must be going."

Amazed at the sound of compassion and empathy in his voice, Julie grasped his hand. He then gently led her off the porch. With determination, she forced the memory of his clenched jowl face and cold assessing eyes from her mind. The couple walked hand in hand to her pickup where they continued to chat for several minutes. She enjoyed their visit, once she saw that the man she had growing feelings for was in his normal state of mind.

Maybe, it was irrational and too much to hope for and maybe she was intentionally blinding herself, but at this moment Julie was putting tonight's episode behind her and moving on.

Returning to the city, she found herself with a headache. Unable to concentrate, she sat at her desk and stared blankly into thin air, her headache intensifying. She had barely closed her eyes when she suddenly jumped at the sound of her phone ringing. She snatched up the receiver and heard Chase's voice.

"Hi. I hope I didn't interrupt anything. I forgot to tell you, Tonka's almost out of food."

"I'll get some, thanks."

"I miss you."

"That's nice to know. I miss you, too." She enjoyed their short talk. It was pleasant, and she felt more relaxed. The call helped to ease her mind and now only a twinge of her headache remained. Although, as she walked down the hall, she was reminded of the day's events, and knew she didn't want a repeat. What she did want and, felt very strong about, was having Chase in her life, so she would help him through this, sure he would eventually stop his abusive actions.

He had told her his early years had been very painful. Among other things, he had endured a bad marriage and divorce. Perhaps, as time went on, she could find the key to unlock some of the misery he'd kept inside.

"Anyway," she sighed. "That's my plan."

After dressing for bed, she picked up her latest magazine lying on the nearby nightstand and settled in for the evening.

The following morning, she lay quietly as a slight smile crept across her face. She wanted her relationship with Chase to stay on the right track no matter what. She knew she loved him but was she in love with him. *Maybe in time, I'll know for sure.* Whatever it was, it definitely was a strong emotion that persisted despite all her logic, leaving her feeling restless and frustrated.

Julie was just hours from seeing Chase again, and she could already feel the anxiety mounting inside her. Finally, she threw back the covers determined to get her day started. As she readied to go, she thought of the many conversations they'd had over the telephone that week. At one point, Chase had come to town to take her to dinner. He was so charming. They laughed a lot and things felt good again.

A short time later, Julie arrived at the farm. Man how much she loved this farm. Turning off the ignition, she heard Tonka's bark long before she saw him come from across the road. "Hi, boy, are you glad to see me today?"

"This boy is," Chase said, from her blindside. He grabbed at her shoulders and grazed her lips with a kiss.

"There's more where that came from." He smiled, showering her with another one. "Oh, by the way, I've made us soup, homemade bread, and I have a lot of other things to share with you, and ..."

"Slow down, you're going to make me drop these groceries."

"It's just that I'm glad to see you. I know it has only been days, but it seems like weeks. We all miss you."

Although she enjoyed his enthusiasm, she hoped he would stay calm, once he understood; she had to work that night and couldn't stay. Oh, well, right now things were good, and she didn't want to spoil the moment. She would have to admit to liking all the attention.

Chase put one arm around her waist and rubbed his stubbly chin whiskers against the tender nape of her neck.

"I'll give you all the attention you want."

She yelped and lovingly pushed him aside. "Quit trying to distract me. By the way, do we have time for a walk before lunch?"

"I guess so, why not?" He grabbed the dog food from the back of the truck. "I can turn the heat down on the soup."

She followed him into the kitchen, aware of his manliness. He was handsome in his own way. A way she liked. "I want to go to the observatory. My last trip just whet my appetite. I really miss it here."

"You realize," Chase quickly added. "You can remedy that situation."

"I know. It's ultimately my choice."

As they walked hand in hand up the hill, the two of them continued to talk. Julie felt a warmth and peace she hadn't felt for a very long time. Chase seemed to be his old self today. She hoped things didn't turn. All of a sudden, she had a spur-of-the-moment challenge.

"I bet I can beat you to the observatory." She grinned. "The first one to reach the bottom step wins."

With great confidence, Chase asked, "After I outrun you and reach the step first, what will I win?"

"It's highly unlikely you will." She laughed. "Still, if by some chance you do, I will clear the table and wash the dishes after lunch. How does that sound?"

"I would like nothing more than to just sit back and watch you work in the kitchen," he said rather sarcastically.

Julie quickly interjected, "Let mine be a surprise. Okay, on the count of three."

Julie had never seen Chase run before, and she was impressed. She's always been a good runner and was proud of it but wondered if this man might actually be faster than her. They were running neck and neck for the first hundred yards. Before long, she began to gradually pull in front of him. This only made Chase more determined, and she felt him breathing down her neck.

Finally, she reached the step first. Chase, being only seconds behind, nearly stepped on her before she could move out of his way.

"That was close," he said, then sat down in an effort to catch his breath.

Julie, fanning herself with one hand and holding her hair off the nape of her neck, sat down on the step above him. Once, her pulse returned to normal, she wanted to know when she could expect her reward.

"How about I start with this?" Moving up one-step to where she sat, he leaned over and gave her a loving kiss causing her to blush.

"And now, if you have enough energy left to climb these remaining steps," he smiled, "we'll continue to the top."

Walking out onto the platform, Julie gazed out over her farm with new eyes. "Oh, how I've missed living out here with all of this."

Then having indulged herself for a few moments, she finally acknowledged, "This fresh country air and, of course, the little sprint we had has made me hungry all of a sudden. Unfortunately, before long, it's back to the city for me, duty calls."

"So you won't stay?" Chase asked disapprovingly.

"It's not that I won't, I can't. I have too many things to do."

Chase's mood immediately changed hearing the words, 'it's back to the city'; however, she could tell he tried to ignore what she'd said while they ate their lunch. His overall body language told her he was disappointed and a bit angry.

Maybe telling him how good things were would lighten his mood. "That was a delicious meal Chase." She pushed back from the table. "My compliments to the chef, I really hate to eat and run but the hour has come. I have an agenda this afternoon you would not believe." The muscles in his jaws pulsed. She didn't like the look on his face, but at least he was trying to understand.

"Let me walk you to your pickup."

Arriving at the driveway hand in hand, Chase opened the door and allowed her to enter. "I really thought today might be the day for you to stay longer."

"I want to but I can't." She reached through the open window to give him a hug. "I know it's hard for you to understand, but I'm not prepared to stay overnight. It's something I'm not ready for yet, maybe down the road."

"Did I ask you to spend the night? No, just a few hours this afternoon would be fine."

"I wish I could. But—"

"I see no reason for you to explain. I understand perfectly."

Did he? No, she saw the color drain from his face and knew he'd read something into her words. He reached through the open window and grabbed her keys dangling from the ignition. It startled her. Watching him place them in his shirt pocket, Julie sank back against her seat with a gasp. Her surprise turned to anger, but she had to control herself. She didn't know what else he might do.

In a restrained tone, she managed to verbalize, "Chase, what is it you want from me?"

For a long moment, he glared at her; much in the same way a snake does before striking. Then he began to relax his taut body. Straightening, he wiped all expression from his face. He muttered a few words she couldn't make out to himself, but didn't speak directly to her.

Julie sat forward and focused her stare straight ahead. She had to squeeze her fingers around the steering wheel in order to stop their trembling. She once thought she really knew and understood this man, but there was a hidden darkness in him that kept surfacing.

Chase pointed his finger at her. "Now, I can handle this situation one of two ways!"

She still didn't look at him. The sound of his voice alarmed her. What was he going to do?

"I will give you an opportunity to get out of this pickup on your own, or I'll drag you out. Either way, I don't believe you'll like the result."

While she continued to hold to the steering wheel, her heart beat hard and fast in her chest. She thought, *if he tried to pull her out, the hold would surely anchor her.*

He placed his hand on the door handle. "Okay. Have it your way." The pickup door flew open in a flash.

When Chase grabbed her arm, her stomach turned. His large hand encircled her flesh completely. She couldn't let this happen. "Wait!" She tried to pull away, but his forceful fingers gripped her with greater intensity. He literally jerked her out of the pickup. This was not the man she had grown to care for. It was as if some unknown force had taken possession of him. "Chase, please!" Panic worked its way to the surface.

He held tight. "Nothing's changed between us, you know!"

She swallowed the lump in her throat. She heard the cynicism and the contempt in his tone, then winced and tried to pull her arm out of his clutches. Again, he tightened his hold. "You're hurting me. Let me go!"

Chase growled with bared teeth, his features animal-like. He pulled her forward as he bolted up the steps of the farmhouse. His firm grasp forced her to comply.

"After, I get you in there," he said, reaching for the screen door. "I don't know what's going to happen."

"Stop it!" Was he really doing this? He'd never manhandled her like this before. Julie fought him every inch of the way, but it seemed she was powerless to whatever had him in its grasp.

Chase slung her into the middle of the living room couch, placed his hands around her throat, and began to choke her. Was this going to be the day she died? No, she couldn't let that happen. But what could she do but fight? She struggled with every ounce of energy to make him stop. No matter how hard she punched him, he was relentless. She was getting light headed, but refused to give up. She began to kick with all of her strength. Finally, she managed to knock a lamp off the end table. It shattered to the floor.

The unexpected sound startled Chase for an instant, long enough to break the spell that had been cast over him. Within that moment, he lessened his grip and quickly stepped back. A horrible, shocked look replaced the rage on his face.

She tried breathing in air. How could he have done this to her?

Momentarily, Chase stood glaring at his hands. He even questioned if they belong to him. "What did these trembling hands just do?" He glanced down at them for the longest time. "I'm really, really sorry, Julie. You must believe me." He started toward her.

Julie held up her hands to stop him from getting closer. "Stay where you are, Chase, I mean it." The fire had left his eyes and tears filled the void, but she still didn't trust him.

"Please find it in your heart to forgive me." Chase dropped to his knees. "I thought I'd forgotten my past, but I have so much anger inside of me, I guess I just couldn't control myself."

"What happened in your past that would make you do something like this?" Julie sat silently and watched the tears stream down his face. Shoulders slumped, he stayed on his knees. "One night I found my wife in bed with my best friend." He wiped the tears from his face. "My whole world came crashing down around me."

She sat for several minutes listening to his plea for forgiveness and the acknowledgement of betrayal in his past. In her heart, it seemed Chase had now become the victim, not her. It was a crazy decision, she knew, but feeling compelled to do everything she could to help, Julie chose to stay and ride out the disturbing storm that had quickly erupted that afternoon.

*As Julie sped away, the chief watched. He hoped the scene that had unfolded made her see that, if he had anything to do with it, this man would have to go.*

On her way back to the city that night, she stared out the window of her pickup at the countryside flashing past her. Her eyes stung with unshed tears. She wasn't sure who she was angrier with, Chase or herself for forgiving him. He had aroused so many emotions in her. All she could think about was how he was able to drain her of her strength and free will.

Julie didn't want to admit it, but Chase had become necessary to her. She wanted him in her life, even though she didn't quite understand this sudden darkness in him. However, after thinking twice, and now that she was away from him, she knew the right thing to do was to stay away.

## CHAPTER 34

Arriving home from the exhausting trip to the farm, the ringing telephone caught Julie off guard. "Huh! Hello."

"Please come back."

"Chase."

"I know you said you forgive me, but in my heart I fear you really haven't. I need to see you to make sure you know how I feel about you. You don't deserve what happened, Julie."

"Chase—"

"Please don't say it won't work between us. It will, I know it will." He paused. "You made the decision not to give me another chance, didn't you?"

"Well, I…I'm confused."

"I understand and I'll make it all better. I promise, just please don't shut me out of your life. Give me that second chance. You said you would. Please?"

Hearing the compassion and sympathy in Chase's voice, Julie took a step back and thought long and hard about their relationship. After considerable validation, she believed that he in fact did deserve a second chance.

"I'll come out on Saturday."

"Thanks babe, I'm looking forward to making it up to you."

On Saturday, Julie put on her brave face and returned to the farm. She pulled into the driveway and spotted Chase. "Good afternoon." She studied her surroundings. "My, you have this yard in really great shape."

"Thank you." He smiled, walked to the pickup, and opened her door. "I just finished mowing not more than ten minutes ago. You have impeccable timing."

She stepped to the ground, and he put his arms around her. She felt good in his embrace. "The air smells so green. I love fresh cut grass." She accepted his kiss and missed the warmth of his embrace, when he released her. The smile she saw in his eyes eased her tensions about coming to the farm.

"Wait just a minute," he continued, "I'll be right back. Here, look at my list. While you are doing that, I will vacuum your pickup. Then I can add that to the list, too."

As Chase detailed her pickup, Julie sat on the front porch and read over his list. He had mowed the yard, burned the trash, fed the guineas, cooked lunch, etc. Although, she was appreciative of his endeavors, she didn't feel the necessity of the lists, but he knew that already.

Chase stepped up on the porch and let her know her pickup was ready. "Did you read over the list?"

"Yes. I did," she graciously acknowledged for his benefit. She knew he wanted a more positive response and saw the anxiousness on his face hoping she'd give more of an answer, but why should she have to do that when she didn't care about the 'list'?

"Well, what do you think?" He held up his hand. "Wait. Don't tell me. If I have to ask, it isn't the same." He sulked and walked away.

She probably should have said more, because now his moodiness was going to start. Was all of this her fault after all? Was she the cause of his abuse? When he returned, Chase had a beer in his hand. Anytime he was disappointed or rejected, he would simply grab one. She began to believe that the spirit on her farm was using Chase's need of alcohol to its advantage. Was the spirit causing his abuse?

*And confirming her suspicion from only a few feet away, the chief simply shrugged his shoulders. It hadn't been his idea to get a handyman out here.*

*Perhaps,* Julie reflected. *As Chase becomes weak, the control of the spirit becomes stronger.* Having lived for some time on this unpredictable farm, she could visualize something as bizarre happening. She didn't like thinking that way but reality was reality, at least out here anyway.

Nonetheless, now being fully aware of Chase's pattern, Julie would try to head off the episodes, but sometimes fell short like she did today. He was definitely breaking her spirit.

Chase had now finished his detailing job and was adding that to his list. Julie left the porch and entered the living room. However, she found herself really wanting to go back to the city. Shortly, he joined her, slamming down his can of beer on a nearby table. The unexpected sound startled her, and she turned to face him. She panicked seeing the look on his face, and he didn't hesitate to take advantage of her vulnerability.

He advanced close. "What you need is a new way of thinking," he said, with his dark brows drawn together.

"Chase, stop it!" Tears of humiliation burned her eyelids. "I don't deserve this kind of treatment. You said that yourself."

"I did?" he blurted out, slapping her hard across the face, forcing her head to turn to the side. "You and your kind deserve that and more." She was stunned and wanted to scream. Her mind felt ready to explode from this sudden outburst. Her jaw throbbed from the blow. She turned her head back and faced him; thus, allowing every nerve to quiver.

Feeling a form of remorse, Chase grabbed her and pulled her close to him, time stood still. After his eyes roamed her tear-ravaged face, he gently wiped away the last lingering wetness from her cheeks.

In disbelief, Julie stood with the lingering pain trying desperately to control the controversy in her heart, and the mayhem in her mind. She said nothing, but questioned silently. Chase's dark eyes were full of secrets. He was like a pendulum swinging from mood to mood.

He reached over and touched her shoulder. Slowly running his fingers down her bare arm, ultimately making her blood run faster, then breaking the mounting tension with words of empathy.

"Julie, I'm so sorry. I don't know what comes over me sometimes."

She hurriedly accepted the blame, though she knew she shouldn't. "It was my fault. I upset you, and I'm sorry."

While trying to regain her composure and at the same time give this, and the other outbursts some thought, Julie had an idea. "Maybe we should seek counseling as a couple."

"Are we a couple?" Taking his gaze from the floor, he glanced into her direction.

Helping this man stay part of her life was very important to her. She wanted to change him, and maybe this is what it would take to make him turn the corner.

"I'm willing to try anything. I just want to get better."

"Good." She was relieved by his answer.

Feeling a load off her shoulders, Julie briefly sat down, rubbed and closed her eyes. It seemed she had only closed them for a brief moment before finding herself going into the bathroom to assess the damage to her cheek. She glanced into the mirrored glass at her fatigued body. Pushing her hair away from her face, she could find only a slight trace of bruising. Thank goodness, it wasn't worse.

Maybe no one would notice. She made her way into the kitchen where she found Chase merely sitting at the table with a cup of coffee in his hand.

"I'm truly sorry." He looked up. "Lately, it seems I can't control my anger."

"Believe me, I've noticed."

"Did I hurt you too bad?"

"I'll be okay." The guilt reflected in his eyes, and his sad smile made her to want to fix everything. She poured herself a cup of coffee and joined Chase at the table. She immediately began to pursue a conversation, which included anger-management sessions along with the need to understand if their once budding relationship could be salvaged. Finally, she was content with their progress and felt it was time for her to return to the city.

"Things will get better, you'll see."

"I hope so. Like I said, I will do whatever it takes," he assured her. "Right now, I don't like the fact that you have to leave, but I concede."

"Thank you. You're the best, you know that?" She was patronizing him again. Her fears were still just below the surface. Being physically abused was something she thought would never happen to her, but now…

"No, thank you for your forgiveness."

Forgiven, but not forgotten. That's what was in her heart and mind as he walked her to her truck. She kissed him lightly before he opened the pickup door for her. "We'll talk soon, Chase."

"Okay. Again, I'm so sorry for hurting you."

She started the engine. "Let's put it behind us and move forward." Was she ready?

As Julie drove up the dusty gravel road, she saw Chase in her rearview mirror still lingering in her driveway, waving goodbye.

Once she was out of view, the recent abusive events ran through her mind. Panic constricted her throat, and she swallowed hard to keep from suffocating. At that moment, she realized she was out of her league. She was virtually paralyzed by fear and doubt. Was she making the right decision? Being frustrated, she turned her radio on. She was just in time to hear the announcer introduce the next song.

"Please don't touch that dial. One of my favorite singers, Jessie Colter, is coming up next singing her classic hit, I'm Not Lisa."

Julie listened intently to the first few bars of music and sensitive lyrics of the song. "I'm not Lisa, my name is Julie. Lisa left you years ago. My eyes are not blue but mine won't leave you, 'til the sunlight has touched your face."

Hearing those lyrics, Julie's eyes welled with tears. "Why does it have to be this way?" she sobbed aloud. The song really brought the focus of their relationship to a head and dumped it right into the middle of her lap.

As soon as she got home, she walked to her den and reached for the phone book. After placing it in the middle of her desk, her fingers nervously went up and down each row searching for just the right anger-management consultant.

Julie desperately needed someone who could enlighten her, someone who could tell her what to do to get help. She sat down in her chair, then began dialing. *I truly hope this is the right thing to do.* She waited for a receptionist to answer.

Once the voice on the other end of the line said hello, Julie made what she hoped to be a life-altering appointment. At the very least, she felt better knowing the first step was set in motion, and she hoped Chase would feel the same.

The following Tuesday afternoon, Julie along with Chase, pulled onto the Ferrell-Haley Clinic driveway. She felt a twinge of nervousness. However, she had forced herself to be optimistic going into this process.

Noticing the mood change in her, Chase placed his hand on her shoulder. "It's going to be okay."

With all her heart, she prayed to the Great Spirit that he was right. An hour later, the preliminary session was behind them. She walked beside Chase and he reached for her hand.

"I truly feel good, and I have confidence this doctor will be able to help me."

"He did seem to listen to every word you had to say."

"Thank you for being here, Julie. I felt more relaxed with you in the room."

"I'm here for the duration. I just want you to get better."

Those one-hour sessions lasted six weeks. Chase acted normal visiting in the city. Although, it was like flipping a light switch on the farm visits. His abuse was on the move. Julie began to dread her visits.

One morning, after she had walked to the farm mailbox, her neighborAlex pulled his truck up beside her. "How's your day go…? He stopped in mid-sentence. "Julie, There are bruises on your face again. You know, this isn't the first time I've noticed them. You need to tell me the truth. Is Chase hitting you?"

"Alex, please, we're getting counseling."

"Counseling, yeah right? A lot of good it's done," he said, slamming the door of his vehicle. "Where is he? I can't and I won't stand by and see you being hurt this way."

Without waiting for a response, Alex headed toward the farmhouse. He swung open the kitchen door and went straight toward Chase. "You low life," he said, throwing the first punch, but his blows didn't stop there. He repeatedly plummeted Chase in the face and body. As the beating continued, the two fell to the floor. "If you ever place your hands on Julie again, I will kill you. Do you hear what I'm saying to you?"

Julie ran into the farmhouse, screaming, "Alex, please stop!" It was as if he hadn't heard her. "Alex! Alex! Stop!" His fist drawn back ready to strike again, he took a deep breath. "You are a sorry excuse for a man." Unwillingly, Alex released his hold and stood.

Chase got to his feet and staggered out of the house. He nearly fell off the porch. Her heart went out to him, but maybe now he knew how it felt. She watched him walk unsteadily to the barn and fought the urge to go after him. Alex's voice pulled her from her thoughts.

"Julie! You need to get a restraining order and get this man out of your life. Why do you continue to stay?"

"I thought I could help him." She sobbed aloud.

"Chase is beyond help, and he has stepped way over his boundary." She heard the frustration in his voice then noticed his injured lip. "Let me take a look at your mouth. At least, I can get you some ice to put on it?"

"No. Thanks anyway." He walked back to his truck. "I'll take care of it later. Just remember what I said."

"I know you're right." Tears streamed down her cheeks.

After having waved goodbye, Julie returned to the kitchen with Alex's words of wisdom still ringing loud and clear in her ears. Then without warning, the screen door suddenly burst open. There standing in the doorway was Chase, torn shirt, bruised knuckles, and a bloody nose. As he began to step in her direction, Julie's heart sank.

Before, she knew what happened; Chase grabbed her and shook her head backwards and forward like a rag doll. While looking at her with hardened and mocking eyes, he pushed her down onto a kitchen chair.

Julie stared up at him in confusion. "Stop it! Get out of my face," she screamed.

With a feeling of real horror, she believed without a doubt, he was going to take her life. As Chase's hands slowly began closing around her throat, he took all her memories and destroyed them one by one. His fingers were strong and slender, their tan color emphasized against her own paleness.

Julie's body jerked in response. "Don't, Chase." She gasped for air. "Please don't do this!"

"Why not, tell me, Julie?" He dragged his stare away just long enough to pick up a nearby coat hanger. Deep lines grooved his mouth. His strong jaw was set, while his smoldering eyes were fixed on her. She glared back at him trying to control the nervous tremors that shivered throughout her body. Then, with her eyes closed, she groaned inwardly. For a split second, Chase lessened his grip.

"You're mad!" She choked, as the hanger began to tighten around her throat again.

He mumbled over the whereabouts of his gun. Being disgruntled with the hanger, he threw it to the floor in disgust.

Although Julie was trembling inside and dizzy with fear, she now sat in total silence, submitting and subjecting her whole being to meet his needs. He had finally broken her spirit, taken her will to live. As her limp body began to slump, Chase removed his trembling hands. His swollen, angry face changed to apathy. He stood looking at her semi-conscious body.

"Oh! What have I done?" He screamed and cried profusely. He tenderly caressed her in his arms and carried her to the living room couch.

"Julie, Julie please speak to me. I never meant to hurt you. He ran into the bedroom and retrieved a pillow from the bed. At the precise moment, he bent down to place it under Julie's head he heard a faint moan.

"Julie, Julie please forgive me," he begged, while pacing the floor. "Oh! My gosh, what have I done?" he repeated over and over.

As Julie lay on the couch, she slowly returned to

consciousness and tried to speak. Only gibberish-like sounds came out of her mouth.

"What has happened to me?" She sobbed uncontrollably into the pillow.

Suddenly, she felt a single raindrop, then two. In disbelief, she slowly turned her face and caught a glimpse of a water bottle in Chase's hand. He was slinging water everywhere. Then retrieving a kitchen towel, he began to mop it up.

Silently observing his behavior, Julie considered the possibility that Chase had totally gone mad.

He then returned to the kitchen, mumbling, "Oh, what have I done?"

Moments later, Julie heard the screen door slam. Being unable to properly process any of the chaotic turmoil presently going on throughout her mind, she raised herself to a sitting position and leaned her head back on the couch. "I'm so confused," she wailed inside, pressing her fingertips to her forehead.

As Julie sat there, she began to rock back and forth before stopping abruptly in a frozen-like state. Afraid to move, she reluctantly turned her head toward the direction of a familiar sound. While rubbing her throat, stumbling over her feet, and heading toward the sound, Julie slowly picked up the ringing phone. She mumbled incoherently into the receiver.

"Julie, what's wrong?"

She tried desperately to make Wapa understand, but her gibberish made absolutely no sense to him, at all

"I'm on my way." He became panicked himself. He had never known her to be this distraught.

When he arrived, he found Julie sitting quietly on the corner of the couch with the receiver lying on the floor. Her face was pasty, her eyes huge, and her neck was bruised and swollen. She appeared disorientated, sad, and very alone. He watched while she put her arms around herself.

He quietly sat down beside her. "It's Wapa," he gently said to her, "can you tell me what happened?"

After pausing, as though she were groping for words, she uttered, "I feel different. It's like Julie has vanished." Motionless and mostly staring out into space, she continued. "Alex came by the farm this morning." She stopped, not wanting to admit the abuse she'd been hiding. Tears trickled down her cheeks. She rubbed her throat and placed her face into the pillow.

"It's okay. Just take your time." Wapa placed his hand on her shoulder. Upon noticing the water on the couch and the floor, he spoke up, "Julie, I can't imagine what you've been through here."

Tossing the pillow aside, she looked in his direction clearing her throat, she continued, "I do feel somewhat better, and my mind is a little clearer. For a while, I felt like someone else when I tried to speak. You know I didn't want any of this to happen. I tried my best to prevent it. Wapa! I couldn't stop him. He was a mad man.

"I know, I know. It's time to put an end to this ordeal and call the authorities. He needs to go to jail."

"But what if this attempt on my life wasn't Chase's fault?"

"What do you mean it wasn't his fault? Where is he, anyway?"

Where had he gone? At that moment, she didn't care. "I don't know. He left. It just wasn't his fault," she repeated.

"No! Julie, don't go there. I'm not letting you take on this burden."

"Wapa, I know Chase has problems, but I can't help but put blame on this farm, whatever or whoever possesses it!"

"I know you believe that, and I truly understand, and that might be what's happening. Even if the spirit has caused Chase's behavior, it doesn't take away the fact that the man himself tried to kill you. I think we need to get some spiritual help out here before it's too late. Let's find out what is really going on around the property."

He took Julie by the shoulders. "I'm going to bring it up again and again until you do something. If nothing else, let me call Night Hawk. He has more experience in this kind of activity than I do."

"Okay." She knew he wouldn't take no for an answer this time. "If you think it's best. It's just that I'm angry. You know how much I wanted Chase in my life and to live out here permanently."

"You're not thinking about staying here are you?"

"No! Just the thought makes the hair rise on my arms."

"I'm glad you've come to your senses. In fact, I insist on following you back to the city. We'll discuss your next move from your house there, or a better idea, why don't you stop by the authorities and get a restraining order?"

"You're probably right." She exhaled. "Even if the farm is somehow responsible for Chase's behavior, I don't want to ever go through this again." She couldn't take the chance of letting him break her spirit more than he already had. Earlier, she'd basically lost her will to live. That was something that wouldn't happen again.

Julie saw Wapa writing something on a piece of paper. "What are you doing?"

"I'm writing a note to Chase telling him to get all of his belongings and be out of the house by morning. I also told him not to try to contact you in any way or he would have to answer to the authorities."

"I think he would have to answer to you, Alex and everyone else in my life at this point."

"On that you are right, Julie." Wapa placed the note on the kitchen table before turning and walking out the door. "Let's get back to town now."

Again, she had to leave her farm on a sad note. Would it ever stop?

Driving to the police station, Julie struggled with her decision to get the restraining order. She knew it was for her own good, but it was a hard decision to make against the one you love. She straightened and went inside the building.

Fortunately, she had held it all together while they filed the complaint but by the time she pulled into her garage in the city, she was beside herself. Once inside the house, she walked to the sink for a glass of water to soothe her sore throat. She was still there leaning against the cabinet when she heard her front door open. Her heart raced. Had Chase followed her? "Whew!" she was relieved at seeing Wapa enter the kitchen.

"Well, how did it go?" He glanced at her face. "You're pale, sit down before you answer"

"For a moment, I thought you were Chase."

"I see. Take a deep breath and relax. Wapa's here."

"Thank you." She loved this wise man. He was a true comrade."

"Now tell me about your visit to the police."

"I did get the restraining order," she replied nervously.

He sat himself at the kitchen table. "Julie, it's best."

"You're right, of course."

"You're making an old medicine helper out of me before my time, you know that?" Wapa alleged with a slight grin.

"I know you're the best friend in the whole wide world." She managed a smile. "And I hope that I'm not really aging you."

"Not to worry. What's your plan, or do you have one?"

"I need to call Madelyn and Alex. They're going to know something has happened if they don't see Chase out feeding the horses in the morning. Anyway, I will feel more at ease calling them instead of having to look them straight in the eye and tell them how foolish I've been." She pondered a moment. "Alex will be relieved I got the restraining order on Chase. After their little, 'altercation', he told me to get one, same as you did."

"You did the right thing. Let me know if there is

anything I can do. Also, if you want to go out to the farm, I'll accompany you."

"Thank you. I'm sure I will be looking over my shoulder for a while."

"How about tonight, will you be afraid to be here alone?"

"No. I don't believe Chase will try anything here." She sounded more confident then she felt, but she prayed she was right.

"Then I'm going to get out of your hair and let you get on with your business."

"Thank you again, Wapa." Julie gave him a hug. "I don't know what I'd do without you."

She followed him to the door and stood watching her dear friend drive out of sight. Then she returned to her den to make those much-dreaded telephone calls.

"Hello, Madelyn."

"Hi, what's up?"

"There was really no easy way to tell her what had happened, so she decided to just say it. "Chase tried to kill me today."

"What? How dare that so and so ....!" Julie could hear her animosity mounting. "Are you in any danger from him now? Are you in a safe place?"

Julie quickly interjected. "Yes, I'm safe, and I'm in the city. I even have a restraining order, so he can't bother me.

"Alright." she said, in a calmer tone.

"Other than a sore throat and a little bit shaken, I think I will be okay."

Before she ended her call with Madelyn, she had informed her of all that had happened, including all the gory details.

"Alright, I can only trust you're really okay, and you better call me in the morning and let me know how you are."

"I'll call."

She hung up and hesitated a few moments before calling Alex. Confronting him with the news was another story. She knew he would be furious with her. Therefore, after inhaling deeply, she slowly and deliberately dialed his number.

"Hello, Alex." She knew her voice quivered, but she couldn't stop trembling.

"What's the matter, Julie?"

"I just wanted to let you know." She took a deep breath. "I got the restraining order against Chase. Right now I'm in the city. Wapa followed me home and everything's under control."

"Did Chase come back and hurt you again? I'll kill him with my bare hands if he did."

Julie could not bring herself to talk about the ordeal. Especially, since she had ignored Alex's warning. She should have left the farm the same time he did, but it was another bad decision on her part.

"No need for that. Wapa left a note telling him to get out. If you would keep your eyes open, I'd appreciate it. Don't confront him, please."

"What did he do to you?"

"Please, Alex, I've been through a lot today, and I'm too tired right now to go into all the details. I will call you tomorrow and explain everything."

"I'm sorry. I am only adding to your stress. I'll keep an eye on things and make sure he leaves. I promise I won't go over there and start anything. Does that make you feel better?"

"Yes, thank you." She hung up, breathed a sigh of relief, and then stretched out on her couch. While lying there, with her eyes shut, she had flashbacks of Chase's hands around her throat, the coat hanger, and the struggle. A cold sweat suddenly popped out on her forehead, and she started to chill. She grabbed her afghan and threw it over her body. "Why me," she wanted to scream. At that moment, the nearby phone rang, startling her. She quickly walked over and picked up the receiver to a deafening silence.

She felt overwhelmed standing there alone, surrounded in total darkness. Suddenly, 'What's up' came blaring through the receiver. A pain shot through her head like a lightning bolt. She blurted out, without giving it as much as a thought, "You can't come near me." Fear engulfed her when she heard his angry voice.

"What have you done? You may live to regret this action," Chase mockingly mumbled, then slammed down the receiver.

Immediately, after hanging up and while in a shocked, trembling state of mind, Julie shouted into the darkness, "I would have never answered that call, not for one second, if I had known it was from Chase!"

Julie had a restraining order, but would it really keep him away? And what good would it be in putting her life back together, a life she feared would lie in shambles for a very, very long time.

# CHAPTER 35

Two weeks had past that brought little peace. Julie sat starring at a blank TV screen and wished her mind could shut down the same way the machine did. It seemed nothing helped to relieve the tension going on inside, not even the thought of returning to the sanctity of her farm, which in the past had a soothing effect on her. She wondered if it would ever again after the episode with Chase.

Having stared long enough at the blank screen, she walked over and pulled back the window curtain. Noticing the gentle, splattering of raindrops on the windowpane, she became melancholy for just a moment. She released the curtain and proceeded to turn on the nearby radio, if nothing more, for a temporary distraction. She soon became lost in the melody of one of her favorites, *Blue Eyes Crying in the Rain.*

As she sat there emotionally lulled by the music, an intense tone caused her to jump. She picked up the receiver and again found herself subjected to silence. Stop the madness she wanted to scream.

At last, a click. With the irritating sound of a dial tone in her ear, she slammed down the receiver. She feared the worst; yet, at the same time, tried to rationalize it could have simply been a wrong number.

In a last-ditch effort to calm herself, Julie prepared a cup of hot tea. However, shortly after taking a sip of the freshly brewed beverage, she was interrupted by the slam of a car door echoing throughout her mind piercing every nerve in her body to its limit. Who could that be? Her heart raced as she stumbled to the window. An unfamiliar car vanished around the corner. Bombarded with visions she wished she could stop, she finally accepted whoever it was had nothing to do with her. Was she ever going to feel safe again?

She sat back down on her chair, pulled up her knees against her chest, and rested her head on them, swaying forward and backward. By now, it took everything she had to keep from surrendering to the hysteria going on inside.

She knew she'd sat there for several hours but couldn't bring herself to move. Earlier that morning, she had opened some of the windows. Now, the afternoon shadows had begun to lengthen, and a cool breeze was blowing throughout the house

Rubbing her arms against the chill, she thought how trusting and undemanding she had been with Chase. How could she have ever anticipated any good to come out of a relationship with a foundation rooted in violence? Trying to dismiss the entire perplexity of her situation, she picked up a novel that was lying on the end table and diligently began to read. It was hard to focus on the words, but she finally relaxed, temporarily laid the book aside, and retreated to her bedroom. Her eyes scanned the room, but her thoughts were somewhere else. As she lay down, she finally fell into a fitful sleep.

The following morning, she woke with a stiff neck and a slight headache. She attributed it to the late night dreams and nightmares which she wished would stop.

She then came to terms with her negligence to tell Bailey of the chaotic happenings of the past weeks. Why had she been putting it off? She knew exactly why. A lecture from her friend was in store, and probably rightly deserved, but today she felt like getting everything off her chest and there was no other friend she would rather have a lecture from.

She stretched, got out of bed, and made herself a cup of coffee. The hot liquid was just what she needed. Relaxing in her chair, she picked up the phone and dialed her friend's number.

"Hello."

"Good morning."

"Well, good morning. Long time no hear from."

"I know. I'm sorry."

"How's everything in your world?" Bailey anxiously asked.

She smiled at her friend's 'always positive' sounding voice. "Well…"

"Uh oh. What?"

Realizing by Bailey's response the woman knew her way too well. "I've put off calling you."

"Because…?"

"Things haven't been going too good 'in my world', as you say."

"What do you mean?"

"I don't like to admit it, but you were right all along." She gave a weary sigh. "Are you ready?"

"I'm listening."

She closed her eyes, took a deep breath, and let it out. Recounting the events would only make them fresher in her mind than they already were, but she had to talk about it. "Here goes the entire ugly truth."

As her friend unraveled the unbelievable and bizarre events of the past weeks, Bailey listened intently. Julie was glad she let her finish without interrupting. Since it had taken a moment for Bailey to say anything, Julie wondered *had they somehow gotten disconnected.*

"Bailey?"

"Oh my, friend, why are you still hanging onto that place?"

"That's an answer I can't give you. I'm not sure. But, that's not the half of it," Julie persisted.

"That would be more than enough for me! What else is going on, if that's not all of it?"

"I feel...I feel...it's kind of like I'm on the outside of my body looking in."

"How do you mean?"

She didn't know how to explain it, but the feeling wouldn't go away. "Well, for example, yesterday I went to prepare my favorite casserole, and it was as though I had never made the dish before. I know it sounds ridiculous, but it was like someone else was in my head, and they didn't know the recipe. All I could do was stand there and watch. Like right now. Even though I'm in the city, I feel a strange presence or something."

"I'll say it again, Julie. You need to sell that farm. Especially if these feelings are following you into the city. That place brings you nothing but misery."

She thought of the happy times she's had on the property, too. "Not always."

"No, not always, but when they're bad, they're really bad. Think about it."

"I know you're right. Perhaps, I should explore that option."

*Tears began to trickle down the chief's once confident face. That is not an option he wanted to shout to the top of his lungs. He only wished she could really hear him.*

# CHAPTER 36

A month has passed since Chase's attack. Julie was desperately trying to get her life back together, but she still didn't feel like herself. Work helped, and she was glad to have something to do with her time in the evenings. Daytime, however, was still lonely and to top it off, this morning something didn't seem right.

Her mind kept going to the farm. She missed it so much, but mostly she was missing her dog today. Images of a young Tonka, running around happy and free, came into her mind and she smiled. If only he could be that way again, she knew she was only dreaming. Maybe she'd make a trip to see the old companion that afternoon.

She placed a load of clothes in the washer, heard the phone ring and went to answer it hoping she didn't meet silence on the other end. So much time had passed since she'd gotten a silent call, she didn't even know why she'd thought about it. "Hello."

"Hi, Julie, it's Madelyn."

"Hi." Her heart skipped a beat. If her friend was calling, something was wrong. "What's up?"

"I'm so sorry to call you this way," Madelyn began.

Her intuition kicked in, and she knew what the call was about. "It's Tonka, isn't it?"

"I'm afraid so."

"I'm on my way." She locked up and headed for the farm. Tonka must have passed over her on his way to meet the Great Spirit to show her he could run again. As she pulled into the driveway of the farm, tears welled in her eyes. What a happy time for her dear K9 companion, but a sad time for her.

Madelyn was waiting for her to arrive. Together they made the much-dreaded walk to the sacred ground to bury Tonka. He had lived more than a long, contented life, but that thought did little to comfort her. What was most comforting was to know where he was, he could run again without pain. Walking away from her devoted dog's burial site was nearly unbearable.

She wiped at her tears as they descended toward the house. Hoping against all odds, she had just made a good decision. "Madelyn, after having talked with Bailey a few days ago, I pretty much decided to sell this place."

"What?"

Nodding her head, she cleared the lump in her throat. "Yes, because of everything that's happened here."

"Well, Julie, I–"

She held up her hand to stop Madelyn's statement. "However, today I realize I simply can't do it. I love this place too much. I have a buyer standing by to purchase my nightclub, there's no reason why I can't live out here again, especially if I'm alone."

"Well, that's unexpected news I must say, but good news nonetheless."

Her wants had changed over the last few weeks. "You know, I've pretty much lost interest in my previous lifestyle. The nightclub, having a boyfriend, I mean I don't want to socialize with people much anymore. I'm withdrawn and very much content living by myself." Julie then paused for a brief moment. With some brightness returning in her heart, she knew what she needed to do before she left the property today. "Nothing has been touched on this farm since Chase left. Today, I'm going to remedy that. I'm going to make some changes around here." Madelyn couldn't help but smile at seeing her friend's eagerness.

"Tell me what I can do to help."

Within a couple hours of that decisive moment, the pair took a step backwards and admired their accomplishments. They had cleaned, completely rearranged the furniture, pulled back the curtains and opened the windows to let fresh air drift through the house on the breeze. It looked like a new place.

Julie was so pleased with everything. Happiness didn't seem to be out of reach now. "Thank you." Julie gave Madelyn a hug. "You don't know what this means to me. I know my Tonka has gone on to a better place, and I'll miss him, but I can't wait to come home."

"You're welcome, and I can't wait to see your pickup sitting out here in the driveway again."

The following morning, Julie carried a duffle bag in one hand and a small cooler in the other. She eagerly walked into her garage, excited about the thought of returning to the country. Today she would be taking the first step in that direction.

Shortly, the farm came into sight and before turning off the key, she couldn't resist honking her horn, just a couple of times, to let Madelyn know she was home. Before long, she was not only trekking up the hillside, but also climbing to the top of her observatory, totally lost in the moment. The grass, the flowers, the fields, the trees, and the sky were as beautiful as ever.

Julie threw up her hands and shouted at the top of her lungs, "Why would anyone want to live anywhere else?"

*"Indeed, why would anyone want to," echoed the chief. The deeply grooved lines in his features seemed to*

*disappear as the light from the sun glanced across his face, for he finally found a form of peace. Julie was back on the farm and his heart soared. What more could he ask?*

Checking her watch and feeling a twinge of hunger, Julie walked down the steps from the observatory and headed back in the farmhouse. After setting her cooler on the table, she enjoyed the lunch she'd prepared earlier; along with the solitude she was absorbing. While sitting there meditating, it struck her how quiet it really was inside her head without the constant worry over Chase. She was finally able to shut thoughts of him out of her mind.

Although, she'd found a form of peace, she couldn't help but think of her all-time sidekick, Tonka. What she missed most this morning was his running around the corner of the farmhouse to greet her. Her thoughts were brought to a standstill from the ringing telephone.

"I figured I would find you there. How's Julie today?" She was delighted to hear her dear friend Wapa's voice on the other end.

"Julie's happy to be back on the farm, but she's still trying to identify the new her. She still doesn't quite know who she is these days."

"Okay, I wasn't expecting that kind of response. I figured you'd be feeling more oriented after you recuperated. I know at the first of your ordeal with Chase, you felt out of sorts, but what's going on now?"

"You've seen me a couple of times since then, right?"

"Yes."

"Did I act differently or do anything strange that you can recall?"

"How strange are we talking? At times, I think you're a little eccentric but that's just you."

"As absurd as it may sound to you..." She couldn't believe she was about to say this. "I think a walk-in came into my body that day Chase choked me; someone's spirit entered without my knowledge. It would explain a lot about how I feel inside."

"A walk-in, huh? I definitely feel you were a victim that day." Upon pausing a moment, Wapa added, "Now that I think about it, I have noticed some changes in you. They didn't stick out in my mind 'til now, though."

"How so?"

"Well, you seem to be more passive than usual and quite a homebody these days. More laid-back and you did surprise me putting your nightclub on the market."

"Why didn't you say something?"

"I never made the connection. Walk-ins usually happen at the point a person doesn't want to live anymore. The person's soul just doesn't want to carry on with life's plan, and people who have near death experiences take on a totally new identity."

"That's me, I feel exactly that way." Excitement built within her. "I mean, I sat in that chair with the coat hanger wrapped around my throat digging in, and I felt life draining out of me. I had no desire to live. He took everything away from me at that moment. Now things are starting to make sense."

"I can't believe I didn't put two and two together before. I'm trying my best to process this whole analogy 'walk-in' theory of yours, my friend." He cleared his throat. "You know, Julie, a walk-in can come during a traumatic time and can go undetected. However, you have seen the signs and that's a good thing. I have an expert at my disposal, you know that. All I have to do is make a call."

"I recognize and accept the fact it's my fault I haven't told you about this sooner. I've put it off way too long. Maybe an appointment at this time would be a wise thing to do."

"I totally agree. So, let me get a confirmation. You want me to call Night Hawk."

It was hard for her to accept that another spirit besides

hers might be inside her body, but the presence was too strong to be ignored. "Yes."

Soon Wapa called her back. "The meeting is set for February 16$^{th}$."

"Only days away, I can't wait!"

Wapa was on his way to pick her up for the meeting. The last few days, she had become more and more excited about possibly feeling like herself again. She looked at the beautiful gift she'd decided to give Night Hawk, sitting on the coffee table. It glistened in the sunlight that streamed through the window. In the few days she had it sitting there, she had already started feeling better. Maybe she would get one like it for herself as this one stood apart from the ones she already had in her collection.

Wapa pulled into the drive and honked. Hearing the noise, Julie stepped outside the door and waved to acknowledge his presence.

"I'm excited!" she said, within reach of his vehicle. "Oh, no," she stopped and snapped her fingers. She was about to leave the most important thing behind. "Wait, I'll be right back." She ran inside and grabbed Night Hawk's gift then ran back. "I'm so energized this morning. I almost forgot Night Hawk's crystal. I sure hope he likes it."

Wapa studied the unique shape of the gift and smiled. "I believe he will."

Soon they found themselves being directed to a small room to the left of Night Hawk's living room which contained several Indian artifacts. Since it was customary to bring a gift, Wapa brought an Indian wand with a red-tail hawk claw that he made, holding a clear crystal. Julie had found her gift for Night Hawk on a trip she made to the Smokey Mountains.

"It's nice to finally meet you, Julie," Night Hawk said, joining them and extending his hand. "Wapa has told me you have need of a reading."

She couldn't believe she was really here. It was too good to be true. Her mind was in a whirl. "Yes. I'm not sure where to begin." Julie heard the excitement in her own voice and felt it deep inside. "I'm part Cherokee, and I'm fascinated with Indian culture. Once, I was in a shop in Oklahoma, when an Indian woman came up to me and said, 'Honey, you shouldn't be ashamed of your gift.' Then she walked on past me. After thinking about her comment, I associated it with the animal, spirit reading cards Wapa had given me." She watched the tall, handsome Indian man move with the grace of a leopard, walk over and sit down.

"I'm not surprised with that incident." Night Hawk nodded his head. "After Wapa called to set up this meeting, I went downstairs. On my way, this deck of cards fell from the nearby shelf." Holding up a deck of medicine cards, he continued, "I then had a vision of an Indian chief who appeared to be strong and powerful. I'm thinking that message was for you."

Julie took a deep breath. Her heart pounded and she wanted to know more. However, she just sat back in her chair not wanting to influence the shaman in any way.

"What other concerns do you have?" Night Hawk asked, while shuffling the medicine cards and placing them one at a time on the table.

Julie hesitated a brief moment. *It's now or never. Breathe in, relax, and tell the man everything.* "Some time ago," she proceeded. "I dreamed about a farm I wanted to own someday. It reminded me a lot of my aunt's land I knew as a child. The following morning, I found it advertised in the newspaper. Something compelled me to move forward with the purchase." She twisted her hands together, unable to relax. "It gives me peace of mind that I cannot find anywhere else when I'm out there, but at the same time, it destroys my happiness."

"You feel this way because?"

She met the older man's wise gaze, needing to lay it all

out on the table. "For example, several of my male friends who have come to the farm have met with off-the-wall tragedies. I know this must sound ridiculous to you. However," she said, trying to not hold anything back, no matter how stupid it might sound, "I'm convinced a spirit, of sorts, is behind all this chaotic behavior. When I was a small child, I often sensed I had a protective spirit surrounding me. Now, as an adult, I'm second-guessing myself. It now seems mostly bad things occur." She didn't tell him who she thought the entity was, she waited for his response. She noticed how serious he had suddenly become. She squirmed, just a little, waiting for his comment.

"That's what I was saying earlier, Julie. I have that same suspicion, and the cards also reflect you will never be able to leave."

She wasn't sure that was totally right. If she really set her mind to leave, she probably could. "Wow!" Julie said, sitting straight in her chair. "And the strange thing is I don't really want to. In fact, I just recently moved back to the property."

Night Hawk laid down another card then looked up. "Your cards indicate you carry the spirit of a medicine woman."

"I hope that's true," she said. "Wapa has already given me my own medicine bag." That was news that made her happy. Deep down inside, she'd felt she was a medicine woman already.

Wapa joined the conversation. "The things you're telling Julie don't surprise me at all. I've also felt the medicine woman presence."

"Oh, one more thing," Julie interjected as though she had almost forgotten the main reason for her visit. Her blood quickly rushed to her face, and she felt flushed. It was like reliving the choking all over again. It took her several moments to calm down. Neither of the men in front of her said a thing. They had sat patiently waiting until she was able to gain control and convey how she thought Chase's attempt on her life had set her in a new direction. "I'm not sure, and I don't want to believe it, but I feel like I have…well…I don't know…a different spirit?" She watched as an understanding expression crossed Night Hawk's face before he spoke.

"Our physical body is not us. It is only a container for us. We existed as a spirit before the body that we now occupy was born. You very well could have had a spirit-changing experience. Your new spirit could have work to do in the material world for a variety of reasons, and this change can be either temporary or permanent."

Night Hawk met her gaze again. "I feel it would be a good idea for me to make a visit to this mysterious farm of yours. What do you say? Perhaps it would help me gain perspective. I hesitate right now to draw any further conclusions."

Nothing would please her more than for this wise man to visit the farm to see what he felt while on the property. "Yes, I would like that very much. You've been a big help. I'm so glad Wapa insisted I come here today."

"And I look forward to seeing you again. The next time will be on this farm of yours." He smiled, stood, and led them to the door.

# CHAPTER 37

Julie woke up this morning in a relaxed, stress-free mode. She thought about her photo album. She had neglected it long enough. Today, she would bring it up to date. After preparing her morning coffee, she sat at the kitchen table with the album and some pictures she wanted to put in it. This was going to be a task, but one she looked forward to finishing.

Hours later, she placed the last picture in her album. All day, looking at the pictures, her emotions were all over the place. They spun like a top out of control. Now the mission was complete. She closed the book and heard the phone ring.

"Hello. Do you know who this is?"

It couldn't be, could it? Her heart took off at a galloping speed. She hesitated before responding. Caught off guard by his voice added to her already heightened emotional state, shocked with an electrical current would be more accurate.

Finally, she managed to find her voice, "Of course. It's Drew." She swallowed hard and tried to calm her rushing pulse. "I never thought I would hear from you again. What's going on?"

"You've been the focus of my thoughts for some time

now," he continued, briefly clearing his throat. "Every day for weeks, to be exact, I've picked up the phone and before I completed dialing your number, I would hang up, no backbone I guess; nevertheless, bottom line, I want and need you in my life. The sound of your voice dances in my head. I need so much to kiss and hold you. I miss you, Julie. Miss you so much. You're my only love."

She didn't know how to handle this sudden revelation he'd had. "Drew, I–"

"Before you say anything, would you please just answer a question for me?"

Curious as to where this was going to lead, she said, "Okay. What?"

"Do you have any feelings left at all for me?"

Not waiting to show signs of weakness and a shaky voice, she tried her best to ignore his flattering words and quiet her galloping heart. "You must know," she began in a matter-of-fact tone, "it took me a long time to move on with my life after you left."

"Julie, I'm so sorry. I know I've done a lot of stupid things in my lifetime, and letting you go is one thing I have lived to regret."

"How is your health?" Julie asked, in an attempt to change the course of conversation before her old feelings came crashing down on her.

"I guess okay. At least, I come to work every day but Sunday."

"I'm glad to learn that."

"Well, I'm on my lunch break. Thanks for not hanging up on me. By the way, is it okay, if I call you again sometime?"

Her mind told her to say no, but her heart said…"Perhaps." She said goodbye and hung up. "Well, that was totally unexpected." She needed to sit down before she fell. "I hope his call doesn't send me right back into a tailspin of the previous magnitude." Oh, great, now she was talking to herself.

She thought of how Drew had been able to break her heart in the worst possible way, and she couldn't allow that to ever happen again. However, that didn't stop her from wondering what today's call was really all about.

It had been a week since Julie received Drew's call and by then, she had dismissed him from her mind. That evening, just after completing her late afternoon chores, a decisive and persistent knock drew her attention. She opened the door. Drew stood there leaning against the framework.

"Evening," he casually said, "may I come in?"

He had caught Julie off guard...again. She stood and stared at him. Her pulse raced, and she had to consciously close her mouth. She'd forgotten how handsome he was.

He stood to his full height. "I'm sorry if I startled you, and I apologize for not calling."

With a quick glance toward her driveway, she noticed he had driven his dad's car, and that's how he managed to get the upper hand, so to speak. She hadn't heard the usual approach of his bike, and it saddened her not to see the Harley sitting in her driveway. Oh how she missed that sound.

"You're probably wondering why I'm here. Well," he gave a slight hesitation just before blurting out. "I just wanted to see you in person and tell you you're the one I love." He cautiously waited for a response.

Julie felt it took a lot of courage on his part, so she stepped back and motioned him in. She watched him take a brief moment to look around the room, it seemed in the hopes of bringing forth past memories. He looked awkward and unable to touch any of them.

Trying not to be drawn in by his face-to-face confession of his love, she wanted to enforce her feelings. "You know, Drew, I'm in my fifties now and drastic changes have been made in my life since you've been gone.

"I understand," She trusted he knew nothing of the changes or happenings she'd gone through after he left. He didn't need to know either. "During our separation," Julie continued as she sat on the couch, shaken by his company. "I've tried to move on with my life."

The passion in Drew's eyes was a painful reminder of the love they'd once shared and secretly, Julie wanted him to take her in his arms, to kiss her, and consequently make her forget the past. Nonetheless, she couldn't conceive what the future held for either of them, if anything at all.

"You know I love you. You're the only woman for me. I've changed, Julie."

As the conversation went on, his pleas for reconciliation didn't fall on totally deaf ears. Before long, warm tears trickled down her cheeks, she wiped at their wetness. However, she made up her mind Drew wasn't coming back into her life so easily.

"Drew, let's not put ourselves through any more heartache. Please understand, like I said, I have moved on."

He checked his watch. "I guess it's time for me to go."

"Yes, I think so."

He stood and before she knew it, Drew had pulled her into a standing position, put his arms around her and pulled her close. It was a challenge for her to pull free. A technique of his she was all too familiar with. He tried to kiss her. She turned her face. While still standing in his embrace, she did offer her cheek. He seemed okay with her gesture.

"I need to be going." He gave a slight grin. "Thanks for seeing me."

As Julie stood waving goodbye to the man she had imagined to be a permanent fixture in her life, her knees wanted to buckle. She had stood her ground and was letting him walk away. Hoping, she could hold to her plan, she closed the door.

Following that evening, Drew continually called and pleaded for the opportunity to come back. She had feelings for him and with each call; it became harder to say no. So, after several of his persuasive phone conversations, she agreed to allow Drew to come to the farm for a visit.

After hanging up from one of those persuasive calls, Julie shook her head and walked over to the refrigerator to find something to eat. While trying to decide, a familiar Wanda Jackson song played in the background. "Right or wrong I'll be with you… I'll do what you ask me to… For I believe that I belong, by your side right or wrong."

Was this an omen of what was to come? "Oh, no," Julie said aloud. "I have to stop listening to the radio. I'm getting paranoid."

Like it or not, Julie was anxious and nervous in the days preceding Drew's visit. Finally, she woke up from a restless night of sleep; the day had arrived. Soon she heard the familiar roar of the Harley coming down the dirt road, and it sent cold chills up her spine. How she had longed for that sound to reach her ears again.

Julie quickly went outside. Her mind was filled with compassion as she felt the air in her lungs take flight. Regaining her self-control, she managed to say 'hi' over the loud roar of the engine.

"Man, it feels good to be here." Drew pulled his key from the ignition and inhaled the scent of the country air. Then while he removed a small black duffel bag, Julie caught sight of the teasing gleam in his eyes.

"You're traveling mighty light these days," she jokingly said, while at the same time, she noticed how much more pale and thin he looked since his surprise visit a few weeks earlier.

"I feel like a bird out of a cage." He glanced in her direction. "Well, can I at least have a hug?"

Julie didn't hesitate rushing into his open arms. At that moment, nothing else mattered. She had allowed him to

246

come see her, and she was going to enjoy the time they were together. Her feelings were on her sleeve.

*The chief would prefer Drew stay in the cage that he had just referenced. He wasn't welcomed here. The way Julie peered up at him made the chief's anger boil.*

*Even though the two standing in front of him may be happy with this reunion, he could only take it in stride. He wanted the man to take himself, and the Harley, on down the road without any assistance from him. However, if not, he had a well thought-out plan of his own.*

"I've waited a very long time for this moment," Drew whispered as he breathed in her familiar scent.

The couple stood embraced in each other's arms with neither one wanting to let go. Still stunned by the control of the chemistry, Julie looked into his eyes. "I've never stopped caring for you." She laid her head on his shoulder.

"Ditto, but you already know that."

Moments later, Drew gazed into her eyes. "How about we build a campfire on the hill tonight?"

Julie smoothed back strands of his hair and smiled. "I would like that."

She wanted to sit by the fire with him more then she wanted to admit. However, the tremble she felt inside made her realize she would have to take it slow, step-by-step and day-by-day. Right now, though, she was going to live for the moment.

Julie ended their embrace and missed the warmth of his arms around her. She noticed the uncertainty in his eyes waiting for her answer. "Let's put your things away and get ready to build the campfire." His laughter was contagious, and she couldn't help but join in. It had been a long time since she'd truly laughed.

"Wonderful!"

They went to the top of the hill and built a leaping

campfire. Above them was a black velvet sky with sparkling stars and a large round moon.

Throughout most of the evening, they tried to catch up on what seemed like a lifetime ago.

Julie's heart was full. She felt excited and calm at the same time. She was so glad to see Drew, to touch him again. She wanted to say so many things.

She took his hands and studied them for a period of time. Seeing the reflection of his eyes through the yellow flame, she said, "Drew, I never told you this before, but one of the first things I noticed about you were your hands. They are so strong and masculine."

"Really." Drew moved in closer. "Tell me more."

Then Julie heard a faint gasp, only vaguely realizing it had come from her own throat as Drew's lips met hers.

# CHAPTER 38

Julie and Drew had enjoyed twenty-four hours together. They were inseparable, yet something was gnawing at her. Drew had been pleasant enough but her gut told her something just wasn't right, but what was it? Having had a picnic, she was anxious for them to ride the four-wheeler to the river for a swim.

She couldn't wait to get there and plunge into the cool depths of the water. She didn't know how long she swam before she climbed out and dried herself off. Feeling tired from the swim, she collapsed onto a nearby blanket, and then eased back, savoring the pleasure of doing nothing.

"Hey, you can't give up already?"

She smiled. "You don't think? Hide and watch me." She giggled then closed her eyes before she heard Drew's voice again.

"You're mean to me. You know that?"

"Not mean, just a bit lazy. This blanket and I are having a good time relaxing." The next thing she knew, her body was being sprinkled with cold water. Without hesitating, she sat up straight like she'd been shot.

"What's wrong?" Drew stood looking back at her. "I was just shaking the excess water out of my hair. Sorry." He grinned.

Quickly changing the subject, he proceeded to say excitedly, "Guess what? I almost forgot to tell you about my great aunt, Mary Lou, who unexpectedly stopped by the family business. It had been a really long time since I had seen her and while we talked, she brought me up-to-date on my family's history. She's like the family historian, and I learned one special bit of knowledge."

Now realizing a nap was out of the question, this peaked Julie's curiosity. "Like what?"

"Well, it appears you're not the only one with Indian heritage. My great, great grandmother was half Cherokee. I never knew that."

"Well, that explains why you enjoyed the rituals of the past."

"Yes, I was really glad to learn that. Now, the Indian ceremonies we have will take on new meaning for me," he bragged.

"That is good news," Julie agreed whole-heartedly. "We're more alike than I ever imagined."

"I've always felt I belonged here on this farm. I've told you that before."

"Yes, I remember. Hey, look over the top of those trees. The last rays from the sun are disappearing, and the air is getting a little chilly. I think it's time to get out of these wet clothes."

After loading everything onto the four-wheeler, Julie took her place on the driver's seat. "Hop on and we'll head back to the farm."

They reached the house and within minutes, they had changed into dry clothes and retreated to the top of the hill where they spent the larger part of the evening huddled beside a small campfire.

"This is my all-time favorite place to be." Drew watched the coals of the fire glow in the darkness of the night.

"No. It's my all-time favorite place." Her mind was off in another direction, not focused on the small campfire at all. She was more concerned with the turmoil going on deep down within the pit of her stomach. She wished she knew what was bothering her.

After returning to the farmhouse that evening, a restless night was in store for her. She tossed and turned into the wee hours of the morning, then got up and sat in her sofa chair.

Her thoughts went back to the last couple of days and began to realize what her problem was. Even though she had had a wonderful time with him, the old Drew was gone. Who was this man who had returned to the farm claiming to be him? He hardly looked or acted like Drew at all. It was something she had felt just below the surface, but didn't want to admit.

She heard him stirring and went into the kitchen to start breakfast. She soon noticed he was acting fidgety and uneasy.

"What's wrong, Drew? Can't you sit still?"

"Is it that obvious? I guess now would be as good a time as ever to tell you."

The look on his face told her what he was going to tell her wasn't good. "You mean you forgot something?" She glanced across the table in his direction.

Drew dropped his head and stared at the floor. "This is hard to talk about." He pressed his fingers into his forehead. "I didn't want to tell you but I know I have to."

"What is it?"

"I basically had to quit my job."

"But your dad is your boss. Did he fire you?"

"I wish it was that simple. I don't know what is wrong with me. One thing is I can't seem to get enough sleep. I'm tired all the time."

"What are you going to do?"

"I don't know. I was hoping you could help. I feel sick inside."

Hearing this news, Julie was devastated. "Drew, I'm so

sorry. I never thought you would have to quit your job because of illness."

"I've been to the doctor. There's nothing wrong with me physically. I think I was just missing you." He took her hand. "Do you think I can stay here until I get to feeling better? I'll get rested, then go back to work."

Her thoughts ran wild, but she wanted to help." She wished she could turn back the hands of time for him, but that was impossible. Suddenly, she became sick to her stomach. At best, she could now account for her uneasiness. "Sure."

As days changed to weeks, Drew slept more and more. It got to the point where he woke up only long enough to eat, then back to sleep. Since Julie was not mentally or emotionally prepared to deal with yet another crisis; especially, of seeing the one you love in such a state of mind, she made the decision to call his uncle.

She dialed the phone and on the third ring, he answered. "Hi, this is Julie, Drew's friend."

"Of course, how are you?"

"I'm fine, but…"

"Has something happened to my nephew?"

Yes, something had happened to him, but she didn't know exactly what it was but wondered if it was related to the farm. She filled him in on Drew's sleeping habits and how he'd lost more weight. Being with her wasn't helping. "I can't stand by and see Drew deteriorate like this. Please come and take him home. Maybe you can convince him to see a doctor."

The following day, at her request, Drew's uncle came. Julie knew the Harley sound that used to bring her such joy would soon become a distant memory.

Drew pulled her into his arms. "I really don't want to go, but I know it's for the best."

"Yes, I believe that, too. I want you to get help and get

well."

"I thought being here would do the trick," he said, climbing inside the truck. "But I thought wrong."

"You gave it your best shot," she said, holding her emotions at bay. "That's all we can ask."

"I'll miss you, Julie."

"Me, too. She leaned inside the vehicle and gave him one last kiss.

They had said goodbye before in their relationship, but that didn't make it any easier. Neither of them ever wanted to believe there wasn't a future for them. Time had done its work, and she and Drew had both given up struggling against the dictates of fate. They now acknowledge that which cannot be altered.

While Julie's aching heart fell into pieces inside her chest, she stood and watched the Harley fade from sight one last time. Her heart was heavy with grief. She went inside to lie down and found herself staring at the ceiling. Her mind was like a battleground though her house was ghostly quiet.

*Although, outside near the old Oak the chief had a sense of peace. Julie was his once again. A smile began to emerge. He loved his ever-controlling force on this intriguing, alluring, and still yet mysterious farm.*

# CHAPTER 39

It was a lonely Friday night. Momentarily, Julie had stopped to glance out her kitchen window, a mere distraction. If nothing more, focusing her attention on the prestigious old Oak often brought her a form of peace and comfort.

Somehow this evening felt different. Julie noticed how the night had a gloomy appearance and dead leaves were blowing back and forth in a disturbing fashion. The wind had an issue with deciding the direction it should be going. *Pretty much like me right now*, she thought.

As she stood there, her attention drifted from the dead leaves toward the shabby-looking moss growing on the north side of her barn. Disheartened with life and the gloomy situation outdoors, she left the confines of the window view, retrieved her photo album, and sat back on her recliner.

Thumbing through the pages, she remembered her first encounter with Drew; especially, those baggy sweats she was wearing the day he spoke to her from across the fence. While trying to commit from memory actually how long ago that had been, her phone rang.

She picked up the receiver. "Hello."

"Hi. How are you this evening?"

Drew's voice sounded weak, but it brought a slight smile to her face. "Actually, I was lost in a moment of you and me." She laid her album aside. Without thinking how it might sound, she asked, "What does love sound like to you?"

"Where did that come from?"

"I don't know, just wondering."

"Hmm... Love sounds like Julie to me."

She closed her eyes and savored his words. "I miss you so much." His voice seemed to be millions of miles away, and she reached into her heart and mind to bring him closer. When she did, she felt connected to him more than ever.

"I miss you, too."

She didn't like how frail he sounded. It worried her. "How do you feel? I mean, really feel?"

"I'm feeling much better today."

"That's wonderful." Though she questioned his answer, she didn't want to push the issue.

"Julie, I want you to know I love you. My heart trusts you. My heart believes you. It's my mind that causes us all our trouble. I beg you to help me heal my mind. The more you talk to me, the more I understand and trust. Please hang in there, and we will make it together."

"I'm trying." Her eyes burned with unshed tears.

"Tell me what you're wearing right now."

She giggled at the question and decided to go along with the game. "I'm wearing short, red satin pajamas."

"No, I'm being serious. You know what I really miss is seeing you in a pair of faded overalls, your dark hair tied back with a red ribbon, while you're sitting on your tractor. I long to be on your farm with you again."

"I want that, too. More than you realize."

"That's good to hear...Oh; by the way, I called and talked with my children today, my sister, and my parents. I told them I was thinking about them, and I love them."

"That's great news. Were they all doing fine?"

"Yes, and everyone was pleased to hear from me. I'm glad I felt like visiting with them. You know, Julie, I've been all over the world in my lifetime, but I have never felt at home anywhere more than I do on your farm. I wish I was there right now."

"First things first, let's take one-step at a time."

"I want to pick up where we left off."

"Me, too, but it's too soon."

For an endless moment, Julie lost sight. In reality, she knew spending her life with Drew was now only a dream, a figment of her imagination. She closed her eyes and fought back the emotion building inside. Then with great effort, she opened her eyes and found herself staring blindly at a painting on the wall. Drew's question pulled her attention.

"You know what I often think about?"

She tried to combat the pain in her heart. "No."

"The hours we spent around the campfire planning our home. I regret not getting to build it for you."

"I miss that part too, but we can still make plans." Why did she keep saying these things? She knew it wasn't going to happen. Was it to give him hope? Maybe it was so she could hold on to the last thread of the dream. "You know, I'm not bad with a saw and a hammer. With your supervision, there's nothing we can't accomplish."

"I'm not so sure about that. My body is so tired and worn out."

She noticed that he struggled to talk. It saddened her to think he was so physically and mentally weak.

"I have tried to fight the curse of your farm. I thought I could win, but I feel I have finally lost the battle. I can no longer win in life, but in death I'll be on even ground with the spirit of your farm."

How could he be thinking this way? She couldn't allow it. "Oh Drew! Don't talk like that. You're going to live to be an old man." She tried desperately to emphasize that over and over to him. She had to redirect his thoughts. "And we're going to get to build our home together. I just know it."

"That's what I like about you, your positive attitude and outlook on life. That and, of course, a million other things."

Her worry about him didn't take away the pleasure of how he felt about her. She couldn't help but smile at hearing his comment. There were a million things she liked about him, too. But there were so many things that needed to be fixed as well. She heard him take a deep, tired breath. "I'm sorry, but I need to say goodnight. However, before I hang up, I'd like to leave you with this reflective thought: If you remember nothing else of me, know I always, always will, and forever continue to love you. I'll have you in my heart for eternity."

"Ditto," she said, as she gently wiped at a last-minute tear beginning to trickle down her cheek.

## CHAPTER 40

The Saturday evening, following Drew's Friday night call, the phone rang and Julie was hesitant to pick it up. She swallowed the lump in her throat, not understanding the feeling she had inside. "Hello?"

Hearing the message coming through the receiver from Drew's sister frightened and horrified her. This was all terribly wrong.

"I'm so sorry," Cathy said. "I never wanted to call you this way."

Julie's heart sank at the words. "No!" she cried out hysterically.

"I went by Drew's this morning to check on him." Cathy hesitated and cleared her throat. "Drew didn't come to the front door." She started to sob. "I went inside. The first thing I noticed was a prescription bottle lying on the floor."

"Oh no!" She couldn't believe what she was hearing.

"I'm so sorry, Julie." She was barely able to get the words out.

Julie heard the panic in her own voice and fear griped her insides like a vice. Tears marked her cheek. "Drew can't be gone."

Julie had to fight to maintain control as waves of sadness, frustration and anger threatened to come over her very being. "No! No! This can't be real. I just talked to him last night."

"Yes, we all talked to him yesterday."

"I know, he told me he called his family."

"Julie?"

"Yes." She wiped a tear and stifled a sob.

"Mom has requested your presence at his memorial. Will you come?"

"Yes." How could she not pay her respects?

Frustration and sheer anger destroyed her control. It seemed like eons ago since she'd received the overwhelming call; however, a frantic glance at the clock, through tear-filled eyes, showed only minutes had elapsed. She finally laid the phone aside and slumped back on her couch, emotions running wild. Here she was left alone again to deal with a shattered, broken life on a farm she couldn't fully grasp or comprehend.

# CHAPTER 41

A sick feeling of dread knotted Julie's stomach as she drove to Drew's hometown for his memorial. Arriving at the church, an icy-cold feeling encased her body. Before stepping out of her pickup, she fought to keep control. Shortly, she spotted Cathy in the crowd and walked across the street to join her.

"Julie, I'm so glad you're here."

She accepted his sister's hug, and they walked the remaining distance side by side. Upon entering the little church, Julie was escorted to the front pew to join the rest of Drew's family. Within minutes, the church's choir began to sing 'The Master of the Wind'. The song seemed to fill the sanctuary with a cherub-like sound. It was during this surreal moment her mind started to wander. Oh, how she wished and how grateful she would be if she could only have a second chance with Drew. She stared at his picture, merely feet away surrounded in a collage of beautiful colors, unable to look away.

Lost in her own world, it wasn't until the eulogy began that Julie's mind was brought back to the present. While listening to Drew's tribute, tears filled her eyes. By the time the last person paid his respect, she was wiping away an emotional stream.

Shortly thereafter, the congregation began to sing 'There's Just Something About That Name'. As they sang this beautiful, mesmerizing hymn, those attending respectfully began to file out of the church. *What a beautiful acknowledgment of Drew's life. He would have been proud.*

Outside the church, Cathy pulled her aside. "Do you know Drew left me with specific instructions?"

"What? No. I had no idea."

"Well, I promised my brother I would fulfill his wishes, but at the same time, never believed I would be standing here talking to you like this. His dream, you know, was to build you a new home, marry you, and live happily ever after on the farm."

"Yes, we talked a lot about that."

Cathy then hurriedly spit out the words. "Drew has requested an Indian burial ceremony on your farm."

"Really!" Julie took a sudden step backwards, while at the same time, tried to grasp what the woman had just told her. "I didn't know," she said tearfully. "Although, I know how much he loved my farm, but..."

"Would you like some time to process all of this before making a commitment?"

She wiped the tears from her cheek. "No, it's not necessary. We have talked about death on more than one occasion, and now that I think about it, maybe in his own way, he was preparing me for this very moment."

"You know his birthday is coming up in a few days. It will just be Mom and me. If it's acceptable with you, we could have his ceremony then."

She felt disconnected and dizzy from the entire ordeal, but she couldn't say no. It was what Drew wanted. "Okay."

"Thank you for that, and thank you so much for coming today. It means a lot to Mom and all of us."

Her mind was reeling beyond control while she made her way back to her vehicle. She opened her door and fell against the seat. Her trembling legs had finally given way. She was unaccustomed to their stiffness.

As she drove alone the eighty miles back to the farm, her thoughts were not only riddled with the pain of Drew's death but also his dying wish.

## CHAPTER 42

The next few days, Julie was preoccupied with Drew's burial arrangements. Her steps carried her blindly, heedlessly across the stones that dug into the soles of her shoes. More than once, she tripped over moss-covered tree roots.

Suddenly, a gust of wind from out of nowhere blew a strand of hair in her eyes. She swished it back and, in so doing, looked down and saw a Raven's feather lying in her pathway.

*Hmm.* She reached to pick it up. *This feather wasn't here earlier this morning, but how appropriate. It will fit nicely into Drew's ceremony.* With the feather in her hand, she walked across the field and looked toward the heavens. Twilight was beginning to veil the earth.

Shortly after returning to her house, she prepared for bed, overwhelmed with emotion knowing tomorrow would be one of the hardest days of her life. She would definitely need all the courage and strength she could muster.

With only brief intervals of sleep the night before, she woke up anxious. Glancing outside she saw a slow steady drizzle the early morning clouds brought. Somehow, the rain seemed fitting, cleansing the air and giving it a spring-like quality.

Just before 9:00 a.m., Julie heard the dreaded knock on her front door. It was time. Inhaling deeply to keep her composure, she greeted both Cathy and Drew's mother. Together they began their trek up the long pathway to the top of the hill to honor Drew's life and fulfill his last request of an Indian burial.

Julie's emotions lay scattered in every direction. She was scarcely aware of what she was doing. Somehow, she managed to keep herself together, though she trembled so bad the Raven's feather nearly fell from her hand during the ceremony.

Drew's ashes were scattered from the top of the hill with its campsite, wooden observatory, panoramic view, and magical powers, to the bottom of the hill with its ever-flowing, never ending babbling brook. They were also placed in secret and sacred places known only to him and Julie.

Drew had at last returned to the place he committed to spend eternity, this place he called home.

As a final touch to his ceremony, Julie planted a deep, red rosebush from Linda's floral in her front yard so it could grow, flourish, and be admired for many years to come.

With the planting complete, the women said their goodbyes. Julie's heart now lay broken into a million pieces; however, she felt somewhat comforted in knowing that she had fulfilled Drew's final wish.

## CHAPTER 43

As Julie stood in the darkened shadows of her bedroom, she fought the emotional ache surging through her. Bits and pieces of her life with Drew were disarrayed to the point of confusion and mayhem. She couldn't stop thinking about him. While frantically trying to gather herself and understand this chaotic turmoil, she collapsed on her bed. Her body refused to move any longer, and her mind needed a rest. How could she go on?

Hours later, she knuckled the sleep from her eyes and made her way to the telephone. She had finally come to the conclusion she needed help finding out whatever or whoever was causing her life havoc on the farm. It was time she allowed Night Hawk to visit. His presence was not a luxury but a necessity.

She picked up the receiver and dialed Wapa's number. Hearing his voice on the other end, she closed her eyes and drew in a calming breath. "Could you please tell Night Hawk I'm ready for his visit?"

"Are you sure? How long has it been since his offer?"

Brushing the hair from around her eyes before answering, she gave a sigh. "Perhaps a moon or two but now Drew's death has just about pushed me over the edge with the farm."

"Are you okay for now?"

"I guess." She sat on the edge of the bed. "My nerves have quieted some. It's just that I'm having difficulty putting his death into perspective. I'm trying to make sense out of this horrible tragedy. You know," she said, fighting back the tears, "I keep wondering what it was I missed. Was there a way I could have saved Drew? Is this somehow my fault?"

"Julie! Stop thinking like that. The events on your farm are far beyond either of our understanding capabilities. The one having that expertise is Night Hawk. His visit is the right thing to do. I will talk to him."

"Thank you." She hung up and busied herself with nothing in particular just to try to occupy her thoughts. That afternoon Wapa's call came.

"Is next Friday okay for Night Hawk?"

Relief flowed through her body. "It's perfect."

"I am glad you finally are letting me send Night Hawk to help you."

"I am anxious and excited." She hung up, knowing she could always count on her friend to be there for her.

At last, the next Friday, an unfamiliar car pulled into Julie's driveway. A tall, good-looking man stepped out. She recognized Night Hawk right away. "Hello."

"Hi. It's good to see you again. Hmm. This is the mysterious farm causing all the upheaval."

"I'm afraid, so. It's nice of you to come." Julie extended her hand. "I assume Wapa told you about the latest." His handshake was firm, and she welcomed the warmth and wisdom his touch brought.

"He told me you feel you may be somehow instrumental in the events happening here."

"I don't like to think that way, but it seems so." She pointed to where they would be going to have their fire. "If you're ready, we'll go up on the hill to continue our discussion."

He nodded. "Okay, lead the way."

Once they arrived on the hilltop, Night Hawk stopped and studied his surroundings. "It's really quite pleasant and peaceful up here."

She was pleased he liked it. "Yes. This is where I spend a lot of my time. It's my sanctuary from the outside world. Look into the sky... It's magnificent, don't you think?"

"It's glorious."

"I'm glad you were able to come tonight, especially because there's a full moon."

"I had it on my calendar so I would be sure to remember."

Julie showed Night Hawk where she previously placed the seven different types of wood needed for the fire. Before long, he had built a cozy blaze. He removed sage and tobacco from his medicine bag and sprinkled it onto the fire. A blue flame shot up, licking the wood, which threw shadows into the approaching darkness.

She seated herself next to Night Hawk before going into detail the need of his visit. While he observed and listened intently, the fire reduced itself to a mere glow in the tranquility of the darkness.

The wise man stood. "Let's take a walk."

In the calmness of the evening, as the big, orange, round-shaped moon lit their path, the pair walked across the farm like two silhouettes disappearing into the shadows. Soon Night Hawk's voice drew her attention.

He glanced at her but kept walking. "Julie."

She met his gaze but couldn't recognize the look on his face. "Yes?"

"I don't want to frighten you, but there is a very strong and powerful spirit out here. The spirit of the Indian chief of which I spoke of at your reading. At this moment, he is listening and watching. He is rather tall, strong, and possesses far more power than me."

Julie stopped and drew a deep breath. "I knew it."

"The good news is..." Night Hawk turned toward her. "I don't fear for your safety, yet you've become an important part of his life." He shook his head. "I cannot see this chief ever letting you leave this place."

It was true after wondering all these years, final confirmation. She had known there was something...or someone. "Thank you," Julie nervously responded while managing to keep her emotions in check. "I needed to know for sure."

"Just remember, he is very powerful. When I came out here tonight I had planned to come again to see you, but I found more than I bargained for."

Shaken, she turned toward him. "What do you mean, more than you bargained for?"

"I mean, I don't think any man is powerful enough to overcome the control of this chief's will. There is nothing more I can do."

This saddened her, but she had his validation tonight and proof from those men who had previously suffered from his wrath. "Maybe, if I had listened to Wapa about contacting you sooner," she said, "I would have been better prepared to have met this challenge."

He placed his hand on her shoulder. "I must say, you have survived years of his chaos pretty well. The things you thought were only in your mind have, and are really happening. Remember, though, no more personal visits from me. One night on your farm is more than enough."

*The chief listened intently and smiled. It was about time someone gave credit where credit was due. A slight smile crossed his weathered face.*

## CHAPTER 44

Julie woke the following morning to an irritating sound she felt and assumed was coming from her alarm clock. She had recently accepted a part-time position at the convenience store down the road, but she didn't think she had to work today. The job did little more than afford her the opportunity to give her mind a rest from the craziness of the farm.

Seconds later, she was able to differentiate the sounds. "Hello."

"Good morning," came the reply. "How's it going?"

"Oh, Bailey, I'm still reeling from Night Hawk's visit last night. Thanks for asking. Speaking of that, he confirmed there's a powerful spirit living out here, nothing less than that of a chief."

"Julie! How much more time are you going to spend on that farm?"

Pretending she hadn't heard Bailey's question she sat up in bed. "I just had a thought. How would you like to take a trip with me?"

"I don't know... What do you have in mind?"

"Nothing dangerous," Julie answered, noticing the concern in her friend's voice. "I would just like to gain additional insight about the one who has chosen to take up residence here. Maybe do a little research on the land."

"Well, that doesn't sound too risky. In fact, it might be fun. Does this trip include lunch?"

"Yes, there's a wonderful little restaurant called Nifty's Café, it's just around the corner from the Genealogical building."

"Okay, what time should I arrive?"

"Why don't you be at my place about 10:00 o'clock?"

"See you then."

Being the early morning person she was, Julie looked at the clock and realized she had overslept this morning. She had only made it to the kitchen, when her phone rang out again. Thinking Bailey had forgotten something, she answered, "Yes."

"I haven't even asked the question, yet." came a voice through the earpiece.

Recognizing the caller's voice, Julie said. "Oh, Cody, I'm so sorry. I thought you were Bailey.

Julie had only been on her new cashier job at the convenience store a few days, when a customer initiated an introduction to her. Before long, she realized Cody was an old schoolmate from high school.

How's your morning going?"

"It's somewhat confusing," he answered. "I was wondering if you were going to be home tonight."

"Sure."

"I have something puzzling to share with you."

"Okay," she replied, thinking Cody was sure acting somewhat strange this morning. "We can build a cozy fire, roast wieners, and eat a few marshmallows. It's going to be a perfect night to be sitting around a little campfire. What do you think?"

"I'm not so confident," Cody barely mumbled before the receiver went dead. Julie hung up the phone, not fully understanding his call, but contributed the anxiousness in his voice to his poetry writing. Tonight he probably wanted to share another one of his quirky little poems with her.

A few hours later as the sun was setting, Cody pulled into her driveway.

"Hi," Julie greeted him. "Ready to watch a few stars come out?"

"I think so,"

"Well, let's trek up the hill and get the fire started." Before long, they had a cozy little one blazing. They sat around it waiting for the star formations to fill the sky along with watching the cinders slowly drift out of sight. Cody seemed a little restless but hadn't indicated his reason for coming over tonight.

Once they finished their meal and put everything away, Cody thanked Julie for allowing him to come over. "Between eating those hotdogs and marshmallows," he spoke up, "I've sat here and ate enough charcoal to last me a very long time."

"I'm glad you came tonight," she smiled in his direction. Cody had become a good friend, and she enjoyed him stopping by whenever he wanted.

At last, Cody reached into his shirt pocket and removed an envelope. Julie had noticed it earlier in the evening and felt she had been right all along. He had written her another poem. They were usually no nonsense ones, but Cody often brought a new flair or meaning to simply sitting around a campfire.

"There is something I need to mention to you," he said, rather seriously.

"Okay," Julie nodded her head. This wasn't his usual way to introduce his poetry to her but....

"Well, I went to bed last night," he began, "at my normal time, and soon found out I couldn't sleep. Suddenly, I felt a compelling urge to write a poem. As you know, sometimes my poems sound a little corny."

"She nodded her head." She couldn't help but give a slight smile. She had been the recipient of a few of his previously written poetry attempts.

"Anyway," he continued. "I got up and sat at the table and began to write a rather-lengthy, serious poem as fast as I could. The words kept coming and coming and coming. I didn't know what to think. It was hard to get all the words down on paper."

Julie could hear the anxiety building and mounting in his voice. She was getting concerned.

Cody suddenly blurted out. "I honestly believe this poem was written for you."

*That was an odd statement.* It took her aback. "I don't quite understand Cody; of course, I believe you wrote the poem for me. You've written several we've shared together sitting right here, not unlike tonight."

"Julie, that's why I've been a little nervous and fidgety, I did and I didn't write this poem. Maybe after I share it," he tried to explain, "you will understand. I hope so, anyway."

"Alright, I'm ready," she said, positioning herself comfortably around the fire.

"Smoke rising from the chimney looked warm from the hill. Light snow was drifting through air cold and still."

Julie sat listening and thinking what a beautiful poem Cody had written this time, and as he continued, she was definitely getting lost in the sound of his voice. So, what had made him so nervous tonight? Julie didn't quite understand. She was letting her mind focus on his face while he continued. "Please don't judge me in this search of my past, for in my heart I believe I've found you, my love, at last."

"Oh, my gosh," she said, jumping to her feet. "What just happened?"

By now, Cody was standing right in front of her with facial expressions, weird features, and off-the-wall emotions that were changing moment by moment. "Julie, I love you."

"What! No! Stop it! Stop it!" Julie shouted at him. "You're freaking me out. That's enough."

"What's your problem, Julie?"

"Your face," she pointed. "It resembles that of an Indian chief. That's the problem."

"I'm not responsible," he shouted back at her. "I tried to tell you that earlier. Weren't you listening?"

Having finally gained some control and composure of her thoughts, Julie was finally apologetic to Cody. "I do believe you," she tried convincing him. "There's just so much that goes on out here I can't explain. I wish I could."

"I have to leave now, I'm emotionally drained. I don't want to be used anymore."

"I'm so sorry."

"Me, too. Here, this envelop belongs to you."

"I'll walk you back down the hill. Maybe things will seem different tomorrow."

"They're going to have to look a lot different as far as I'm concerned."

"I totally agree." Julie waved goodbye, and hugged her arms against the sudden coolness of the night.

The image of Cody's face kept haunting her over and over. Even as she lay in bed that night, his words kept echoing in her mind.

It would be early dawn before Julie could even think about her body relaxing. She had to get some rest. She had made early plans for the day and didn't want to cancel out on them.

At approximately 9:50 a. m., through bloodshot eyes, Julie watched Bailey pull into her driveway.

"Ready for your adventure?" Bailey anxiously asked at seeing Julie standing in the doorway.

"How about a cup of caffeine first. I mean coffee," Julie asked, hoping for a 'yes' answer.

"If we have the time, why not? Julie, you're looking a bit tired this morning." Julie shook her head, Bailey always told it like she saw it.

"Thanks. I didn't sleep much last night. Once we're on the road, I'll share the reason for these bags under my eyes."

Julie poured Bailey a cup of coffee, and they sat long enough for each of them to enjoy a cup. By then, Julie noticed it was 10:30 a.m., and time for them to be on the road. Julie pulled her kitchen door shut.

"Once Bailey had fastened her seat belt," Julie said, "You're not going to believe this one. Bailey, you remember those silly little poems that I share with you? The ones Cody keeps writing."

"Yes."

"Well, last night he shared a rather serious, puzzling one, causing these bags under my eyes." She quickly looked into her rear-view mirror to see if they were still visible.

"You still have a trace. It must have been some poem. How serious was it?"

"I'd say pretty serious. He told me he went to bed one evening and felt compelled to get back up to write it."

"So, what did it say?"

"Something about smoke rising from the chimney and lives falling apart. I can't remember exactly. I've been quite emotional since he read it to me."

"Sounds intriguing."

"I don't know about intriguing. I just know the poem has knocked me off my feet. There was no way possible for Cody to know the things he mentioned in that poem. He referenced the Raven's feather in Drew's ceremony, and Phantom not being able to walk on four hoofs…"

"Oh, my gosh, that's creepy."

"That's not all."

"Go figure. I'm listening."

"The more he read, the more uncomfortable it made me. By now, the embers of the fire were dying, and I wasn't listening to his words anymore. I was mesmerized with a transformation happening to his face. It was like…like…"

"Don't stop now, my interest is piqued."

"It was like he was taking on the persona of an Indian chief right in front of my eyes." She glanced at Bailey, whose eyes were wide open by now in disbelief.

"That can't be."

"It happened. I promise. I had to tell him to stop. He was freaking me out."

Bailey shivered. "You're freaking me out, right now. Look at my arms."

"I'll stop talking about it then."

"No way, I have to know the full story even if it does bother me."

She smiled at her friend, glad she wanted her to continue. She had to talk about it until it was all out of her system. "Cody didn't understand why I wanted him to stop reading, so I told him. He still claims he didn't compose it."

"He didn't? Who did, then?"

Should she tell Bailey what she truly thought? It was now or never. "Believe it or not, I think it was the chief that Night Hawk confirmed was on my farm. Since Cody writes poetry, he would be the perfect person to put the words on paper and then share the poem with me."

"That's unbelievable, but I guess it could happen."

"It could and it did. Oh, we're here already," Julie said, seeing their destination right in front of them. "We'll have to finish the mystery of the poem later."

She pulled into the parking lot of the Polk County Genealogical Society archives building, switched off the ignition, and turned her attention toward her friend. "And Bailey?"

"Yes."

"One more thing. I believe, without a doubt, it's a love poem."

Bailey shook her head. "You and your farm never cease to amaze and intrigue me."

What ease she had listened to her was amazing. "That's all you have to say?"

"What else is there?"

"Nothing, I guess, I just thought you'd be startled or mystified or something."

"I didn't say I'm not. There's just nothing I can do about it. I've run out of descriptive adjectives. You've heard all of them before: creepy, aggressive, powerful, scary, etc..."

Julie joined in her friend's laughter. "Let's eat at Nifty's then we'll go on."

"Sounds good to me.

Julie pulled in front of the brick building. "Are you ready to continue this journey?"

"I guess. We're here."

"Let's go inside, then." Julie followed Bailey through the door.

"Good afternoon," a man greeted, "My name is Charles. How can I be of service today?"

"I'm interested in locating written documentation of the Indians that lived in Polk County. Especially, any that may have lived on my land."

"There's very little actual early Indian information recorded," Charles confirmed, "however, I can verbally tell you they were here alright."

"That's exciting isn't it, Julie?" Bailey asked.

Julie was excited and disappointed with the response Charles had given. She wasn't going to give up, not just now any way. "Yes, but I was hoping to find that information in print."

Upon directing them to sit at a long wooden table, Charles continued, "Let's see if we can uncover any helpful written information." He walked over to a gray file cabinet and removed a manila folder from one of the drawers. Handing Julie a page, he asked, "Is this beneficial?"

"Let me see." She took the document from him. "This

does show there were Indians in Polk County during the time in question. Although," she added, rather disappointed, "it doesn't indicate they were Cherokee." She glanced at the frail looking man. "Charles, in your opinion, could they have been from the Cherokee tribe?"

"Anything's possible, I guess. However, let's see what else this folder might contain."

Shortly, Charles looked up and noticed his co-worker had returned from upstairs. Looking in her direction, he motioned to get her attention. "Mallory, can you show these ladies the article your grandfather is in? They came in looking for information on the Indians that once lived in Polk County."

Mallory walked across the room to another file cabinet and returned with a similar folder. "This folder contained a published article from the Bolivar Herald, dating back to July 6, 1939." Handing the article to Julie, Mallory smiled. "I hope this piece of history will be beneficial. However, I want you to know my grandfather was one of the white men involved. I apologize for any heartache this might cause you. I do not agree with what the white man did."

Julie kept her fingers crossed. "Thank you, I hope it's beneficial, too. Thanks for your help."

According to the article, the government had bought up all Indian rights to the land, but there was no mention of what tribe the Indians were from. She glanced up at Bailey. "Nothing about Cherokees. It's so sad that since the Indians chose not to leave voluntarily after they were paid for their land, the white man felt the necessity to stand guard with deer rifles; ultimately, following close to their heels to insure they left without resistance." One of the men just happened to be Mallory's relative.

Bailey patted Julie on the shoulder. "Yes, that is sad."

She closed the folder and sighed. "I guess we're finished here. I'm ready to return to the farm."

She stood and returned the folders to the main desk.

"Thank you, Mallory and Charles, for your help today." She and Bailey left, and Julie closed the door behind them.

While walking back to the pickup, Bailey spoke up, "I've been thinking. Maybe your purpose in life is to be an Indian advocate. Have you ever given that any thought?"

"No." Julie hesitated. "But maybe you're right. I'll give that some thought." She placed her key into the ignition. She had always tried to do what was right for Indians and their ways. Maybe her friend was right. "Before we leave, is there any place here in town you would like to go before we head back to the farm?"

"No, not that I can think of. I'm just trying to soak in all the information I learned and read about this afternoon. I think milling over the archives today was quite fascinating."

"I totally agree."

Before long, they were nearing the farm. Seeing her driveway up ahead, Julie said, "I'm glad our search wasn't a total loss. I want to especially thank you for going with me today. I have gained more insight into this mysterious farm of mine. However, I won't rest until I can find out more about this chief who has gone to such great lengths to protect, communicate, and make contact with me."

# CHAPTER 45

The following morning, Julie woke up thinking about her and Bailey's research adventure. The puzzle pieces to her mysterious farm were beginning to fit little by little. While walking into her bathroom, still puzzling over her protector's heritage, the thought popped into her head about Bailey's comment of her being an Indian advocate.

"Maybe I have been. Huh, wouldn't that be something?"

Brushing her hair this morning with more vigor than usual, Julie was startled by the squawking of her baby guineas. She pulled back the bathroom curtain and smiled. It was merely Madelyn's dog, Apollo, rounding them up. Julie gave a sigh of relief it wasn't an intruder. Looks like the babies had simply gotten out of their pen again. Hopefully, they would soon be old enough to take care of themselves, but right now, Apollo needed her help.

After closing the gate behind the babies, she patted the dog on the back. "Good job."

The air was crisp and clean. A gentle breeze dispersed the clouds, and the land reverberated with power. Whatever lay ahead would challenge her on every level, and she was definitely up to it.

She was feeling relieved of some of her heartache. Maybe it was the knowledge Night Hawk had given her about the chief's spirit, or maybe time was helping her heal from the loss of Drew. Whatever it was, she welcomed it.

She looked up just in time to catch a glimpse of her mailman driving around the bend in the road. "Ah, there goes Fred." As she made her way down the long lane to her mailbox, she hoped he'd filled it with intriguing mail. There is a slim to zero chance that a new adventure could have its beginnings that morning, but one never knows.

She stood at the road's edge sifting through her mail for that fascinating letter, when she spotted a cloud of dust rising above the road. Soon, an old Ford pickup came into view. Seeing it pull to a halt just inches away, she allowed herself a small smile.

"Good morning. I just moved here from up state. I'm Billy, and this is my dog, Jake."

Julie extended her hand. "It's a pleasure to meet you." She surveyed the rugged-looking cowboy, and then petted the dog on the head. "You, too, Jake."

"The pleasure is all mine. You take care now, you hear."

Billy tilted back his black cowboy hat, exposing his sparkling, blue eyes and eccentric grin. Suddenly, she felt like flirting. "I will, cowboy, I will." She smiled as she watched him drive away.

*She pondered with an ever so slight grin on her face, while the chief watched from the old oak, arms crossed, with a threat of anger burning inside him. The cogs twisted and turned in his mind. He was not to be reckoned with.*

# EPILOGUE

Nearly ten years had lapsed since Julie's search for answers to her complicated life. This morning, Julie found herself searching for an answer to that gnawing, lingering, *go or stay* question she and Bailey, well mostly Bailey, had discussed throughout her entire stay on the farm.

A cool breeze blew across the porch and redirected her thought. She picked up the afghan beside her and wrapped it around her shoulders. As she began to swing lightly, she glanced around at the beauty of the countryside. Her gaze rested a moment on Drew's red rosebush. It often lifted her spirits just to watch the petals, which at times, seemed to move ever so slightly on the seemingly alive yet unpredictable farm of hers. Looking at it now brought back so many memories.

*What would I be doing today, if I had only said 'yes' to just one of Drew's proposals.* She was so enthralled thinking about her missed opportunities with him, it took her moments to notice the unidentified car which pulled into her driveway and did a quick turnaround. In a short amount of time, the incident triggered a memory of a similar one that occurred over a year ago. She was sitting on the front porch just like she was today. From nowhere, a car pulled in her driveway.

*A gentleman quickly stepped out and said, "Julie, I presume. You probably don't remember me, but I've been searching for you a very long time. In fact, you're on the top of my bucket list. Until I get a kiss from you, I cannot remove your name."*

*Not particularly wanting to kiss a total stranger, but realizing at the same time, he surely was someone from her past, she answered, "Well, I can't be that person that keeps you from completing your bucket list, now can I?"*

Shaking her head at the craziness of it all, she took a big swallow of iced tea and pulled the afghan tighter around her shoulders. She glanced down at the large, rather old, photo album in her lap containing pictures and memories of yesteryear. She gently opened the cover to view its content. She had hopes her answer to the *go or stay* question would be somewhere between these pages.

"Whew!" She noticed the slight tremble in her hands, and realized her mind-set was different today. Could she, at age sixty-five, face the reality of what she might uncover by choosing to do this? She was about to find out.

Fortunately, a picture of Tonka was the first to catch her attention. She couldn't help but smile. He weighed ten pounds the day the picture was taken. She remembered how he would come running around the corner of the farmhouse as soon as he heard the sound of her pickup approaching.

Turning to the next page, she looked at a picture of Wapa's old bread van. He finally had to retire it. She felt everyone, at least once in his life, deserved a friend like him. Although, she was still haunted thinking about the day he called with distressing news.

*"I have terminal cancer."* Her knees had buckled beneath her. *"I would like you to hold my hand when I cross?"*

Remembering the call like it was yesterday, a tear came to her eye. She had thought nothing in her life could compare to Drew's request of an Indian burial on her farm, but she was wrong.

Wapa's call had literally brought her to her knees. Over the years, she had called him on many occasions; especially, when she felt desperate and alone. He never failed or disappointed her. This time, the shoe was on the other foot. A lump formed in her throat. She sobbed and reflected on their friendship. She hadn't been able to fill the void in her heart since his passing.

After several minutes of silence with non-stop tears, she noticed next to Wapa's van was a picture of Brody. He was standing in front of her nightclub. He had been and still was her soul mate. Over the past few years, they both worked for the same employer and had remained friends through thick and thin. Their bond was still as tight as it was the night the music stopped.

On the following page, she studied her wedding photo. She and Slate standing together, both dressed in pink. She had imagined they would grow old on this farm. Realizing the depth of his love, tears again flooded her eyes. Slate was the glue which had held her life together, a little known fact even to her. Until that moment, she hadn't fully comprehended their many conversations, even those after their divorce were conversations of his love and devotion.

Missing him was an understatement. Now, he had passed away one early morning from a heart attack after one of those conversations around the campfire. He had been her protector ever since the night they met at the lake.

She quickly closed the album. Her emotions were at an all-time high. She found herself in the midst of an anxiety attack. She wanted to shout, moan, cry, run and die in an effort to erase her pain. It all hurt so badly. So many facets and so much tragedy hovered over thirty-five years of her life. Why had she been chosen to endure this kind of existence?

Realization hit her. She had never taken the time to stop or slow down long enough to allow herself to properly grieve for those most important people she'd lost in her life. It was time to face the ugly reality of it all; no longer hiding, ignoring, or sweeping debris under the rug.

She sat back in the swing with the determination to sit there long enough to see this endeavor through, no matter the agony her heart and soul went through. Opening the photo book one more time, through swollen eyes, she tried focusing on a picture of her dad standing beside Spook. He had lived several years after moving from the farm. She still missed him. However, she has only to look out her kitchen window to visualize him working on the barn he built for her. A diabetic complication was listed as his cause of death. He passed away never really knowing all the farm drama.

Her mother had out-lived her dad by several years. She had been a cancer survivor. She and Julie had some good times together through the years. However, she passed away before Julie received the validation of why she had singled her out to be left with a family member. She was never told if her mom loved her on the same level with her other children. This was something she had so longed to hear.

The picture of Spook also brought memories of Blake. She owed Blake so much. She hoped to one day be able to locate his whereabouts and let him know what a mistake she had made for blaming him. Her horse accident was not his fault.

Julie wiped at the wetness of her tears, leaned back once again, and closed her eyes. Images of Shawn formed behind her lids. How could she ever forget? He was forever scarred from the mysterious light that had taunted both of them on his trip to the farm. At this time, Shawn lived by himself with no one special in his life. "I hope someday, you'll be able to take control and find happiness," she breathed.

She raised her head and glanced at her new shop. Her

mind flooded with recollections of Kail. One day, he called and wanted to come back to the farm. She agreed and they had such a good time. He came to see her from that day forward for several months. During that time, he built her the shop. After it was built, Kail left again. He no longer called or visited. "I still don't fully understand, your eccentric behavior, but it's not for me to judge." She was just glad they'd had the time to spend together.

Turning to the next page, looking at Chase's picture made her shiver. The thought of him sent cold chills down her spine. "I still look over my shoulder, for fear you will return to the farm one day," she said. She had cared deeply for him. However, he was the one man responsible for the most drastic change in her life. Because of his actions, her life was forever altered by a walk-in. Though she'd learned to accept it, she lived her life one day at a time, through someone else's eyes.

*What if those eyes belong to none other than Rising Starr? It would definitely explain a lot and bring this interesting journey full circle. If that were true, after all the centuries cloaked in mystery, the infamous legend would end. But wait, how much validity can be placed on this assumption? For you see, if you were to glance over at the old Oak right about now, you would observe a slight mischievous smile beginning on the somewhat alluring, always in charge, powerful chief's face, and he isn't confirming or denying anything.*

Having gone through nearly every emotion possible this morning, Julie laid the album aside and stood. A gasp caught in her throat. On the floor, lying in plain sight was a faded envelope. "Oh, my gosh." She reached to retrieve it. Her hands trembled. So, this was where she had stuck the chief's poem. How many times she had searched for it and thought the envelope containing the words was lost forever.

Shortly after that night on the hill, when Cody had given

the poem to her, she learned about the chief's heartbreak and ultimately his centuries-old legend. After all the tragedies she'd been through on the farm, how could she not believe the tales of his legend?

She sat on the swing, envelope in hand, and thought back to the various times she felt his presence and the impact he had on her life for several decades. Leaning back, she still couldn't fully understand or comprehend the scope of it all.

There were comforting and tragic times. She shivered thinking about the power this chief possessed over her, yet the compassion and patience he had with her at the same time. He had gone to such great lengths to give her the rather unorthodox compelling writing she held in her hand.

She was glad for it as it had helped her accept and acknowledge the journey she had been destined to follow. Now she wondered how her decision today would be received by the powerful always in charge dominant one.

With her future on the line, she tucked the faded envelope back between the archive pages for safekeeping, stood then stepped off the porch. What if the chief had other plans for her? She didn't want to think that way. There was already enough on her mind.

It had definitely been a trip this morning going through the pages of the archives, and she has yet to deal with her negligence in calling Bailey, but she hadn't received her conformation on the new property. She had contacted a realtor and there was a nice 25-acre farm barely outside the city limit that she was waiting for the bank to get back with her on. After all, the deal might blow up in her face. She hoped not.

Glancing across the road at Madelyn's farm, trees lay on the ground like wounded soldiers. Since Madelyn's passing from cancer, and Alex having moved away, the area was but a mere image of itself. In a way, it reminded her of the devastation she witnessed the first time she laid eyes on her own farm.

Making her way to the barn she shuddered, thinking about the magnitude of it all. Once inside, she removed the very old, dirty 'For Sale' sign wedged back in the corner. It was covered in dust and cobwebs. She looked at it and wondered why she had kept it all this time. "I guess I kept it just for this day."

She washed away all the debris and touched up the black letters with paint before leaning the sign against the barn to dry. She returned with a hammer in her hand, got the sign, and began a walk, she had never visualized she would be taking. It was not a long walk but a life-altering one.

Originally, her plan was never to leave the farm and like Drew, upon her death, her ashes would be strewn alongside his. However, here she was going out to the edge of her yard with a hammer and a for sell sign.

Before she hammered the marker in, she took one last look around. She wondered if the chief would ever allow her to find real love. Would she be able to permanently move away from the spirit and the mysterious farm that had deceived her and held her captive for so many years?

She placed the sign on the ground and hammered on one side, then the other. From out of nowhere a loud burst of energy rocked the ground. It jolted the sign like it was the projected target, and sent a shockwave through the hand she held on to it with. After another boom of thunder the once velvet, blue sky turned a sinister gray. What was happening? Had she indeed angered the chief this morning with her decision to leave?

Her pulse pounded as she ran inside for shelter. She reached the kitchen and glanced out her window. From the sudden downpour, streams of water rolled from the hillside. She hugged herself against the bone chill of her thoughts. Her anger grew and she lashed out. "Please stop this!"

No sooner than her plea was out, through the pouring

rain she saw a zigzagged, blinding flash of lightning come from the sky. Thunder cracked a defining roar when the bolt struck the center of the Oak atop the hill. Her heart threatened to stop beating.

She stood helpless and watched, in horrified terror, the old tree that meant so much to her being maliciously attacked. Heartbroken, she witnessed the long-standing, mighty old oak spread it's splintered and wounded branches. Her world stood still and she forgot to breathe. Then, after moments of silence, just long enough to say its goodbyes it seemed to moan as it cracked apart then fell from its long-held prestigious position.

Julie sank to the floor, inconsolable. Night Hawk's words echoed through her mind. *I cannot see this chief ever letting you leave.*

# DEDICATION

## ABOUT THE AUTHOR

Native to the Ozarks, I graduated from Central High School and attended SMSU. In 1962, I gained part-time employment with Lily-Tulip, a cup company built previously in 1952. It would be thirty-seven years later when many employees of the company and I were caught up in downsizing.

Widowed the year before and still too young to retire, I needed a source of income so I decided to attend a local junior college. I worked toward a certificate in 'Office Systems Technology'. The three English classes, within the certificate requirements, personally demanded a lot of my time writing articles.

Since a friend of mine always had a story to share, I turned to her for my writing inspiration. Before long, she suggested I write her life's story. I declined. Writing a book was never in my wheelhouse or on my bucket list.

Jumping ahead sixteen years you can see she won. I hope you enjoyed the intriguing, out of the norm, bizarre ups and downs of my friends mysterious life that is wrapped inside the cover of DOMINANCE.